MW00905753

Much Ado about
MACBETH

Randy McCharles

Much Ado about

MACBETH

Randy McCharles

TYCHE BOOKS LTD.

Much Ado about Macbeth
Published by Tyche Books Ltd.
www.TycheBooks.com

Copyright © 2015 Randy McCharles
First Tyche Books Ltd Edition 2015

Print ISBN: 978-1-928025-29-0
Ebook ISBN: 978-1-928025-30-6

Cover Art by Stefan Lorenz
Cover Layout by Lucia Starkey
Interior Layout by Ryah Deines
Editorial by Andrea Howe of Blue Falcon Editing

Author photograph: Leonard Halmrast

All rights reserved. No part of this book may be reproduced or transmitted in any form or by any means, electronic or mechanical, including photocopying, recording or by any information storage & retrieval system, without written permission from the copyright holder, except for the inclusion of brief quotations in a review.

The publisher does not have any control over and does not assume any responsibility for author or third party websites or their content.

This is a work of fiction. All of the characters, organizations and events portrayed in this story are either the product of the author's imagination or are used fictitiously.

Any resemblance to persons living or dead would be really cool, but is purely coincidental.

This book was funded in part by a grant from the Alberta Media Fund.

Government

Dedication

This novel was inspired by my high school days, a trying yet magical time for everyone involved: students, teachers, administrators and, of course, parents. I did take drama in high school and Simon Riordon (the younger version) bears a strong resemblance to one of my teachers. High School is where I was introduced to William Shakespeare, but the greater drama was in the lives of fellow students and their families. Today, as an adult, I have a more realistic vision of the teachers, who during my school days appeared to not have lives outside of teaching. Imagine my surprise when I discovered that they were people too. From the heart of a student of life, this novel is dedicated to educators, parents, and students everywhere. All the world's a stage, and we its players; and nowhere is this more true than in high school.

Contents

-Act I-

Scene 1: A Desert Place

LIGHTNING DANCED ACROSS the leaden city skyline, a gleeful counterpoint to the echo of grumbling thunder. Beneath the burgeoning storm, in a vacant lot surrounded by aging, smog-shrouded buildings, three hags huddled together, looking much at home amid the long, wild grass and windblown trash. In the nearby rush-hour streets, traffic lights twitched from yellow to red to green, and the horns of irate drivers and the shriek of too-worn brakes joined the hellish song.

The first hag raised her thin, grating voice to be heard above the clamour. "When shall we three meet again? In thunder, lightning, or in rain?"

The second hag groaned in exasperation. "Cripes, Agatha. It's the twenty-first century. Must you keep quoting those tired, worn-out lines?"

"Sisters!" crabbed the third and final hag. "Speaking of tired, worn-out lines, you two have this same argument year after year. Could we just get on with it so that we can get back indoors?" She looked up at the darkening sky. "My corns tell me it's about to rain."

"Well," harrumphed Agatha, who towered above the others but was so thin that she sometimes seemed to pass through doors without opening them first. "If your corns say it's going to rain, then who am I to argue?" As if in answer, a large raindrop splatted onto her overlarge and crooked nose.

Gertrude, the second hag, suppressed a smile. It was no wonder she stood shorter than Agatha. She was horribly misshapen, with one shoulder much higher than the other, and a back so crooked that her chin was buried in her chest. "Very well, the short version. Where will this season's supplicant meet us?"

The third hag, Netty, stood no taller than a child and tended to sound as if she were screeching, even when speaking softly. What she lacked in height, however, she made up for in girth. "At the Dairy Queen." The onion-shaped hag grinned through missing teeth while tapping her fingers together with excitement.

"The Dairy Queen?" Agatha's craggy face darkened to match the sky.

"Well," said Netty. "The nearest heath is 140 miles away, and our supplicant claims that school bus passes don't cover that distance. I settled for the Dairy Queen across from his school."

"School!" Gertrude's ancient eyes danced with fire. "We haven't entertained a university supplicant since . . . Oxford, 1872." The rumpled witch rubbed her grubby palms together. "I do love universities. Students are so vain. Almost as vain as the professors."

"Don't get your hopes up." Netty rolled her head on her round shoulders. "We're not talking university."

"What, then?" asked Gertrude. "College? Trade school? Fine arts? Please tell me it's fine arts."

Netty's voice came as little more than a whisper—screeching still, but a whisper. "High school."

"High school!" Agatha and Gertrude crowed together.

"Is that even legal?" asked Agatha.

The other two gave Agatha a blank stare.

"We're witches," Gertrude murmured in the soft, reasonable voice that was her trademark. "Everything we do is illegal. Otherwise, what would be the point?"

"Whatever." Agatha scowled at Gertrude. "You skipped over when. As in: When shall we three meet again?"

"Right," said Gertrude. "I got confused by Netty's corns."

"Don't go blaming my corns!" The squat hag wagged a plump finger in her deformed sister's face. "It's your own fault. You're the pin-up girl for that attention defy . . . defa . . . defi— Oh, that AC/DC thing where you can't keep your thoughts in a straight line."

Gertrude stared at Netty. Then her lips moved. "What was the question again?"

Netty smiled.

"When," thundered Agatha, "shall we three meet again?" The tall hag's words were punctuated by loud claps of actual thunder.

"Later today," Netty said quietly. "After school."

"Right, then," said Agatha. "We meet again at the Dairy Queen after school. I'm glad that's settled. Now we can adjourn and go indoors for a nice hot cup of tea."

Agatha's two sisters began hobbling away.

"Where are you going?" demanded Agatha.

Netty looked back and screeched against the storm. "We're adjourning."

"We have to say the words," Agatha called back.

"No," murmured Gertrude, her soft words somehow penetrating the wind. "We don't."

"Frizzle frazzle," Agatha mumbled then hastily uttered the closing words: "Fair is foul, and foul is fair: Hover through the fog and filthy air."

While scuttling to catch up to her sisters, the tall witch muttered, "You'd think that after doing this for four hundred years, it would get easier."

"What?" Netty screeched at her.

"I said—" began Agatha, but her words were drowned out by a sudden downpour.

Scene 2: The Play's the Thing

PAUL SAMSON ALWAYS enjoyed this time of year. First day of school. Classes not yet started. Nothing gone wrong. Yet.

He stood alone in Ashcroft Senior High's five-hundred-seat auditorium, wearing his traditional teaching attire—Paul Stewart sport coat, corduroy pants, and Calvin Klein penny loafers—waiting for his grade-twelve students to arrive for the first drama class of their final year. As he always did when standing in an empty auditorium, Paul felt at peace. Through the drawn-back curtains, he could see out into the risers, row upon row of empty theatre seats, the stage itself bereft of props and backdrops. So quiet. If only every day, every moment, could be like this.

"Sir?"

Paul looked at his watch then turned to consider his senior-year assistant, Lenny Cadwell. Somehow the boy had crept up on him.

"You're early, Lenny."

"Yes, sir."

Lenny Cadwell was Ashcroft's rising star. Rail thin; straight, black hair that tended to get in his eyes; and handsome in a standoffish, bad-boy way, Lenny was polite and efficient offstage and a flaming prima donna when in front of an audience. He was exactly the kind of actor no director in his right mind would hire. All efforts to rein him in had not so much failed as gone unnoticed. Lenny was one of those rare people who saw and heard only what he wanted. To everything else he was blind, deaf, and dumb. Of all the candidates from last semester Paul could have chosen as his assistant, Lenny had ranked dead last. Unfortunately Lenny was also the only senior student who took drama seriously and, therefore, the only real candidate. Paul was stuck with him.

"Well, what is it, Lenny?"

"Class will be starting soon," the boy said. "Do we know what play we will be putting on this term?"

Well, so much for peace. Drama for grades ten and eleven was like a still pond, the only disturbance being the actual students, all of whom thought they were born actors and didn't need any actual training. Grade twelve, by comparison, was a whirlpool, a maelstrom of decisions and consequences that threatened each year to drag Paul down into oblivion. While the tenth- and eleventh-grade curricula had lists of approved plays from which to choose, twelfth grade was another story. It was up to Paul to select plays that would both challenge and best use the skills of the students, most of them now in their third year of drama instruction. But with so many brilliant plays to choose from . . .

Well, Paul always hated making the choice. And no matter what he chose, someone would disapprove—usually quite loudly.

Even so, Paul had spent the summer mulling over the question of which play his twelfth-grade class should perform for first term. He had narrowed his list down to a dozen popular high school plays that he felt would illicit the least objection. Then he had run out of time. Since breakfast, he had reduced the list to three by the simple means of following his whimsy. But whimsy went only so far. He still had two choices to eliminate.

"Well, Lenny? What play do you think we should put on?"

The boy stared at him, surprise breaking his wonted unruffled expression. Paul had to force himself not to laugh or smile. He couldn't remember ever asking Lenny his opinion. Not once.

But Lenny recovered quickly, his prima donna persona taking over. "How about *Tony and Tina's Wedding*? It's been playing at the Carousel Dinner Theatre forever, so it must be good."

And that was why Paul rarely asked students their opinions. He ran the fingers of his right hand through his thinning brown hair, an alternative to strangling the idiot would-be actor. Never mind that *Tony and Tina's Wedding* was not a play. It was dinner theatre. And a musical.

Calmly Paul said, "That it is playing now, right now, downtown, is precisely why we would not do it here. We want to put on a play that people can't see somewhere else. Something that they haven't seen recently."

Lenny gave him the look that said *I don't understand what you are talking about, so I am forgetting it right now. See? Forgotten.*

"How about *Grease*?"

Another musical. Was that all kids cared for these days? Musicals? Paul shook his head. "And which of our third-year students can sing? Can any of them sing? And what kind of lesson does *Grease* teach, anyway? Give up being straight laced and join a gang?"

Again, Lenny gave him the look.

Paul drummed his fingers against his lips. "A lesson. That's what we need. Something that educates as well as entertains." He ran his remaining three plays through his mind then began reviewing the nine he had capriciously dismissed. Did any of them teach a lesson?

"How about—?" Lenny said, but Paul shushed him.

"Wait, wait, something's coming." Paul remembered how last June several eleventh-graders, some in his own drama class, had been suspended for cheating on their final exams. Summer school had caught most of them up, but several were repeating eleventh grade. The affair had blemished Ashcroft's reputation, but Paul was more concerned about the cheating itself. None of the students had felt bad for doing it, only for being caught. Surely there must be a play about the evils of cheating.

"Sir," said Lenny. "It's almost time."

"That's okay, Lenny." Paul found himself slowly nodding his head. "I have chosen our play."

"Sir? What is it?"

"*Macbeth*!"

"Who?"

Paul considered the twelfth-grader. "One of Shakespeare's most famous plays?"

The boy's face blanched. "Shakespeare."

Paul spoke through gritted teeth. "You can't be an actor without performing at least one of the Bard's plays."

Again the look. Wisdom: in one ear, out the other.

A bell rang and the doors at the top of the auditorium banged open. Students began dribbling down the aisles.

Paul gave Lenny a penetrating look. "Go visit Mrs. Shean in the library. Ask her for *Macbeth*. She should have several copies of the Penguin Popular Classics paperback edition. We'll see how far we can read today."

Scowling, Lenny slouched off to do as he was asked.

Scene 3: Full of Scorpions Is My Mind

"ARE YOU OUT of your mind?"

Winston's beady eyes looked ready to explode, which, for Ashcroft High's principal, was his normal look. Paul decided that the overweight and habitually unhealthy-looking administrator's expression would look great on a production poster. He just wasn't sure which production. Perhaps *Mutants from Mars*?

"What, um, seems to be the problem?" Paul asked.

Winston gave him a one-word answer. *"Macbeth."*

Paul whistled. Word traveled fast. Class had ended ten minutes ago.

"I found out five minutes after your class started," Winston said, apparently reading his mind. "I know everything that goes on around here."

Everything except half a hundred students cheating on their exams, Paul mused. "So what's the problem with *Macbeth*? Schools have been teaching Shakespeare forever. You can't get more classic than Shakespeare."

Winston tugged a handkerchief out of his rumpled suit coat pocket and wiped his face. "The parents will revolt. We can't have a school play about something as inappropriate as witchcraft."

"Witchcraft?" Paul's heart almost stopped in his chest. It hadn't even occurred to him that the brief appearances of the witches would be an issue. It's not as if they flew on broomsticks, sacrificed goats, or performed magic in the story. *Macbeth's* witches were little more than cryptic fortune-tellers.

"Macbeth isn't about witchcraft. It's about cheating. Remember cheating? *Macbeth* is the most appropriate play we could put on right now. As for witchcraft, that's merely the plot device the play uses to facilitate cheating. If anything, the play is antiwitchcraft."

Winston shook his head and had, in fact, had been shaking his head the entire time Paul had been speaking. "The parents don't look that deep. All they see and remember is 'bubble, bubble, toil and trouble.' They'll surround the school with pitchforks and picket signs."

Paul sighed and decided that correcting the flawed quote from the play would not be helpful.

The school principal smiled. "Why don't you put on *Romeo and Juliet* instead?"

"Romeo and Juliet?" Paul echoed. "A play about teen sex and suicide. The parents will accept that?"

Winston burst out laughing and dabbed at his face again. "You're right. A horrible topic. The parents love it, though. Most popular Shakespeare play for high schools, I understand."

"Well, I don't understand," Paul said. "And I'm a parent. I'd quit before I directed a high school production of *Romeo and*

Juliet."

"I'm not asking you to quit." Winston folded and tucked the handkerchief back into his pocket. "And you don't have to do *Romeo and Juliet*. I'm only asking you to reconsider *Macbeth*. Be forewarned. If you proceed with that play, you will regret it."

"ARE YOU OUT of your mind?"

Paul had stepped out of Principal Winston's office, only to be cornered by Elizabeth Cadwell, president of the Parent-Teacher Association. She was also the spitting image of her son, Lenny, only thinner and paler. And from Paul's past encounters with the *gorgon lady*, as she was adoringly dubbed in the teacher's lounge, the fruit didn't fall far from the tree. Paul was not surprised to see her. Winston might think that he knows *everything that goes on around here*, but the gorgon lady was usually three steps ahead of him.

The human lizard repeated her question. "Are you out of you mind?"

"Apparently." Paul wagged his head. "Winston just suggested that I put on *Romeo and Juliet* instead."

The gorgon smiled. "What an excellent idea. The parents will love *Romeo and Juliet*."

"Especially the sex scenes," Paul said.

The gorgon lost its smile. "The what?"

"You know, thirteen-year-old kids defy their parents and sneak out for hanky-panky. I much prefer the sex over the suicides."

"The what!" The gorgon's blanched face turned an ugly red. "Are you screwing with me? Because if you're screwing with me—"

"Or," Paul said, "we could do *A Midsummer Night's Dream*. Great costuming, though skimpy at times. And dancing! Oh, the dancing!"

"That . . . doesn't . . . sound . . . too bad," the gorgon admitted.

"And the orgies." Paul clasped his hands together. "Think of the fun the kids will have."

"Orgies!" the gorgon shouted then froze and looked around.

Mrs. Kennedy, the school secretary, was smirking into her sleeve. Several students sat in the waiting area, staring at the gorgon in disbelief. Then they laughed and mimicked her.

"Orgies!" they cried and pressed the backs of their wrists to their foreheads. "Orgies!"

Paul sighed, wishing they were in his drama class.

The gorgon wagged a finger in Paul's face. "We'll see what Winston has to say about this!" Then she turned and barged into the principal's office.

"You don't have an appointment!" Mrs. Kennedy called after her.

As Paul walked away, several of the students saluted or rose from their seats to give him a high five. Apparently the gorgon was as popular among the students as she was among the teachers.

Scene 4: What Fools These Mortals Be

"DOUBLE, DOUBLE, TOIL and trouble . . . Is he gone yet?"

Netty made one final slurp through her milkshake's straw then rolled her bulbous head to peer toward the door past Agatha's narrow, yet towering, shoulder. "Aye, Sister."

"What a schmuck," said Gertrude. "Do these mortals never learn?"

All three witches cackled, drawing looks from a nearby table of teenagers.

Agatha let out a long, rancorous breath. "If they did, wouldn't our lives get boring?"

"How many Macbeth pretenders does that make?" asked Gertrude. "We've been doing this shtick how long? The story has to get old someday."

Agatha shook her wrinkled jowls. "So long as they put on the play, there will be actors looking for a leg up. And frankly, this last actor needs all the leg he can get."

"He's just a lad," said Netty. "Hasn't even come into his own yet."

"And now perhaps he never will," said Gertrude.

Netty pursed her fleshy lips. "He did accept the bargain."

"Perhaps he'll find his way," said Agatha.

The other two looked at her.

"Well, there's always a first time," Agatha rasped.

All three witches fell silent and shook their heads.

"That drama teacher," said Netty. "Not much of a challenge."

Gertrude chuckled. "Can you believe it? He thought *Macbeth* was his idea."

"A morality play about cheating?" Agatha chortled. "Oh, yes. *Macbeth* is the first play that comes to my mind."

"So susceptible to suggestion." Netty poked at her teeth with a gnarled finger. "I was hoping for a bit of a tussle."

"Were you?" asked Agatha. "We've had hundreds of years of experience at this. That drama teacher's had . . . what? Forty years of mortal coil? And face it; mortality isn't as coiled as it used to be."

Again, the three witches cackled.

"People have gone soft," Gertrude said. "This job isn't a challenge anymore."

Netty nodded. "Used to be we'd have to use lies and illusions to trick people into making mistakes."

"Now all we have to do is point." Agatha pointed a long, skinny finger across the table, as if to demonstrate. "Damn disappointing in my book."

Again, silence.

"I'm going to do it," Agatha said, breaking the awkward moment.

"Do what?" asked Netty. "Rain down curses upon The Bard's Play and everyone involved?"

"Maybe later. I was talking about today's special, the poisonberry Blizzard. I'm going to give it a try."

Gertrude snorted. "You need glasses. The sign says *boysenberry*, not poisonberry."

"I'm a witch," said Agatha. "I can't wear glasses. You ever see a witch wearing glasses?"

"Well, I—" Gertrude began.

"I'm talking real witches. Not those Wiccan wannabes."

Gertrude drew a long breath in through her nose. "If you put it that way, then no, I haven't seen a witch wearing glasses. Though I have witnessed my fill of stubborn, half-blind witches who can't tell a broomstick from a coat rack."

"I rest my case," Agatha said then frowned.

"If you're purchasing a Blizzard," said Netty, "get an extra spoon. I want to sample a taste."

"Make it three spoons," said Gertrude. "Heh. I've always been fond of boysenberry."

Agatha grumbled as she rose from the plastic bench seat. "The things you put up with when you're a witch."

Scene 5: Under a Hand Accursed!

"*MACBETH*. THAT'S NICE, dear."

The words shocked Paul into immobility. "You know, you're the first person today who hasn't told me that I'm out of my mind."

Sylvia, Paul's wife of twenty years, looked up from her magazine and cast him a familiar smile. "What was that, dear?"

The shock began wearing off. "I said, you're the first person today who hasn't told me that I'm out of my mind."

Smile still in place. "I gave up telling you that years ago. If you don't know by now . . ."

"Fine, fine. Supper—"

"Is in the fridge."

"Is Susie home yet?"

"Been. Gone."

Paul sighed. "I never tire of domestic bliss."

"Me neither," said Sylvia, her nose back in her magazine.

Paul sighed again and went into the kitchen to inspect the contents of the fridge. Whatever supper Sylvia had alluded to escaped him, so he made himself a peanut butter sandwich and retired to his study.

The study was Paul's refuge. His Fortress of Solitude. It was also a mess.

Sylvia hadn't entered the room in years, having told him that if he wasn't going to keep it clean, then neither was she. Books and boxes lay on every available surface, including the floor. Papers lay strewn everywhere, as though a hurricane had made a mad dash about the room. There were cups and plates and occasional silverware, some of which hadn't seen the kitchen in days.

Paul's desk was the cleanest area in the study. Not that *clean* was an apt description. Organized shambles came closer. Everything on the desk was currently in use. If it wasn't, Paul would place it elsewhere, such as on the floor.

Even so, with the start of a new school year, Paul knew that he would have to clear his desk. He took a bite of his sandwich then picked up several books he had planned to read during the summer but hadn't gotten to. A survey of the room revealed four bookcases with not an inch of spare capacity. No wall space for a fifth bookcase, either. Spotting a reasonably stable stack of books on the floor, he added those from the desk and watched a moment to see if they would topple. When they didn't, he frowned at some papers that lay across his computer keyboard. Unable to remember what they were for, he added them to a pile of similar papers on the spare chair. Then he stacked several small plates, including the one with his sandwich, and placed them on top of the papers on the chair, promising himself that he would take the dishes to the kitchen. Later.

It was enough to get started. He took another bite of sandwich and peered about the room.

In addition to books, papers, empty dishes, and some clothing, his study was awash with boxes of scripts, many with *Ashcroft Senior High* stamped on them, some from other schools, most with no stamp at all. Paul had been collecting scripts for almost twenty-five years. In all that time, he had never developed anything remotely akin to a filing system. As a result, it took forever to find a loose-leaf script of *Macbeth*.

When he finally found one, he ran his fingers through the remains of his hair and mentally kicked himself. How could he have forgotten? And neither Winston nor the gorgon had even mentioned it. There, below the title, in only a slightly smaller font, were the words *The Cursed Play*.

Paul dug through his desk drawer for a bottle of correction fluid and, fingers trembling, obliterated the warning. He didn't believe in superstition. What modern person did? But he couldn't deny the play's history. Countless renditions of *Macbeth* had been plagued by accident, tragedy, and even death. *Macbeth*'s reputation as The Cursed Play was well earned, and anyone who knew anything at all about Shakespeare was aware of the curse. He was aware. Yet he had forgotten.

Then again, perhaps the curse should be forgotten. Though he had never before directed *Macbeth* himself, he had seen several productions that had gone off without a hitch. He couldn't help but believe that the accidents were a self-fulfilling prophecy. Was that it? Ignore the curse, and it ignores you?

None of his students had mentioned the curse. Many claimed never to have heard of *Macbeth*, though he found that difficult to believe. Even with computer games and texting, is it possible to grow up ignorant of Shakespeare? Even so, after today's read-through of the Penguin edition, they seemed eager enough to anticipate cast assignments. Well, as eager as disinterested students taking an elective course could be.

Curse or no curse, it was too late to back out now without looking the fool. And he could just see the gloating look on the gorgon lady's face. He would never give her that pleasure. No, The Cursed Play it was, and if anyone complained, he would simply ridicule them as superstitious. It was about time that he turned the tables and became the ridicul*er* rather than the ridicul*ee*.

With the skill and concentration of a surgeon, Paul worked his way through the script, writing up a list of roles as well as some production notes. Unlike the paperback edition from the library, the production script included stage directions and plenty of white space for performers to mark their lines and write in notes. When he was done, he turned the stack of sheets over and almost choked when he saw the title page.

The Cursed Play glared up at him, with no evidence of the correction fluid he had applied earlier. *It flaked off*, he told himself. *The bottle is old*. But he saw no sign of any flakes, and the Liquid Paper had seemed fluid enough when he had applied it.

Paul opened the word processor on his Mac computer and typed up a new title page, excluding the subtitle, and printed it on his inkjet printer. He crunched up the original page and threw it into an already overflowing wastebasket.

The paper, ink, and font of the new page didn't match the rest of the pages, but no one would notice. Tomorrow he would take the loose-leaf script to Mrs. Shean and have her make thirty stapled copies.

Scene 6: What Noise Is This?

PAUL ARRIVED FOR the second day of classes and found the Ashcroft-Tate Auditorium almost filled to capacity, which was surprising as there were five hundred theatre seats and only thirty students in his class. Three hundred of the occupants were misbehaving, shouting into cell phones, engaging in loud conversation with their neighbours, or fidgeting with the contents of purses or briefcases. All of them were near Paul's age. That left the students, sitting in the front two rows, calm as angels.

Paul didn't even have to look around. "Mrs. Cadwell, I see you've been busy."

The gorgon lady did not stand up from one of the seats, but instead stepped out from behind a backstage curtain and swaggered across the stage like a queen—a drama queen. She was a poorer actor than her son. "This play must be stopped!" she demanded.

The Parent-Teacher Association occupying the seating area cheered.

The Ashcroft Senior High School PTA was renowned as the most active Parent-Teacher Association in the country. It also had the rare distinction of having no teachers among its members. There were times when Paul felt convinced that many of its members did not actually have children attending the school. The PTA seemed to exist for the sole purpose of making teaching near impossible, and for the most part, they were astonishingly good at it.

This did not deter Paul. He strode toward centre stage and waved his hands for quiet. "This play," he echoed, "hasn't even started."

"Nor shall it," said the gorgon. "The PTA won't stand for it." Again, the PTA cheered. Some stood and she basked in the standing ovation.

Paul again waved for silence and didn't speak until he got it. He glared at the filled theatre seats. "We're not going to have much of a discussion if you keep applauding every word Mrs. Cadwell says."

The PTA cheered.

Paul shook his head. Dumber than the students.

The gorgon lady motioned her followers to silence and immediately received it. "We don't need a discussion. We are just here to inform you that there will be no play about witches, no Macbeth—"

"But I want to do Macbeth!" shouted one of the students. He rose from his seat and faced down his mother.

"Lenny?" The gorgon lady looked at a loss for words.

"We read the play yesterday, Mum. It's cool. It's not about witches. It's about war. And castles. And intrigue. It's a James Bond play."

The rest of the students shouted support for their classmate.

Not the argument Paul would have made, but coming from Lenny, it was probably more effective than anything he could have said.

The gorgon lady looked dumbfounded. She glanced at the PTA and opened and closed her mouth, but nothing came out. Her eyes roved over the front two rows of shouting students then glared at Lenny. She seemed to reach a decision. "We'll speak about this at home, young man." To the PTA, she smiled and called, "We have delivered our message. There shall be no Macbeth. Our work here is done." Then she turned to Paul and wagged her finger. "This isn't over."

Paul sighed. "Of course it isn't." He could read on the gorgon's face that she already had a Plan B in mind.

The PTA left the theatre looking confused and shouting questions at Mrs. Cadwell, who answered them all by holding one hand palm out and shaking her head. Some few looked blank faced at Paul. One, an older man who looked as if he might have slept through the protest, asked, "So that's it, then? No Macbeth?"

Paul shrugged a reply, and the man turned to follow his tribe of lemmings up the aisle.

After the chief obstruction to their children's education had shuffled out of the auditorium, Paul retrieved the stapled scripts he had brought from the library's copy room and gave them to Lenny to hand out. "Yesterday we read the words of the play. Today we'll read them again in conjunction with stage directions. As we do, try to imagine yourself on the stage going through the motions of the characters."

"When do I get assigned my part?" asked one of the students.

Paul let out a deep breath. "In due time. After we all get a better sense of what the parts are." He dreaded the response he would receive when he told them they would have to audition for parts. He could already feel the lead balloon landing on his head.

Scene 7: Cruel Are the Times

THE PTA WAS meeting in Paul's living room. Or so it seemed. At least, his house felt as crowded as the Ashcroft-Tate Auditorium had been that morning. But Paul knew that it couldn't be the PTA because the strangers in his home were cheerful rather than angry. Paul assumed that there must be times when the PTA wasn't angry, such as when they plotted to re-create the school system in their own image, but Paul had never been present for one of those times.

Sylvia also looked more cheerful than usual. "Paul! Don't you dare sneak off to your hidey-hole. Come say hello."

Paul led his wife to a quiet corner of the hallway and spoke in a hushed whisper. "I don't know any of these people."

"That's because every time they come over, you hide in that office of yours." "They" were the Hinton Valley Realtors Society, of which Sylvia was a member.

Paul put on his best hangdog expression. "But you'll just spend the evening talking shop. I'll be a wallflower."

Sylvia forced a smile. "If you join us, we'll have something to talk about besides shop."

Paul hated social gatherings, making small talk with strangers, and being made to reveal his ignorance regarding real estate. Sylvia had somehow managed to combine all three in his living room. He shook his head. "Can't this time. I have to prepare for classes tomorrow. Start of the year and all."

Sylvia's smile drooped into a glower. She shook her head slowly then turned back to her guests.

It had been a while since Sylvia had given him the glower. Paul knew his wife hadn't been fooled; as a drama teacher, he had more prep flexibility than most high school teachers. He could easily spend some time at her work party. Guilt gripped his stomach as he hurried into his study, forgoing his ritual foraging in the kitchen. He'd wait until the gathering ended or hunger overtook him, whichever came first.

Laughter from the living room echoed in Paul's ears as he worked on putting together the list of cast, understudies, technicians, and ushers. Most of his thirty students would want to perform on stage, but there were only eight roles of substance and fifteen minor parts. That left seven students who would not get to perform. Two or three of those seven would be unsuitable even as stagehands and would be delegated the duty of usher and possibly receive a failing grade.

Paul hated to fail anyone, but he always had a few students who signed up for his course believing it was an easy ride, that they could do nothing and receive an *A* for their lack of effort. Even those who did the bare minimum in first- and second-year drama, squeezing by with a *C*, somehow felt they could do even less in third year. They wouldn't audition for the larger roles. Or if they did, they wouldn't try to get the parts. Then they would sleepwalk through the bit parts or be relegated to moving props.

A burst of laughter erupted from the living room, piquing Paul's curiosity. He cracked open the study door to try to hear what was so funny.

"And then he agreed that perhaps we needed a plumber after all."

More laughter.

Gossip. Four things in the living room that Paul hated.

He reclosed the door as a fresh wave of guilt roiled through his stomach. He really should spend a few minutes with Sylvia's coworkers.

It was after Susie was old enough for Sylvia to return to work that Paul noticed that their family was drifting apart. Paul had his teaching, Sylvia sold houses, and Susie had her friends at school. Rare was the time that any of those lives intersected anymore. Paul had no idea what to do about it, and it was killing him.

Other teachers at Ashcroft had told him that this was normal, a phase of family life that hit everyone. It would last until Susie's first child was born and he and Sylvia became grandparents.

Fawning over grandchildren would draw them together again.

Paul couldn't even imagine Susie having a child. She was seventeen. Still a kid. And people were getting married and having children later in life than when Paul and Sylvia were wed. Would their marriage last until Susie had children? The thought of losing his family tore him up inside.

Would spending a few minutes with his wife's friends from work make Sylvia happy? Or would he embarrass himself so badly that they'd encourage Sylvia to leave him? Paul could never find a right answer.

The only thing Paul knew that he was any good at was teaching drama.

He finished making his cast list in descending order of lines spoken then added a few audition lines for each role, focusing on dialogue that exemplified the passion and personality of each character. After reviewing his list carefully, he performed the part of his job that he was most uncomfortable with. He opened the Web browser on his computer and logged into the school homework Web page.

Paul considered himself a Luddite when it came to computers. After much pain and anguish, he had learned to use a word processor, which was essential these days for teaching in a public school. Even so, the Internet still put the fear of God in him and no part of the Internet more so than the Ashcroft Senior High School Web site.

After much poking and prodding and starting over several times, he found the page for his third-year drama class and, on the second attempt, managed to upload his audition list. He checked his watch and found he had posted the list ten minutes before he had told his students it would be available. Success!

Tomorrow he would learn if any of them had bothered to check the list and practice the lines. It would be interesting to see if he had correctly guessed which student would audition for which role.

With no good reason to further avoid Sylvia's friends, Paul found himself trembling at the thought of trying to make small talk with a bunch of strangers. Maybe he'd make himself a sandwich first.

Scene 8: The Vile Blows and Buffets of the World

NEXT DAY AT class, Paul was relieved to discover that the PTA was not waiting to lynch him in the auditorium. Perhaps Lenny was good for something after all. Maybe he had convinced his mother to find some other failure of the school system to repudiate.

While the students wandered in, Paul set up his folding director's chair and pulled his Cecil B. DeMille megaphone from the locked cabinet in the backstage storage area. He didn't need either of the stereotypical accoutrements, but the students always seemed to expect them. Theatre was, after all, theatre.

"Audition time," he said through the horn, and the students stopped their chatter. "You are all third-year students. In the past, I assigned you roles based on what I thought would help you best. But now I have to prepare you for the real world. Out there, no one is going to call you up and offer you the lead in *Tony and Tina's Wedding*." He glanced at Lenny. "If you want a role, you are going to have to audition for it. Auditions start now."

The groans in the room were silent yet visible on his students' faces.

"First up is the role of Macbeth, Thane of Glamis, a brave and loyal man who succumbs to his ambitions and commits murder. In essence, he falls off the straight and narrow and cheats to get what he wants. Who is trying out for the role?"

Several boys stepped forward, the quickest of whom was Lenny. Paul was not surprised.

"Okay, Lenny," Paul said. "Let's see what you've got."

The twelfth-grade student struck an impressive pose, his expression one of fear and perhaps even desperation.

"It will have blood; they say, blood will have blood:
Stones have been known to move and trees to speak;
Augurs and understood relations have
By magot-pies and choughs and rooks brought forth
The secret'st man of blood. What is the night?"

The class offered some halfhearted applause.

"Thank you, Lenny," Paul said through the megaphone. "Kim,

how about you?"

Kim Greyson, an athletic boy with sandy-blond hair, stepped forward and gave a poor and obviously unpracticed imitation of Lenny's pose. He spoke the words with little emotion and stumbled on "secret'st." It wasn't the worst Paul had seen.

"Thank you, Kim. William? You're up."

William Page's performance was marginally better than Kim's, but he stuttered the lines and got lost after "magot-pies" and was unable to finish. After William's classmates stopped laughing, Paul said, "Good try. John?"

The final applicant for the role twisted his foot against the floor and said, "I, uh, think I'll try for a different part."

Paul was not surprised. During the previous two years, Paul had watched John Freedman habitually bite off more than he could chew. At least he had backed off early this time.

"Okay. Fine. Next up is Lady Macbeth, Thane Macbeth's ambitious wife who pushes her husband to commit murder, only to suffer a mental breakdown over it and commit suicide. Who wants the role?"

Two girls stepped forward. One was Gemma Henderson, whom Paul expected to not only try out for the role but win it. The other girl was—

"Susie? What are you doing here? You're not in this class."

Susie Samson, Paul's daughter, who had never shown any interest in drama and had not taken his class in grades ten and eleven, stepped forward and handed him a slip of paper. "I have a note." It was from Principal Winston.

Paul scanned the note quickly then read it through more carefully. When he was done, he counted to ten; it wouldn't do to show his anger in front of his students. Then he said, forgetting to use his megaphone, "Susie will be joining our class for the rest of the year. Gemma, you can go first."

Gemma Henderson was not so much an actress as she was an outgoing person, a girl who thrived on being the centre of attention and knew how to smile and make her eyes big on demand to get it. Excellent skills to have but not enough on their own to make someone a good actor. Gemma struck a pose, not unlike that struck by Lenny playing Macbeth.

"Out, damned spot! out, I say!—One: two: why,

then, 'tis time to do't.—Hell is murky!—Fie, my
lord, fie! a soldier, and afeard? What need we
fear who knows it, when none can call our power to
account?—Yet who would have thought the old man
to have had so much blood in him?"

Paul had to think about this one. It wasn't bad, but something
about Gemma's performance screamed newscaster. And it was a
little too . . . cheerful for a woman cracking under mental strain.
Still, Gemma was his best student among the girls by far, and
with luck would develop a little more range as she worked with
the part.

"Very good, Gemma. Okay, Susie, do you think you can do
what Gemma did? You're at a bit of a disadvantage having never
taken drama before."

In answer, Susie jumped straight into the scene, rubbing her
hands as though truly bloodstained and speaking the words
haltingly, moving her head and arms as though haunted. Even
her tone carried a hint of a Scottish lilt. When she was finished,
the class just stared at her.

Once Paul recovered from shock at his daughter's surprisingly
good acting, he realized that he had seen Susie's performance
before. It was a relatively decent imitation of Jeanette Nolan's
role as Lady Macbeth from the 1948 film version of Orson
Welles's *Macbeth*. What Susie lacked in experience, she made up
for by doing her homework.

"Thank you, Susie," he said through the megaphone. "Next is
Banquo, Macbeth's companion whom he murders."

Scene 9: 'Twould Have Anger'd Any Heart Alive

PAUL WAS RELIEVED to find Susie at home after school. She knew
better than to disappear after dropping that bombshell on him in
his class. He suspected she had already said something to her
mother since supper was waiting when he arrived and Sylvia and
Susie were already at the table. Spaghetti, one of Paul's
favourites. He couldn't remember the last time the three of them

had sat down for supper together. It disappointed him that it took a note from the school principal to make it happen.

Sylvia was unusually talkative, full of vim and vigour about last night's realtor gathering and how much fun it was.

"The housing market has been dead for months," she said. "Getting together for socials is the only excitement we get these days."

Susie twisted her fork, collecting a dainty spiral of spaghetti dripping with tangy sauce. "Jo-Ann said her dad had a good time."

Susie's friend's dad was also a realtor. She went on to talk about some clothes Jo-Ann had bought, which led to a discussion of Susie's shoes, which somehow led back around to the realtor gathering and how to properly freeze leftover spaghetti.

Paul sat patiently through it all, enjoying his spaghetti and garlic toast. He even opened a bottle of red wine, which he shared with Sylvia.

When they finished eating, Sylvia said, "I suppose we had better discuss what happened to Susie at school yesterday."

"To Susie?" Paul said. "The note I read said Susie started another fight."

"Dad! How come I always get the blame?"

"It takes two people to fight," Sylvia said.

Paul waved a hand. "Fine. Fine. Why don't you tell us what happened?"

"Victoria Whitcomb!" Susie snarled. "She kicked me playing soccer. Again. So I kicked her back."

Paul had heard all this before. From Susie. From Sylvia. From Principal Winston. From Angela White, Susie's gym instructor. And from Victoria's parents. He knew that what he was about to say, Susie had heard before. Why hadn't it sunk in? Maybe he needed to be more blunt.

"Victoria Whitcomb," Paul said, "couldn't kick a soccer ball if it was the size of a Volkswagen."

Both Sylvia and Susie stared at him for several moments then burst out laughing.

"I can't believe you said that!" Sylvia whispered.

"I never would say that," Paul said. "Not on school property, anyway. But I'm not speaking right now as a teacher. I'm speaking as a parent. And as a parent, I'm suggesting that

Victoria Whitcomb has no business playing soccer or any other sport, for that matter. She kicked you, Susie, because she missed kicking the ball. She always misses kicking the ball. She tries. Dear Lord, she tries. But it's just not in her. She's a menace—to the other players and to herself."

Susie was still smiling at her dad's diatribe when Paul dropped the other shoe.

"You know this as well as I do, so you should know better than to kick Victoria back. That is why you get the blame."

Susie dropped her smile. "Yeah, I know. I didn't mean to kick her. It just hurt and I got angry and I struck back without thinking."

"Did you tell Ms. White that?" Paul asked.

Susie shook her head. "I just told her that Victoria kicked me first."

"The school should have called us in," Sylvia told Paul. "Or you at least. You work there. They shouldn't just be able to pull Susie out of P.E. Maybe we should call Mrs. Cadwell. She'll sort this out."

Paul put up his hand again, this time not in defeat. "The last thing I need is to owe Mrs. Cadwell a favour. I'll sort this out with Winston myself and get Susie back into gym class."

"I don't want to go," Susie said.

"What?" Paul and Sylvia spoke at the same time.

"I liked dad's class today. I think I want to stick with drama."

"Susie," said Sylvia, "you were never interested before. No matter how much I begged you to take your father's class."

"You begged?" Paul said.

Sylvia ignored him. "And you've always liked sports. You really enjoyed playing basketball last year."

"Sports are okay," Susie said. "But I've been there, done that. Watching everyone try out for parts today was fun. And it's fun pretending that you're someone else. 'Out, damned spot!' And I don't get to swear playing sports." She held up both hands. "Kidding. Really, guys."

"Well," said Sylvia. "If you're sure. Paul, are you okay with this?"

Paul had to think for a moment. Being pulled out of P.E. and put into drama class—Paul's drama class—as punishment didn't say a lot for drama as a subject or Paul as a teacher. And it could scar his daughter with all sorts of stigmas she hadn't even thought about yet. But he couldn't very well say any of this and expect agreement.

"If that's what Susie wants," he said, "I'll support it. Besides, I'm delighted to finally have my daughter in one of my classes."

Scene 10: Receive What Cheer You May

PAUL SAT WITH his finger poised over the Enter key. He was tempted to turn off his computer and announce the cast assignments in class tomorrow. But he also knew that most theatre companies these days no longer took the time to notify actors of audition results individually. Instead, they posted the cast list in the most impersonal way possible. If Paul was going to teach his students how theatre worked in the real world, he was going to have to play by the real world's rules, no matter how cold they were.

He also knew that when his students saw the list, there would be tears, arguments, fits, and for many, relief. It was impossible to make everyone happy, especially when so many of the auditions were . . . not very good.

There were too many roles for boys and not enough for girls. Many roles had no more than four lines, though that didn't stop half his class from auditioning for them.

Paul himself wasn't happy with many of the assignments. After two years of drama coaching, most of the students were still a long way from being even remotely employable as even the lowest of low-rent actors. But he supposed that was true for all high schools. If you were serious about being an actor, you had to enrol in an acting school, something Paul should have done himself when he'd had the chance. If he had, he might now be on the stage instead of behind it. But it was too late for regrets now.

He was surprised and pleased at how many students had tried out for the major roles. Even his daughter had auditioned for Lady Macbeth, the biggest surprise of all. It was said that seventeen is an age of change, when teens begin putting their childhoods behind them and look toward becoming adults.

Maybe he was seeing that in his own classroom. Perhaps some of his students would make him proud with this play. He knew his daughter already had.

"Let the chips fall where they may," Paul said. He closed his eyes and lowered his finger. When he opened his eyes again, the cast list, along with understudy and stagehand assignments, was posted on the third-year drama homework page. The list included two ushers who were guaranteed a *D* for the class if they slept their way through the term. He closed this thought in true Shakespearian style. "Tomorrow is another day."

As he turned out his office light to go join Sylvia in the living room and watch some TV, he heard a muffled whoop emanate from his daughter's bedroom. Paul couldn't keep a smile from brightening his face.

Scene 11: What's Done Cannot Be Undone

THURSDAY FOUND PRINCIPAL Winston sitting behind his desk, a cold fire simmering in his piggy eyes and perspiration beading down his cheeks. "I understand you haven't changed your mind about the play."

"That's not why I'm here," Paul said. "Susie was in a fight on Tuesday, and instead of calling her mother and myself to meet with her guidance counsellor, you expelled Susie from P.E. and assigned her to my drama class."

Winston's expression didn't change. "You were told the last time your daughter was caught fighting that if it happened again, she would be expelled from P.E."

Paul shook his head. "I could argue that what happened with Victoria Whitcomb wasn't a fight but I won't. I can see that your mind is made up. Ashcroft High has lost a star athlete. So be it. I'm here about your putting my daughter in my drama class. You know that she has no interest in drama, just as you know that she would rather die than sit in one of her own father's classes. This is cruel and unusual punishment, and I demand that you remove Susie from my class immediately."

A slow smile spread across Winston's face. "I could do that."

He leaned forward over his desk. "In fact, I will do that. If . . ." He left the word hanging for a long moment. "If you abandon *Macbeth* and choose a play that will get Elizabeth Cadwell off my back."

Paul leaned forward and rested his hands on the top of the visitor chair in front of the principal's desk. "This isn't even about Susie. It's about me." He straightened and, taking a cue from the gorgon lady, wagged a finger in Winston's face. "This is low, even for you."

Winston reached across his desk and slapped Paul's finger away. "I'm the principal and I'll do whatever it takes to keep the peace. And right now, the biggest threat to peace in this school is that blasted play. Have you considered *Death of a Salesman?*"

Paul stepped away from the desk and opened the door to the outer office. "I won't give in to blackmail," he said loudly, ensuring that Mrs. Kennedy and anyone in the waiting area would hear. "And we did *Death of a Salesman* two years ago." He slammed the door and leaned against it.

The three students sitting in the waiting area looked at him with blank expressions. Mrs. Kennedy, sitting behind the secretary's desk, nodded and offered a thin-lipped smile. "I thought your class did a bold performance of *Death of a Salesman.*"

"Thank you," Paul said before walking toward the auditorium. He wasn't sure if *bold* was a compliment or a criticism.

Then he smiled. If Winston had had any plan at all to pull Susie out of drama, it would never happen now. Susie was in for the long haul, exactly what she said she wanted.

Scene 12: Let Not Your Ears Despise My Tongue

WHEN PAUL ARRIVED at the Ashcroft-Tate Auditorium, several of his students were already there. He had expected Lenny to be waiting, but so too were Kim Greyson and Gemma Henderson. The three of them were arguing over a copy of the cast list one of them had printed out. When they saw Paul, all three began shouting at him at once.

"And so it begins," Paul whispered and raised a hand for silence. Eventually he received it. "I'm guessing that you are unhappy with your assigned roles."

They all started shouting again, but Paul looked at Kim Greyson, and the three fell silent.

"Kim," Paul said, "you auditioned for the role of Macbeth and got it. I'm surprised to see you here."

"But I shouldn't have got it," the boy answered. "Lenny did much better than me during the audition. He deserves the role."

Lenny remained silent but nodded in a cool, I-told-you-so manner.

Paul smiled. "Yes, he did. But I need Lenny to play Macduff."

"I didn't audition for Macduff!" Lenny's voice and manner were the perfect rendition of a petulant child. "Macduff is boring."

"Macduff is the hero," Paul said. "He cuts off Macbeth's head."

"He's still boring," Lenny said.

Paul sighed. "The issue is that no one auditioned for the role of Macduff, and it is a major role. Three students auditioned for Macbeth and only one can have that role, so one of the remaining two has to play Macduff. You"—he pointed at Lenny—"are that student. I've made you Kim's understudy, so you still get to learn and practice the Macbeth role. You just won't be performing it on stage."

"What's the point in that?" Lenny demanded.

"What about me?" Gemma interrupted. "I'm supposed to be Lady Macbeth. Instead I'm a witch!"

"I'm sorry, Gemma." Paul cringed at what he had to say next. "But Susie's audition for the role was much better than yours."

"It was, you know," said Kim.

Gemma bared her teeth at him. "Even if that's true, don't you need Susie to play Lady Macduff? She's the hero's wife who comes to a tragic end!"

"No," Paul said. "I need Susie to play Lady Macbeth and I need you to play Witch Number Three."

By now the bell had rung and the rest of the class was wandering in. Paul could tell from their conversation that many of them had not checked the school Web site and were only now learning of their assignments. He motioned them all to take seats in the folding chairs on the stage and pulled his director's chair close in front of them. There would be no megaphone today.

"You've all received your assignments for the play. Some of you are happier about them than others."

"Favouritism," someone whispered from the group. If Gemma thought she had fooled him, she was only fooling herself.

"Welcome to real life," Paul said. "Most actors who audition for a role do not get it. Sometimes they are offered a chance to try out for a different role, but usually they get no role at all. This is where the phrase 'out-of-work actor' comes from. You may be still be working, waiting tables in a restaurant or washing dishes, but you are not acting."

Low grumbling sounds emanated from the students.

"Fortunately for you, the school requires that not only do I have to fill all the acting and support roles from this classroom— I can't look for better actors and stagehands elsewhere—but I also have to give all of you jobs. So none of you will have to wash dishes until you can find another play to audition for."

Paul gave each student his best piercing gaze. "This is the easiest audition you will ever win."

"But you have me down as an usher," said one of the students.

A heavy sigh left Paul's lips. "Tell me, Trevor, what roles did you audition for?"

Trevor shrugged. "I didn't try out for any. I thought you'd assign me something."

"Exactly. No one is going to offer you a role in a play unless you try out."

"I could be an assassin."

"Your classmates auditioned to be assassins," Paul said. "And they got the parts. You—" Paul looked down at his printed copy of the cast list. "—are the understudy for Assassin Number Three. You will learn and rehearse that part, but on the night of the performance, you will be an usher."

"If I'm just going to usher, why should I learn the part?"

"Because you never know," Paul said. "That's the whole point of understudies. Come performance night, Allan may be home sick and you will be called upon to take his place." To the whole class, Paul said, "What's our motto?"

Thirty voices recited without enthusiasm, "The show must go on."

Paul let it slide. "Okay. For today's class, we'll do another read-through of the play. Only instead of taking random turns, you will each read your assigned part and get more comfortable with it. I want to hear you read with passion, just as if you're reciting the lines on the stage. Tomorrow we'll do it again with the understudies reading. Let's begin."

Scene 13: Something Wicked This Way Comes

AGATHA LET OUT a heavy sigh. "I miss my cats."

Gertrude let out a softer sigh. "I miss my hedgehogs."

Netty let out a loud burp. "I'm ordering more fries."

"Oh, my," said Gertrude. "We've been eating junk food for four days straight. You can't want more."

Netty's eyes chased each other around their sockets then stopped as if reaching a conclusion. "I like Dairy Queen fries. And you're one to talk. You seem pretty fond of the Dilly Bars yourself."

"That's different," Gertrude said. "Ice cream and chocolate never get old."

"Perhaps we should just go home," Agatha said. "I never signed up for a life of burgers and ice cream."

"I suppose you'd rather be dining on gall of goat and slips of yew," suggested Gertrude.

"And nose of Turk and Tartar's lips," Netty added.

Gertrude ran a gnarled finger down one side of the laminated card. "I think I saw Tartar's lips on the menu."

"O well done!" said an apparition standing beside their table. It was possible that she was one of the Dairy Queen staff come to take their twelfth food order of the day, except that Dairy Queen didn't wait on tables. Neither did their uniforms consist of dragon skin and iron spikes.

The apparition continued. "I commend your pains; and every one shall share i' the gains. Yada yada yada." Then she swung herself onto the plastic bench next to Netty, and now there were four witches sitting at the window-side booth.

"By the pricking of my thumbs," said Gertrude. "If it isn't Hecate, come to share in the glory of our work without actually doing any of it."

For a witch, Hecate was rather pleasing to the eye, with the shapeliness, bone structure, and milky complexion of a supermodel. None of the three hags believed it was her true appearance, but that she had stolen it from a magazine, or possibly a comic book titled *Wonder Woman*.

Hecate's grin displayed perfect teeth and ruby lips. "It is good to be the boss. Word in the underworld is that someone is putting on The Bard's Play. I assume that is why you three are slumming it in this dump."

"You should try the fries," Netty suggested.

Hecate sniffed the air. "I think not. Hell smells better. What stage is your venture at?"

Agatha rubbed her skinny hands together. "The thespian has acknowledged his destiny."

Gertrude wagged her gnarled chin. "And now we await the inevitable claim that we haven't lived up to our side of the bargain."

Hecate snorted, her delicate nostrils flaring. "Mortals are so eager to latch on to destiny, yet they always fail to understand it." Then she stood. "I'm off to Hell to ensure a suitable place awaits your thespian. Keep up the good work." Then she was gone.

"She really should have tried the fries," Netty said.

"Who?" asked Lenny Cadwell, sliding into the seat Hecate had just vacated.

"Our bo—" Agatha began.

"A coworker," Gertrude said, cutting off the tall witch.

"Another witch, then." Lenny flicked his hair out of his eyes and tried to appear disinterested.

"Arguably," admitted Netty.

"What is it you wish from us this time?" Agatha asked. "Is the starring role in your school play not enough?"

Lenny slammed the table with his hand. "It is enough. And it's what you promised."

"Then what is your complaint?" asked Gertrude.

"My complaint? I have no compliant. I just dropped in for a burger."

"I recommend the FlameThrower GrillBurger," suggested Netty. "It's got zing."

Gertrude snorted. "She's eaten three since breakfast."

32

"Are you sure you don't have a complaint?" insisted Agatha.

"Well," said Lenny. "Since you ask. You said I would get the starring role."

"Yes?" chorused all three witches.

Lenny stood up, awkwardly as he was still sitting in the booth and it wasn't designed so people could stand. "I didn't get the starring role. He made me the freaking hero!"

"In truth?" Agatha waved for Lenny to sit back down, which he did. "Usually the starring role is the hero."

"Or heroine," said Gertrude. She twisted her deformed neck to look up at Lenny. "Did you wish to be the heroine?" She cast him a gruesome smile. "That can be arranged."

Lenny blinked a few times, uncomprehending. "No. No! In this play, the starring role belongs to the villain. I want to be the villain."

Netty laughed. "Well, they do say that villains have more fun."

The other two witches joined in the laughter, and it quickly degraded into cackling.

Lenny sat through this, frowning.

"Oh, go on," Agatha said at last. "Go on home and do your homework, or whatever it is you kids do these days when they let you out of school."

"You wish to be the villain," Gertrude said. "The villain you shall be."

"Just like that?" Lenny asked.

Agatha glared at him "Yes. Just like that."

"We're witches!" Netty crowed. "It's what we do."

Lenny left the table, looked back at them once, then headed toward the door.

"Now," said Gertrude. "Where were we?"

Agatha scratched a wart on her nose. "I believe we were plotting magical illusions and dark destructions."

Gertrude wagged her misshapen head. "No, that wasn't it. Ah! Ice cream and chocolate. Time for a Dilly Bar."

Scene 14: Out, Out, Brief Candle!

PAUL COULDN'T REMEMBER the last time the family had sat together for supper two nights in a row. Neither could he remember the last time he had seen Susie so happy. He smiled and helped himself to more carrots while Susie recounted to her mother how she had waxed elegant, yet manic, as she read Lady Macbeth's lines in class. She went so far as to begin acting at the dinner table.

In mid stanza Susie broke off and demanded, "How come I have to die offstage?"

Paul looked up from his carrots and saw his daughter staring at him with wide eyes. "What?"

"I die offstage. That ponce of an errand boy marches out and announces that I'm dead. Can a death be more boring?"

"Where did you learn a word like *ponce*?" Sylvia asked. "I'm not certain what it means, but I'm pretty sure you shouldn't be using it."

"Seyton is not a ponce," Paul said. "He's Macbeth's servant. He's supposed to act subservient."

"Whatever," Susie said. "He doesn't even say how I die. Do I poison myself? Does someone kill me? Maybe Seyton kills me. Perhaps he's secretly in love with Macbeth—"

"Seyton is not in love with Macbeth," Paul said firmly, cutting into his pork chop with perhaps more gusto than was warranted. "It's not that kind of play. The truth is that it doesn't matter how Lady Macbeth dies. What's important is Macbeth's soliloquy regarding death. His realization that life is fleetingly short and, in the grand scheme of things, quite meaningless."

Sylvia looked confused. "That can't be what he means. In the next scene, Macbeth is outnumbered and fighting for his life." Sylvia nodded. "Oh yes, I've read *Macbeth*. Who hasn't?"

Paul and Sylvia both turned to look at Susie.

Their daughter turned her face back and forth between them. "What? I've read *Macbeth*. Just this morning."

"Well," said Sylvia. "You're taking drama at school. Most of your schoolmates will never read the book."

"But they will see the play," Susie said, grinning. "And I'm

Lady Macbeth!"

Paul returned to his supper as mother and daughter continued discussing acting. Never in his wildest dreams had he envisioned such a scene playing out in his dining room. It was music to his ears. Even the part where Susie tried to explain what a ponce was in terms that her mother wouldn't get on her case for.

Scene 15: A Thing Most Strange and Certain

FRIDAY MORNING AND the school corridors were silent and empty as Paul made his way toward the Ashcroft-Tate Auditorium. He loved it when class was in session. Students busily learning facts and methods that seemed to them as utter uselessness but which, in later years, would serve them well. After twenty years of teaching high school, it still amazed Paul that the less students knew, the more they felt they had nothing to learn. He supposed that applied to teachers as well. And to the PTA—especially to the PTA. Human nature, then. Just the way people are wired. An idiot has no desire to learn anything, while a genius has an unquenchable hunger for additional knowledge.

The bell rang, sounding much like a fire alarm in the empty hallway, and Paul frowned. He had dawdled and now would have to fight his way through a sea of students the rest of the way to the auditorium. Sure enough, doors erupted all along the hallway, and students came pouring out, racing to visit a washroom before their next class started or outside off school property for a few puffs on a cigarette. Most of them simply wanted to get out of the classroom and feel the freedom of the hallways for a few minutes before finding a desk in their next class.

Paul raised his briefcase over his head as students rushed past him on every side, and he slowed his pace to prevent getting his feet tangled as students dodged in front of him, as though he were just an obstacle to barely avoid running into. As he neared a stairwell, he somehow heard, above the talking, the laughter, and the rush of passing students, a *thump, thump, thump, aghh!* The river of fifteen- to eighteen-year-olds suddenly froze. All heads turned toward the bottom of the stairs, and a hush settled its heavy cloak over the hallway.

Paul lowered his briefcase and held it like a shield. "Make way! Make way!" As quickly as he could, he forced his way toward what everyone was looking at. When he at last reached the bottom of the stairs, he found, lying on the floor, rocking back and forth and holding his right knee, his would-be Macbeth, Kim Greyson.

In an older, simpler time, Paul would have looked around at the gawking students and shouted, "Someone go get the nurse!" But in today's modern world, he simply pulled his cell phone from his sport coat pocket and called the school secretary.

"Mrs. Kennedy, it's Paul Samson. A student has hurt himself. . . . Yes, it looks serious. Better call for an ambulance. . . . Kim Greyson. . . . Yes. . . . Main floor. South stairwell. . . . Yes. Thank you."

He put the phone away and shook his head. "Everyone go to class. Nothing more to see. Kim is in good hands."

The sea of students began moving again, much gentler than before, respectfully giving the injured student a little space but still rubbernecking as they went by. The bell indicating the start of class rang, and the remaining onlookers drifted off so they wouldn't be too late.

"Well, Kim," Paul said.

Kim looked up at him with large, moist eyes and grimaced.

"How did you manage to fall down a flight of stairs that was packed shoulder to shoulder with students?"

"No idea." Kim rocked gently on the hard floor and grunted. "I think my leg is broken."

Paul nodded. "Hopefully it is just your leg. Knees are much more difficult."

"It hurts," Kim said. The boy's eyes shimmered, but no tears appeared.

"Yes," Paul said. "I'm sure it does." But he wasn't thinking about the injury. He was thinking that a student with a broken leg couldn't play a main character, especially not an army general. He'd have to make Kim one of the thanes. Perhaps Angus. Thane Angus has two lines and doesn't move much. The role of Macbeth would have to go to Lenny.

Scene 16: The Shot of Accident nor Dart of Chance

BY THE TIME the paramedics arrived, examined Kim, conversed with the school nurse, then packed the boy onto a wheeled stretcher and carted him away, Paul arrived late to a class of chattering students who immediately quieted as he walked across the stage and sat in an empty director's chair.

"How's Kim?" Lenny asked. Rather than the worry or boredom that exuded from his classmates, the boy's expression carried only hopeful expectation.

"Doesn't look good," Paul said, quoting the paramedics. "Broken fibula. Possible patella damage as well."

His announcement was met with blank stares. Paul sighed. "He broke his leg and may have damaged his knee."

The news elicited a chorus of *ohs* and *ows*. Lenny's face split into a wide grin.

"Yes, Lenny. This means that you'll have to be Macbeth. William, you'll be Macduff. Everyone, open your scripts, and we'll see how far we get before the bell."

Paul only half listened as the understudies read lines. How had things gone from top of the world last night to his play's villain being sent to the hospital this morning? Perhaps the play really was cursed.

No, he couldn't think that way. Accidents happen. Seventeen-year-old boys were constantly hurting themselves. They still carried a sense of youthful indestructibility, taking risks and operating with general inattentiveness until life stepped up and hit them in the face a few times. How else could you explain falling down a flight of stairs that was crowded with students? No curse. Life had simply hit Kim Greyson in the face. Perhaps he'd tread more carefully going forward.

When class ended, a student Paul didn't know entered the auditorium and handed him a note. He didn't have to read it. With a sigh, he headed toward the principal's office.

Principal Winston was old school. He handed out detentions like they were candy and made the students do work as penance. Most of the students in his waiting area were in detention, waiting for Winston to give them an assignment. Completing the assignment usually meant that detention was over. Neither was Winston above pulling teachers out of class, even though the school board gave him grief over it. Paul was certain that the old fart would have teachers serving detention if he could get away with it.

There were three students still in detention when Paul arrived outside the principal's office: Winston's private workforce.

Once Mrs. Kennedy nodded Paul inside, the school principal greeted him with a pronouncement: "Your play is cancelled."

That took Paul by surprise. The production was in its first week. It usually took at least ten days before Winston reached the point where he threatened to cancel. Paul offered his traditional response. "Because?"

Winston grunted. "I would think that was obvious. One of your students is in the hospital. His parents have already called and given me an earful. The play is too dangerous, so I'm shutting it down."

Paul was stunned. That was absurd, even for Winston. "Kim didn't hurt himself in my class. He fell down the south stairwell. Using that logic, you will have to shut down the school, not the play."

It was Winston's turn to look stunned. Eventually he frowned and loosened his tie, which to Paul's eye already looked plenty loose. "He was on his way to your class."

"It could have been any student falling down those stairs." Paul shook his head. "This is just a lame excuse, and I can't think of anyone who won't see it as such. Go ahead and cancel the play. Then you can get thirty more phone calls from angry parents."

Winston let that run through his mind for a moment. "Get out of here."

Paul kept the smile from his face as he left the office and closed the door.

"The drama teacher wins another round?" asked Mrs. Kennedy.

Paul nodded. "That man gets more mental every year."

Mrs. Kennedy chuckled. "Then he'll make superintendent in no time."

Scene 17: Contradict Thyself, and Say It Is Not So

EMPLOYING A PLASTIC spoon, Agatha churned the remains of an extra-large Mint-Oreo Blizzard. "I still can't get used to this concept of weekends off," the tall witch said.

The three hags had changed seats, with Agatha now sitting by the window with her back against the wall. Gertrude shared the same bench, while Netty occupied most of the opposite bench all on her own. It had taken them a week to reach this arrangement. Witches were like cats that way.

"Waste of a perfectly good building," Gertrude said. "Standing empty for two full days out of every seven."

Netty bobbed her round head. "When I went to school, the building never stood empty. Classroom by day. Tavern by evening. Sleep house by night. Used as a church on Sundays."

The other two hags stared at her. "You went to school?"

The onion-shaped hag cackled. "No, I just slept there!"

"What about Saturdays?" asked Agatha. "You said the building never stood empty."

"Got hosed down on Saturdays."

"All day?"

Netty flashed a gap-toothed smile. "Needed lots of hosing."

"Especially since you slept there," Gertrude said, nodding her crooked head.

The three hags all cackled.

Agatha gazed out the window toward the high school across the street. "With no one there all weekend, we'll have to hold off on the curses until Monday."

"Oh, my!" Gertrude said. "Does that mean that we get the weekend off?"

"I've never had a weekend off," Netty admitted. "Wouldn't know what to do with one."

"You could take up cribbage," Gertrude suggested.

"Cribbage?" Netty scowled at the deformed hag. "Is that a vegetable?"

"It's a card game," said Agatha. "With pegs."

Netty looked thoughtful. "You poke the cards with pegs?"

Agatha stared at her. Then she said, "Yes."

"Our Agatha is in a cribbage league," Gertrude said. "Plays most Saturday afternoons. What's that league called?"

"The BCC," grumbled Agatha.

Netty smacked her thick lips together, working her tongue around a loose tooth. "The British Broadcasting Corporation?"

Agatha sighed. "The British Cribbage Congress."

"Well," said Netty. "You certainly don't seem happy about it."

Gertrude chortled. "Agatha must be down in the standings."

Agatha threw down her spoon. "I am *not* down in the standings! I'm in second place."

"Then why so glum?" Netty asked, pushing several fries into her mouth. "Second place isn't bad. Though I'm a bit surprised. A small curse here and a slight nudge there, and you could be in first place. Why aren't you in first place?"

"Because," Agatha said, grating her crooked teeth, "Hecate is in first place."

"You called?" Hecate asked from where she suddenly sat next to Netty on the bench across the booth from Gertrude and Agatha. The senior witch had her midnight hair up, and her dragon skin cloak was studded with diamonds.

"All dressed up and nowhere to go?" asked Gertrude.

Hecate smiled. "I'm off to the opera. *Die Meistersinger von Nürnberg.* One of my favourites."

"I always find Wagner a bit tedious," Agatha said, "especially *Die Meistersinger.* Four and a half hours. What was the man thinking?"

"This one will be three hours," Hecate said. "I'm going to burn down the opera house at the opening of the third act."

"Oh, my!" said Gertrude. "That sounds like fun."

"More fun than cribbage," Netty agreed. "Sounds daft, poking pegs through cards."

"Yes, well . . ." Hecate gave Netty a peculiar look. "Everyone needs a little down time. Cribbage is a good way to let off a little steam."

Gertrude snorted. "Let off a little steam? National competitive cribbage?"

Hecate shrugged. "Never do anything small. And speaking of small, I see your Thane of Glamis coming." As quickly as she had appeared, Hecate was gone.

"I hate that witch," Agatha said.

Lenny Cadwell threw himself down into the space Hecate had vacated. "Kim broke his leg."

"Kim?" echoed Netty. "Who's that?"

Lenny twisted sideways and looked down into the bulbous witch's rubbery face. "My classmate who was going to be Macbeth. Now I've got the role."

"Oh, what a coincidence," said Gertrude. "Isn't that the role you wanted?"

"You broke his leg!" said Lenny. He glared at all three of the witches.

"Did nothing of the kind," refuted Agatha.

"That's right," said Gertrude. "We haven't moved from this spot all day."

"All week," corrected Netty.

"All week," Gertrude admitted. "Well, we have switched seats."

"We were right here sipping cherry colas when the poor lad had his spill," said Agatha.

"At the end of first period," Netty added.

"Poor lad." Gertrude wagged her crooked head. "I understand that a broken fibula can be quite painful. A bruised patella can hurt even more."

Agatha let out a loud cackle then covered her mouth with her hand. "Sorry. I don't know where that came from."

"You're not going to do anything else, are you?" Lenny asked. "I mean, I have the role now. You've kept your promise. No one else needs to get hurt."

"No one else needs to get hurt." Agatha rolled the words off her tongue. "I rather like that line. Do you mind if a borrow it? It could come in handy."

Lenny stared at her. Then he rose from his seat and wandered out of the Dairy Queen.

Once the door closed, Gertrude said, "Not as dumb as he looks, that one."

Agatha stared at her, straight faced, and said, "No one else needs to get hurt."

All three witches burst out laughing.

Scene 18: Now Is the Time of Help

FRIDAY EVENING AND Susie was off somewhere with her friends. Sylvia joined Paul in the dining room for supper, but the energy of the previous two family meals was absent. Missing was Susie's excitement about her newly discovered interest in theatre, and Paul was in a foul mood about Kim Greyson's injury.

He knew that the injury had nothing to do with his choice of play. If he had been forced to do *Death of a Salesman* again or, God forbid, *Grease*, Kim would still have fallen down the stairs and Lenny would now be Willy Loman or Danny Zuko. And Lenny should have the lead anyway. He was a better actor than Kim. Paul was just loath to feed the boy's prima donna attitude. Lenny needed a setback if he was ever to learn anything, but it looked like that setback would have to be something other than not playing the role of Macbeth. The idea that The Bard's Play was actually cursed was ridiculous.

"I was wondering if I could help with the play," Sylvia said from out of nowhere, shipwrecking his thoughts.

Paul's fork froze midway to his mouth. "Help?"

"With the play," Sylvia repeated.

"Er."

"It would be fun." Sylvia smiled.

"I, uh, don't know what Susie would think. I mean. It's bad enough that she has to be in her dad's class. But with her mother too . . ."

"It was Susie's idea," his wife said. "Look, the housing market is in a shambles. I haven't had calls from anyone looking to buy or sell in days. I need something to keep myself busy."

Paul coughed. "I don't think the school is actually keen on teachers bringing their spouses to work. Winston would lay an egg."

Sylvia laughed but whether it was at the image of the Ashcroft Senior High School principal laying an egg or his spouse-to-work comment, Paul didn't know.

"Don't be silly," Sylvia said. "I wouldn't help as your spouse but as Susie's mother. You've had students' parents help with plays before."

Paul bought himself some time by wiping his mouth with a napkin, but he was still at a loss for what to say. "Sometimes that's unavoidable," he began and realized immediately that he had taken the wrong tack. "I mean, most of that help was less than . . . helpful." Even worse.

Sylvia glowered at him. "You're not suggesting that I'd just get in the way?"

"No, no, no," Paul said, though that's exactly what he meant. "It's just awkward for the students when one of them has a parent running shotgun in the classroom." He could see from his wife's expression that he had failed to help matters.

"Susie already has a parent in the classroom," Sylvia said. "I don't know how you can get more shotgun than by being the teacher."

Paul had no choice but to give in. If he kept on the way he was going, he'd be eating his shoes for dessert. "You're right, dear. Of course. And since Susie's agreeable, I don't see a problem. What did you have in mind?"

Sylvia smiled her "score one for me" smile. "Why, set designer, of course. Architecture is my forte."

Set designer? Paul wasn't sure how ten years of putting for sale signs on people's lawns earned you a forte in architecture, but he decided that allowing his wife to take a stab at set design wouldn't be disastrous.

Before he could say anything, Sylvia reached over to the counter and retrieved a DVD still in its shrink-wrapped plastic case. She turned its face toward him. It was the 1971 Roman Polanski film adaptation of *Macbeth*.

"We can watch the movie tonight, and I'll make set notes."

Paul nodded his head. It might be worthwhile watching the film again. "But tomorrow night we'll watch the 1948 Orson Welles version. I think you'll find its set easier to emulate. It also lacks Lady Macbeth's nude sleepwalking scene that Polanski included."

"Nude!" said Sylvia. "Not our Susie!"

"You can't go wrong with Orson Welles," Paul said.

While his wife pontificated on the audacity of modern directors adding nude scenes to PG-13 classics, Paul recalled the other problem with the Roman Polanski version. After his pregnant wife and several friends were murdered by Charles

Manson's followers, the director had dropped his current project and proceeded to develop the film version of *Macbeth* that Sylvia had just purchased. Some people theorized that Polanski had already decided to start the *Macbeth* project, and that it was the play's curse that had given rise to the murders in his home.

The curse again. Paul had the horrible feeling that he wasn't going to be able to escape it.

-ᗩᑕт ΙΙ-

Scene 1: And Thus I Clothe My Naked Villainy

"ATTENTION, EVERYONE." PAUL found that he had to use his megaphone to bring his class to order. Mondays were like that sometimes.

"I hope you all had an enjoyable weekend and that you spent part of it learning your lines."

Grumbling eddied among the students.

"I'd like to introduce Susie's mother, Mrs. Samson. She has graciously volunteered to help us with sets and costumes."

"Hello, everyone," Sylvia said. "I'm thrilled to be here."

The grumbling evolved into a halfhearted chorus of "hi" and "welcome."

Paul continued. "While I walk small groups through some of their lines, Mrs. Samson is going to come around and speak with the rest of you, taking your measurements, and discussing costume ideas. As you know from previous years, our wardrobe department consists of two racks filled with cast-off clothing. Our prop closet isn't much better. We'll be relying on class members to contribute toward props and costumes. Nothing fancy, but the more authentic the production looks, the better your individual performance will be received."

A huge outpouring of breath greeted that.

Paul was neither surprised nor discouraged by the lack of enthusiasm. As with every school production, those students with true interest would eventually put some effort into their costumes and find things at home to enhance the stage. None of them ever did at the beginning.

Lenny put his hand in the air.

"Yes, Lenny?"

"I already have a costume." He held up a gym bag.

Now Paul was surprised.

"Can I go to the changing room and put it on?" Lenny asked.

"Please do," said Sylvia, excitement in her eyes.

"Of course," Paul said.

A few minutes later, the young man paraded across the stage dressed in black boots, black pants, black shirt, and a black cape. A large silver brooch tied the cape just above his heart. In his hand he carried a silver sword. And on his head he wore a thin, silver crown.

The class went, "Ooh!"

"Very good," Paul said. In fifteen years of teaching, he had never seen a boy come in with a better costume. The girls usually did quite well, but the boys rarely made more than a token effort.

"It's very . . . black," Sylvia said.

"I'm the villain." Lenny looked at her with an expression that clearly stated that his attire should be self-explanatory.

"I see," said Sylvia, just as clearly not seeing.

Paul tried to salvage things. "Now let's see the rest of you start working on your costumes. And think about things you may have around the house that may work as props."

Sylvia added, "On Friday, wear some clothing you don't mind getting paint on. We'll be painting scenery flats."

Paul opened his mouth but didn't say anything. You don't get the entire class painting flats. Just four of five are needed. Well, he doubted more than five students would come prepared.

Instead he said, "Let's get started, shall we? You've all read through your lines. Now it's time to think about what props you may want to use to embellish your words. The stage is a visual art. What you do with your facial expressions, your movements, and your props often says more than your dialogue. I expect you all to come up with ideas. Don't go too hog wild. We're not going to use machine guns instead of swords. Speaking of swords, that's one of the few items that we have plenty of in our supply cupboard."

Paul reached into a large, cardboard box he had retrieved

from the cupboard before class and brandished a gunmetal grey sword.

"I already have a sword," Lenny said. He brandished the silver sword he had brought with this costume. Like the ones in the box, it was painted plastic.

"You can use that one, Lenny," Paul said. "The Thanes and the English soldiers will also need swords. Mrs. Samson has thirty large shopping bags, the durable paper kind with twine handles. Everyone take one and write your name on it. These are where you will store your costumes and any personal props for your character. Keep them backstage by the supply cupboard."

Anna Bortolotto raised her hand. "I'm a stagehand. I don't have a costume."

"Not just any stagehand, Anna. You are the *lead* stagehand." Paul reached into a second box and retrieved a blank notebook. "Your job is to keep a list of all nonpersonal props. In your copy of the script, you will make notes for the movement of all the props listed in your notebook. During rehearsal and the public performance, you will ensure that those props are where they should be, when they should be. That includes the scenery flats, tables, chairs, and any other set pieces."

Anna's eyes nearly exploded. "That's more work than acting!"

"You should have considered that during auditions."

"But . . . but . . ."

Paul couldn't keep the smile from his face any longer. "And that's why you have six assistants. But you'll lose three during the performance. Trevor and Jocelynn will be ushers, and Sally will run the lights.

"None of you will need costumes, but you will need to wear dark clothing. Black shoes and pants. Black turtlenecks if you have them. Stagehands must be as invisible as possible. It doesn't hurt for the ushers to wear black either."

From the second box, he pulled out a rolled-up newspaper tied with string. "Does anyone know what this is? Come on, you saw it in second year."

Lenny said, "A fake prop."

Paul nodded. "We'll use these when the script calls for a missing prop." He waggled the newspaper. "The sooner we stop using these, the better. Okay. I have a dozen swords and one dagger in this box. Who thinks they need one?"

Scene 2: With Thy Keen Sword Impress

"GAH!" NETTY SPAT great gobs of chili, cheese, and mystery meat all across the plastic surface of the table shared by the three witches. "This doesn't taste like any dog I've ever eaten."

Agatha stared down her long nose at the mess and managed not to comment.

Gertrude chuckled. "You can't say I didn't warn you. It's a rare fool who doesn't know that canines and cheeses don't mix."

"Netty is a rare one," Agatha said, no longer able to hold her tongue.

The two witches cackled together while Netty fumed and rinsed out her mouth with soda pop.

"I fail to see the humour," said Hecate, who stood suddenly by the table, scowling distastefully at Netty's lunch, even though the senior witch looked little better. Hecate was dressed from head to foot in heavy, grime-stained grey denim, her luxurious, black hair tucked up beneath a hard hat. Thick dust coated her face but failed to mask the woman's elegant bone structure and inherent beauty.

"Been sweeping chimneys?" asked Gertrude. "Heh. Now that's an honest profession."

"Don't be ridiculous," said the senior witch. "There are no honest professions. And chimneys haven't needed sweeping since the invention of the gas furnace. I was paying a visit to the Kunynak silver mine in Uzbekistan."

"Hmph," said Agatha. "Visiting Kunynak is number two thousand six hundred and twenty-seven on my bucket list."

"You have a bucket list?" asked Netty. "Why would you include a silver mine on a list of buckets?"

Agatha ignored the onion-shaped witch. "Some of the silver from that mine is used by goblins to make jewellery." The tall witch lifted a tarnished pendant that hung from a thin chain around her shrivelled neck. "A niece who lives in Kunynak bought this for me some years ago."

"You have a niece?" asked Netty.

Agatha continued to ignore her. "It's the only thing anyone has ever given me. I'd always hoped to visit my niece and the mine

50

someday."

"Well, you can strike Kunynak off your list of buckets," Hecate said. "I turned all of the support beams into kindling and buried the mine under a mountain. There's nothing left to see."

Agatha's fingers froze on her pendant, and her eyes bulged.

"Why would you do that?" asked Gertrude. "Kunynak seems a little out of the way, even for you."

Hecate sniffed. "I had a lover there once."

"You had a lover?" asked Netty.

Everyone ignored her.

"And?" Gertrude asked.

Hecate looked at her. "And he was in the mine when I buried it."

"Oh, my." Gertrude smiled wickedly. "Lovers' spat, huh? He done you wrong? Left you for another woman?"

"None of the above," said Hecate. "I murder all my lovers. Just me being me. Now down to business. How is your curse coming along?"

Gertrude snorted. "We broke a budding actor's leg."

A mewling sound came from Netty. "He lost the lead role and has been reduced to playing Thane Agnes."

Agatha, having partially recovered from her shock and disappointment, let out a heavy sigh. "By Thane Agnes, Netty means Thane Angus."

"Ah!" said Netty. "So you *are* listening to me."

"Hmm," said Hecate. "I never liked Angus. He was always a bit of a ponce. But that's it? A broken leg. You've been on this for a week. I expected more."

"It's just the setup," Gertrude said. "Our candidate is still on the rise. Heh. We haven't begun to knock him down yet."

"Rome wasn't burned in a day," Netty said.

"Yes," said Hecate. "It was." Then she vanished.

"I don't believe it!" Netty said.

"That Hecate murders her lovers?" asked Gertrude.

Agatha snorted. "Comes as no surprise."

"No!" Netty's cheeks shook like jelly. "That Rome was burned in a day. I'm sure it smouldered for at least a week."

Agatha's gnarled fingers fiddled with her pendant. "I suppose we may as well decide what tragedy should befall the play to put our young Macbeth out of business."

"We could break his leg," Netty suggested. "Maybe knock him down some stairs."

The squat hag's two sisters looked at her.

"We did that last week," Gertrude said.

"We told Hecate about it thirty seconds ago," Agatha added.

"Oh." Netty pushed a fistful of fries into her mouth. "I thought I'd seen it done somewhere."

"I do love a good broken bone," Gertrude said. "Perhaps we should break the injured boy's other leg."

Agatha drummed gnarled fingers against her lips. "During rehearsal. A battle scene accident, perhaps. Macbeth could fatally stab him."

"What?" asked Gertrude. "In the knee?"

Agatha shrugged.

"Don't these actors use wooden swords?" asked Netty.

"Plastic," Gertrude said. "Safer than wood."

"Safe!" Netty was so scandalized, she spit out a mouthful of mushed French fries, adding them to the spewed chili dog on the table. "What good is a sword fight if it's safe? Who would waste their time watching grown men hitting each other with plastic tubing?"

"These aren't grown men," Agatha said. "These are schoolchildren. But I agree. I haven't seen a decent gladiator fight in centuries."

Gertrude weaved her fingers together in a show of concentration. "We could replace Macbeth's plastic sword with the real thing," she suggested. "Heh. Fake weapons are accidentally replaced by real ones all the time."

"Like on *Miami Vice*," Agatha said, "when the starter pistol was discovered to be a real handgun."

"Don Johnson!" Netty crowed, causing heads all throughout the restaurant to turn. "So dreamy! I mean," the bulbous witch lowered her voice to a soft screech, "he truly brought his character to life."

"Or *Murder, She Wrote*," Gertrude suggested. "The retractable blade that wasn't, so the womanizing stage actor got gutted like a fish."

Agatha nodded.

"My favourite episode," Netty added, "was where the supposed fresh fish was frozen, so instead of catching his dinner, the startled tourist received a pickerel, bang, straight through the heart."

"I don't think I saw that one," Gertrude said.

"So it's settled, then?" asked Agatha. "Netty will swap our Macbeth's plastic sword for a real one, and Macbeth will serve his predecessor a fatal blow to the knee?"

The three witches cackled.

"As soon as the boy's back in school," Netty added.

The other two witches looked at her.

Agatha snorted through her long nose. "The boy's not back in school? It's been three days!"

"If I broke my leg," Gertrude said, "I'd be back on the job in three minutes."

Netty let out a shrill laugh and grinned at her bent and misshapen sister. "If you broke your leg, who'd notice?"

All three hags burst into laughter.

"No matter." Agatha cast a dark gaze around the table. "Our Macbeth shall wield his sword, and the stage shall become watered with blood."

The three witches nodded agreement then looked down at the spoiled tabletop as though Netty's spewed lunch were the blood of drama students. Silence enshrouded the restaurant booth until Netty said, "I'm going to order another chili cheese dog!"

Agatha and Gertrude turned their astonished gaze toward the rotund witch.

"I'll tell them to hold the cheese this time." Netty wiggled one of her loose teeth with her tongue. "And the dog too." She sniffed at the table. "And possibly the chili."

Scene 3: Unwelcome Things

PAUL HAD TO admit that he was getting used to Sylvia's coming to school with him for his morning class with his senior students. Of course, his wife still had her real estate work and other things to do for the house, so they couldn't drive in together, which meant bringing both cars. And since Susie started school sometimes earlier and sometimes later than Paul, she usually caught a ride with a friend.

That all three family members took three different vehicles to get to the same place within an hour of each other screamed dysfunction of some kind. Likely it was the same kind that prevented them from sitting down for supper at the same time. Sometimes Paul wondered what the world would be like if families spent more time together.

The one drawback of having his wife as a workmate was that it had become more difficult to find a parking spot. With Sylvia helping him prepare for class, he could often arrive twenty minutes later than he normally would, meaning he was sometimes the last teacher to arrive at the school. And he needed a second stall for Sylvia's car. But the aggravation was worth it. Twenty extra minutes first thing in the morning was worth an hour at any other time of the day. Paul was enjoying being spoiled.

After finding a parking spot and climbing out of his car, he grabbed his briefcase and waited for Sylvia. His wife parked in the only remaining stall and joined him on the way to the main entrance.

"I'll have a word with Winston," Paul said. "It's the same thing every year. Over the summer, students somehow forget all of the school regulations, including that they aren't allowed to park in the teachers' lot."

Sylvia patted him on the arm. "The students' lot is filled to overflowing. I don't wonder that they park wherever they can."

Paul turned in a circle as he walked, his arm flung wide to take in the whole area. "The school is surrounded by residential streets. It wouldn't kill a healthy, young teenager to walk a block."

"Or a teacher," Sylvia said.

Paul smiled. "I miss the good old days. When I was in high school, perhaps a dozen students drove cars."

"And when I was a teenager," Sylvia said, "I had to walk twenty miles to school, uphill, both directions."

"What?"

Sylvia laughed. "That's what you'll sound like if you tell your classes that, in your day, students walked to school."

Paul laughed as well, knowing she was right, and stooped to pick up a piece of litter outside the school entrance. It was a white slip of paper the size of a book cover. The side facing up was blank. He turned it over and saw what he could only describe as a cartoon witch, complete with long nose; warts; and a tall, pointy hat. Stamped over the witch was a red circle with a diagonal line running through it.

Sylvia looked over his shoulder and read the caption. "Witches are not welcome at Ashcroft High."

"What cereal box did this come out of?" Paul crumpled the paper in preparation to toss it into the recycling bin he knew was just inside the school's doors.

"You don't suppose it has anything to do with the play?" Sylvia asked. "You did say that Mrs. Cadwell has a bee in her bonnet about witches."

"Of course it's about the play," Paul said. "I'm surprised it took Cadwell this long to take another shot at me."

Paul tried to push open the swinging door of the recycle bin lid, but it wouldn't budge.

"Let me," said Sylvia. She grabbed the entire lid with both hands and pulled it off the bin.

Paul's jaw dropped when he saw that the bin was filled to the brim with leaflets. He pulled out three that were in reasonable shape and tossed in the crumpled one so Sylvia could replace the lid.

"Not that Winston won't have seen them already," Paul said as he slipped the leaflets into a pocket of his sport coat. "The things I miss when I come to school twenty minutes late."

Scene 4: And on Thy Blade and Dudgeon Gouts of Blood

THE HALLWAYS BETWEEN the main entrance and the Ashcroft-Tate Auditorium were strewn with leaflets. Paul glanced down a side hallway and saw Jerry Noonan, the caretaker, pushing a broom with a hundred pounds of paper in front of it.

Sylvia put a hand over her mouth. "I can't believe this. That poor caretaker."

Paul sighed. "Students pull stunts like this all the time. It takes an exceptional parent to outdo them."

"Parent? You mean Mrs. Cadwell? Where did she get all the paper?"

"I hope she bought it, and the printing, with PTA funds." Paul grimaced. "If she used school supplies, we'll be printing our play programs on toilet paper."

When they arrived at the auditorium, Paul expected to find a truckload of paper blocking the stage area and possibly the theatre seating as well. The play could well be cancelled by the simple expedient that the Ashcroft-Tate Auditorium would be closed for cleaning. But the stage and seating were untouched.

Sylvia must have had the same expectation. "Has the caretaker been here already?"

Paul shook his head. "No point leaving leaflets here. It would be like singing at deaf people."

The students began arriving after the second-period bell, and Paul was surprised to see many of them clutching familiar leaflets.

"Gemma?" he asked. "What are those papers stuffed between the pages of your script?"

Paul's Witch Number Three grabbed a fistful of leaflets and fanned herself. "Souvenirs, Mr. Samson. I'm going to take some home for my hope chest."

Paul couldn't argue with that. He had three souvenirs of his own, though he preferred to think of them as evidence.

Sylvia murmured to him in a low voice, "If that's what Gemma keeps in her hope chest, I pity her future husband."

"I suspect she meant something else. A scrap box, perhaps."

His wife looked at him, so Paul clarified. "A three-dimensional scrap book? I don't know what kids call things these days."

Lenny Cadwell slouched into the auditorium with more than just his usual disinterest on his face. Paul had expected embarrassment, but what he saw was anger. He tried and failed to imagine what Lenny's next conversation with his mother would look like.

Then Paul found himself feeling an unexpected emotion of his own: guilt. Susie's passion for the play had brought them closer than they had been in years, while Lenny's passion alienated him from his mother. He briefly wondered if there was some sort of relationship karma whose balance had to be maintained.

Since there was nothing he could say or do that would be helpful, he started the class. "I don't see anyone with their prop bags. Please go and get them."

While the students wandered off backstage, Paul continued speaking through the megaphone so they could hear him. "Dress rehearsals won't begin for a while yet, so you don't have to get into costume, but I do want you to get into the habit of keeping tabs on your costumes and props." Secretly, though, Paul just wanted his students to feel embarrassed about hauling out an empty bag each morning and remind them to think about their costumes and personal props.

When the students returned to the front of the stage area, Lenny carried a torn bag in one hand and his prop sword in the other. His anger from earlier had been replaced by astonishment.

"What is it, Lenny?"

Lenny let the ripped bag containing his Macbeth costume fall to the floor and held the sword by the pommel with both hands. "I think this is a real sword."

Paul couldn't help but be amused. This was the best acting he had ever seen from Lenny. "Why would you think it's a real sword?"

"It weighs a ton," Lenny said. "And it cut my finger."

Paul leaped off his director's chair. Even before he was close enough to confiscate the sword, he could see that the blade wasn't hollow plastic. The weapon's design was identical to the silver sword Lenny had bought with his costume, but it lacked the waxy look of plastic.

Sure enough, when Lenny let him take the sword, Paul guessed that it weighed at least two and a half pounds. There was a splash of red along one edge—blood.

He stared at the boy but couldn't see where Lenny had hurt himself. He hoped that meant that it wasn't much worse than a paper cut. "Lenny, please report to the nurse. You'll need disinfectant and a bandage."

Lenny gawked at him. "It's just a flesh wound." Then he smiled as if at a secret joke.

Hardly secret, Paul thought. What drama teacher doesn't recognize *Monty Python* when he hears it? "Even so," he said, "school policy."

As Lenny wandered off, Paul tried to think of what he should do with the sword. He didn't know if his heart could take two stunts in one morning. But who would do something as dangerous as replacing a plastic prop with a real sword? Someone could have gotten hurt.

The obvious candidate was the same woman who had printed the leaflets. The students getting hold of a real sword could get the play cancelled, especially if someone got hurt. Still . . . the gorgon lady might be two geese short of a gaggle, but Paul couldn't imagine her endangering any student, never mind her own son.

He turned to Sylvia. "Get the kids started with the cauldron scene. I'll be back after I lock this in the trunk of my car."

"You're what?" Paul's wife pressed up close and hissed into his ear. "You have to turn this over to the school. I'm not a teacher, but even I know that."

"Technically," Paul whispered back. "But Winston is looking for any excuse to cancel this play. He'll have a heyday with a real sword being found in the auditorium."

"How are you going to keep it from him?" Sylvia demanded.

Paul shrugged. "One problem at a time."

Sylvia was shaking her head in disbelief as Paul turned away. He knew she was right but refused to let the gorgon lady win so easily. Cadwell had to be behind the sword, and if he could prove it, Winston could hardly reward her by cancelling the play.

As he walked down a leaflet-strewn hallway toward the main doors and the parking lot, it occurred to Paul that the sword prank had effected one good thing: it had put a smile on Lenny's face.

Scene 5: This Is the Air-Drawn Dagger

"It's HARDLY A decent likeness," suggested Gertrude. "Heh. Though the artist has captured your eyes."

Agatha twisted her upper lip. "That isn't me. And the eyes are just dots."

Gertrude looked up at the tall witch and smiled. "Your point?"

"My point," said Agatha, "is that I don't wear hats. My hair won't allow it. Netty wears a hat."

Netty snorted, spitting soda across the table. "When I pose for a picture, all they get is my hat."

Agatha further curled her lip into a full-fledged scowl. "You were supposed to give Macbeth a sword. Not leave these . . . unwanted posters all over the school."

Netty picked up the leaflet they had been studying and chewed on a corner of it. "Bah! Tastes terrible. I didn't leave these. I just brought one back with me. Although . . . the likeness does look like Agatha when she was younger. Didn't you used to wear a hat?"

"Well, I didn't make these posters." Agatha looked at Gertrude.

"Not me. It was Netty's turn to curse."

"I did the sword," Netty said. She reached beneath the table and held up a plastic silver sword. She waggled her hand, and the blade blurred with movement.

"I didn't realize you were good with a sword," said Agatha. "I've never seen a blade move that fast."

"That's because it's hollow." Netty stopped waggling her hand and smacked Gertrude on the top of the head with the blade.

Gertrude tensed then frowned. "You couldn't cut water with that sword."

Netty tossed the plastic sword into the air and it vanished. "Weighs less than water too."

Agatha looked thoughtful. "The real sword you left in its place. Does it weigh less than water?"

Netty opened her mouth then closed it. Her eyes wandered around in their sockets and rolled like marbles settling in a roulette wheel. "Shouldn't we order some food?"

Agatha glared at her.

"I've always preferred daggers over swords." Gertrude chuckled. "Easier to conceal about your person, and they get the job done."

"Daggers have been done to death," said Agatha. She picked up the leaflet and scowled. "I did have a hat like this once. 'Witches are not welcome at Ashcroft High.' Sisters, I think we need to find out who it is who doesn't welcome us . . . and say hello."

Scene 6: Thou Liest, Thou Shag-Hair'd Villain!

PAUL HAD BEEN so distracted by the real sword in Lenny's prop bag that he had forgotten to drop by Winston's office and mention the parking problem. As a result, the following morning, he and Sylvia had been forced to park both cars in front of someone's house two blocks from the school and walk in.

"Are you sure it was a good idea to bring that sword home?" Sylvia asked. "I thought the school kept a closet full of confiscated items."

"Water pistols and bubblegum," Paul said. "If I turn in a sword, Winston's going to want to know where I got it."

"Won't Winston hear about it, anyway? That's not the kind of thing that principals don't hear about."

"The sword will be less real if I describe it rather than let Winston wield it about his office." An image of Winston doing just that flashed through Paul's thoughts. The stout man was laughing manically as he spun the sword, double fisted, around the office, smashing furniture and slicing the wallpaper to ribbons.

"Good luck explaining why you took it home," Sylvia said.

Outside the main doors to the school, Paul stooped to pick up a piece of paper. It sported a cartoon drawing stamped over by a red circle with a diagonal line running through it.

Sylvia looked over his shoulder and read the caption: *PTA is not welkom at Ashkroft High.*

Paul ignored the spelling mistakes and stared at the cartoon.

"Hmm," said Sylvia. "Mrs. Cadwell appears to be having a bad hair day."

"That is Mrs. Cadwell, isn't it?" Paul groaned and stuffed the leaflet into a coat pocket. "I thought it might be one of the antiwitch leaflets. With what we saw yesterday, they'll be popping up for weeks. I can't imagine where this one came from. I hope not many were printed."

Paul's hopes were dashed when he opened the door to the school.

Sylvia gasped.

The hallways were a sea of paper, the polished linoleum floor visible only where the tramping of students' feet had cleared a path. The walls were papered with leaflets. As was the ceiling. Amidst the carnage stood a lone student whose expression indicated he had been waiting for Paul to arrive.

"I have a note for you, Mr. Samson."

"Of course you do," Paul said. "Sylvia, please manage the class for me until I get there."

Paul had to guess that the rest of the school fared no better than the entrance. He saw nothing but paper the entire way toward Winston's wrath. As he neared the principal's office, he spotted Jerry the caretaker shaking a broom at a hallway ceiling. Leaflets rained down on him wherever the broom touched.

"Thank God the students didn't use glue," Jerry said. "I don't know what's causing them to stick, but they let go easy enough."

Paul pulled one of the leaflets off the wall, and it virtually fell into his hand. He ran his thumb across the back of the paper and against the wall but found nothing. "Static?"

"Beats me," Jerry said.

Paul had never known Mrs. Kennedy not to have a smile, but as he approached the secretary's desk, he saw that today was an exception.

"This has gone too far," the fifty-something woman said. "Yesterday was too far, and today is farther."

"I agree completely," Paul said, pausing by her desk and nodding vigorously. Agreeing with the school secretary was never a bad idea. "The sooner we find out who is responsible, the sooner that student and Mrs. Cadwell can spend a month in detention."

"Mrs. Cadwell?" Mrs. Kennedy cast Paul a perplexed stare. "But she's the victim."

"She's today's victim," Paul agreed. "But she's yesterday's prankster."

Mrs. Kennedy ground her teeth. "Apparently there are no regulations prohibiting the PTA from distributing leaflets."

Paul snorted. "Distributing leaflets? Is that what that was?"

"You'd better go in," Mrs. Kennedy said. "Mr. Winston is waiting for you."

Winston's face was stormier than Mrs. Kennedy's. And it was only Wednesday.

"Please tell me," Winston bellowed, "that you are not responsible for this fiasco!"

"Okay," Paul said. "I am not responsible for this fiasco."

"I'm being serious!"

"So am I." Paul shook his head. "I was more surprised by today's leaflets than I was by yesterday's."

Winston sighed and leaned back into his chair. "Mrs. Cadwell was responsible for yesterday's leaflets."

"Of course she was. She's the only person in this school who spends more than five seconds thinking about witches. And she's probably the only one who might think that littering the hallways with leaflets will convince anyone of anything."

Winston wiped his face with a handkerchief and frowned. "There's at least one other person who believes in leaflets. The person who retaliated this morning. It wasn't you?"

Paul couldn't believe that Winston regarded him as a suspect. "I consider myself fortunate that I know how to spell *welcome* and the name of the school."

Winston shook his head. "I can only assume that the misspellings are intentional, but for the life of me, I can't imagine why."

Paul had to agree. Not even the worst student's spelling was that bad. "They do make the anti-PTA prankster seem illiterate. Unless . . ." No, it was just too insane to be true.

"Unless what?" asked Winston.

"Unless the anti-PTA prankster is the PTA."

"What?"

"Think about it," Paul said. "If illiterate kids oppose the PTA, that only strengthens the PTA's position."

Winston worked his jaw. "No, I don't buy it. And Mrs. Cadwell was scandalized by the cartoon. None of her people would risk that. Did you notice the hair?"

Paul had to admit that Winston had a point. "Where is Mrs. Cadwell, anyway? I expected her to be here with two beams of wood, several nails, and a hammer."

"Gone home." A twisted smile worked its way across the principal's face. "Said the embarrassment was more than she could endure and that she wasn't coming back until every last leaflet was destroyed." He raised a hand to prevent Paul from commenting. "I know. It's tempting to put a few out each day for the rest of the year. Don't think I haven't considered it."

That was exactly what Paul was going to suggest.

Winston shook his head. "Cadwell may be embarrassed now, but she's not stupid. She'll be in my office by Friday, laying an egg."

Paul sighed. "Yes, she will. I'll ask my students what they know about today's leaflets, but I don't expect a confession." He turned to leave.

"Samson. Cadwell hasn't mentioned anything yet about a real sword showing up in your drama class."

Paul's hand froze on the doorknob. "Right." Paul turned around. "Leaflets aren't this week's only prank."

The principal continued. "A weapon on school property is hardly a prank. I suspect that she will mention it, rather loudly, the next time she barges into my office."

"Perhaps . . ." Paul decided to take a gamble. "Could you mention it before she does?"

Winston's eyes narrowed.

"I didn't come to you yesterday to complain about Cadwell's leaflets. And I didn't come and complain about the sword she sabotaged—"

"Cadwell? She may be crazier than a sack of rabid weasels, but she'd never endanger a student."

Paul made his play. "If it wasn't her, it was one of Cadwell's PTA sycophants. Or a student who helped with her leaflets. I find it more than coincidental that the sword was planted at the same time that the PTA was littering the hallways. Regardless, it was an obvious attempt to sabotage the play, and I hold Cadwell personally responsible. She's the one leading the charge."

Again, Winston worked his jaw. "You want me to tell Cadwell that you hold her responsible for a sword showing up in your drama class? I'm not your bloody mother!"

Damn. Paul had never been much good at gambling. "Just let her know that I complained to you about the prank before she did."

Winston shook his head. "That woman has never taken responsibility for anything, and your accusation is just that, an accusation. She's going to make a counteraccusation that one of your students played a dangerous prank on her son. Oh, yes, I know it was Lenny Cadwell whose plastic sword was switched. I'm not an idiot."

Double damn. Paul shrugged. "It was hardly dangerous. The

metal sword must have weighed five pounds." Just a slight exaggeration. "Lenny knew instantly that it wasn't plastic. His prop bag ripped from the weight before he even touched the sword."

"I was told that Lenny cut himself."

Paul's heart lurched and he made a decision. He had never lied to Winston, not in fifteen years. He'd bent the truth more times than he could count, but he'd never outright lied. Today would be a first. "Paper cut," he said, "from the torn bag. The sword was just a big butter knife."

Winston stared at him, and Paul knew that he was going to demand to see the sword. Paul would have to compound his lie by going out and finding a different sword. One that really was a giant butter knife.

But then the principal shook his head and leaned back in his chair. "Get out of here."

Scene 7: Blood Hath Been Shed

IT WAS TWO-for-One Sundae Day at the Dairy Queen. Business was brisker than normal, and nowhere more so than at the booth at the far end of the seating area. Three hags sat at a table crowded with sundaes, each one with a different combination of ingredients.

"Isn't today Thursday?" Agatha asked.

Gertrude pulled a disk from a ragged pocket and glared at it. "Thursday. Seventeenth day of September. Quarter moon. Humidity twenty percent." Then she put the disk away.

"Wasn't that a sundial?" asked Netty.

Gertrude squinted at her. "What if it was?"

"Sundials are supposed to tell you the time. Not . . ." Netty waved pudgy fingers in the air. "All that other stuff."

Gertrude smirked. "Agatha didn't ask for the time."

"Yes, but . . . it's a sundial."

A wicked smiled creased Gertrude's face. "Heh. I threatened it into revealing more information."

"My point being," said Agatha, waving a gnarled hand over the table, "why aren't these ice cream treats called Thursdays? Why are they called Sundays?"

"Perhaps they make them on Sunday," Netty said, "then put them on clearance on Thursday before they go bad."

The other two witches stared at her.

Then Agatha let out a chest full of air. "That's the first thing you've said this week that made any sense."

Netty offered a wide, nearly toothless grin, and all three witches cackled.

"I hope," said Hecate, appearing on the bench next to Netty and taking in the array of ice cream, "that you are celebrating the destruction of The Bard's Play."

"What's with the uniform?" asked Agatha. The senior witch was dressed in stiff white linen that included an odd-looking starched hat.

Gertrude peered up at Hecate with a crooked smirk. "Heh. Are you going to serve ice cream Sundays behind the counter? I didn't realize the witching business was ailing so badly."

Hecate raised an eyebrow at Gertrude and eventually understood the deformed witch's implication. "This is not a server's uniform. It is a nurse uniform. I'm off to Hinton Valley Hospital."

Gertrude nodded her hunched head. "Pays better than waiting tables."

The three sisters exploded into cackles.

Hecate did not join them. "The only place the witch business is ailing is right here. Tell me that you've cursed the play."

Agatha licked ice cream off a gnarled finger. "Netty gave a murderous student a sword."

Hecate appeared confused. "Shouldn't they already have swords? This is *Macbeth*."

"They have prop swords," Gertrude said. "Fakes. Netty gave our Macbeth a real sword."

"I see," said Hecate. "And how many of his fellow actors did your Macbeth cut to ribbons before realizing that his prop sword was real?"

The three witches looked at each other.

Hecate frowned. "Blood did flow?"

Agatha moved her lips. "There was blood, yes."

Hecate frowned further. "Any fatalities at all?"

"Our Macbeth is a ponce with a sword," Netty said. "He was his own first casualty."

"Well," Hecate admitted. "That's better than nothing. Without Macbeth, the show can't go on."

"He, uhrm, recovered," said Agatha.

"The resilience of youth," added Gertrude.

"It was just a flesh wound," said Netty.

Hecate's nostrils flared.

Netty busied herself with examining the ice cream. "Or so I heard."

"The hospital," said Agatha. "What do you plan to do there?"

Loath to miss an opportunity to talk about herself, the senior witch smiled. "I'm going to swap some medications. Then perhaps I'll spend some time in the maternity ward watching colicky babies." She rubbed her hands together. "I never grow tired of the wailing of children." Then she was gone.

"Raspberry," said Netty.

Agatha looked at her. "What?"

Netty grinned. "I think I like the raspberry Sunday best."

"I agree," said Gertrude. "Let's throw out these other ones and order a dozen raspberry."

"That would be a waste," said Agatha. "I'll eat the other ones."

"Even the caramel?" asked Netty. "It tastes like burnt sugar."

Agatha drew a deep breath through one nostril. "Perhaps I'll pass on the caramel."

Scene 8: Give Us a Light There, Ho!

ON FRIDAY, AFTER a week of running through lines, a few of the students actually knew theirs and could repeat them off book. Of the major roles, Lenny was coming along, as was Susie. Paul could hear Susie each evening in her room, enunciating eloquently and swearing each time she missed a word. William was doing surprisingly well as Macduff, and John Freedman kept stumbling over Banquo's lines. Fortunately Banquo spent more time standing around, listening to Macbeth, than he did talking, so Freedman would probably be okay in the end.

Paul owed much of the students' progress to Sylvia, who, with little to do yet in the way of sets and props, spent each second period helping any students who were struggling with their lines.

Watching Sylvia reminded Paul that his students were just kids. Seventeen or eighteen years old. Younger in his other classes. Paul couldn't remember being that young and, like the rest of the teachers at Ashcroft Senior High, followed a policy that expected the students to behave like adults. It was hardly surprising that teenagers frequently failed to meet that expectation. After fifteen years, Paul still didn't know if the approach was good or bad.

"Who's ready to paint?" Sylvia asked, looking for hands.

Five hands went up.

Paul smiled inwardly while his wife sighed.

"Well," she said. "We may not finish today. We'll start with the castle walls. They should go quickly. Painters, come with me."

Paul made a mental note to give each of the volunteers extra credit then watched the small band troop out of the auditorium toward the arts and crafts room, where Clyde Goodall, the art teacher, had cleared space and set out supplies. During first period, he had enlisted Jerry the caretaker to help him move the third-year scenery flats from backstage, where they had sat all summer, to the art room.

Gemma Henderson, who was not one of the five volunteers, carried a big box over to Paul.

"What do we have here?"

As Gemma set the box down, Paul saw the word *Macbeth* written on one side in felt pen.

"My dad told me to bring this to class. He said it's a box of *Macbeth* props he got from his cousin who used to be an actress."

Paul poked around in the box and found a decent-looking crown, a couple of collapsible bloody daggers, a chalice, a fantastic-looking battery-operated lamp for hanging on a castle wall scenery flat, and a plastic skull.

"I think the skull is from *Hamlet*," he said.

Gemma rolled her eyes. "Whatever."

"Thank your dad for me," Paul said. "These will come in handy." He picked up the box and took it to a shelf in the backstage storage area. The cousin must have been in amateur theatre to have such relatively inexpensive props. But they were perfect for a school play.

"All right, students," he said after returning downstage. "Since you're not painting, you're going to walk through lines."

Groans.

"And I really do mean *walk*. Read-throughs are over. From now on, it's time to act. Leave your script in your bag; you won't need it. If you can't remember your lines, approximate them. If I need to cue you, I will. Let's put some body language behind your words."

"What about those who left with Mrs. Samson?" asked Trevor. "Who's going to say their lines?"

"That would be me, Trevor." To the class, Paul said, "Let's start from the top. Enter three witches."

Scene 9: Eye of Newt and Toe of Frog

SECOND PERIOD ENDED and Paul made his way through the sea of students toward the arts and crafts room to inspect the painted scenery flats and to have lunch with Sylvia before his first-year class in fourth period. He had almost arrived when the students parted to reveal the gorgon lady in all her frightful glory. Paul hadn't crossed paths with Elizabeth Cadwell since her PTA had taken over his auditorium two Tuesdays ago. It had been a blissful two weeks.

"Mr. Samson," the gorgon lady greeted him in dark, icy tones.

"Mrs. Cadwell," Paul returned brightly. "I must say that your son, Lenny, outdid himself turning out a costume for this term's play. He's the talk of the class."

Paul then braced himself for whatever bullets the gorgon planned to shoot him with. Would she accuse him of defamation by means of illiterate leaflet? Or threaten to get him arrested for attempting to murder her son with a sword? When she did neither, Paul's good mood returned instantly.

"Let's cut the pleasantries," said Mrs. Cadwell. "I ran into Gemma Henderson and two of your other students last evening."

"I hope no one was hurt," Paul said.

"What?"

"When you ran into the girls. The last thing we need around here are more injuries."

"Oh no." The gorgon lady wagged her finger at him. "You are not distracting me that easily. They were at Value Village, shopping for costumes."

"Really?" said Paul. "You don't strike me as the Value Village type. What were you doing there?"

The gorgon lady added a sneer to her finger wagging. "I won't be distracted. They were shopping for witch costumes."

Paul put on his best puzzled look. "Halloween is still six weeks off. A bit early to be looking for witch costumes. I'll have a word with them."

Mrs. Cadwell almost screamed. "They weren't shopping for Halloween. They were looking for costumes for your play!"

"Then I must have a word with them," Paul said. "Witch costumes are entirely inappropriate. Pointy hats and warty noses won't do."

"They won't?" said the gorgon lady, looking crestfallen.

"Of course not. Broom-riding witches have no place in *Macbeth*. These are hags we want. Crones. Yes, a difficult thing for seventeen-year-old girls to pull off, but that's what acting is all about. What they want for costumes are rags and heavy makeup. They can probably find these at home. No trips to Value Village required."

The gorgon lady looked like something she rarely was— speechless. If only they could have had this discussion in front of the entire PTA. That would be three public embarrassments in two weeks. What a coup!

Paul stepped around her and continued on his way.

Scene 10: To the Amazement of Mine Eyes

"WELL," SAID SYLVIA. "What do you think?"

One entire wall of the art room was lined with painted scenery flats, eight feet tall and four feet wide. Most of them were granite grey, while several were painted with fields and trees. Three of the granite walls had battlements along the top with a stormy sky peering between the stones.

Paul was near speechless. "You finished them all in one hour?" When he had his students paint, they were lucky to finish three flats.

Sylvia's face glowed. "Once we got started, it went fairly quickly. I don't know what would have happened with thirty students in here. I'm glad most weren't prepared."

"Yes." Paul was still trying to comprehend what he was seeing. "There is such a thing as too much of a good thing."

"What shall we do for lunch?" Sylvia asked.

"I'm not sure," Paul said. "I usually bring my lunch and recover from the morning in the teachers' lounge. There's always the Dairy Queen across the street that some of the students go to."

Sylvia's face brightened even more. "I haven't been to a Dairy Queen in years. Not since we took Susie to one for her tenth birthday. I wonder if they still have chocolate-dipped cones."

With third period well under way, the walk through the school was an uneventful one. The gorgon lady had made herself scarce, and they were outside and across the street without interruption.

At the Dairy Queen, the staff were quietly preparing for the lunch hour rush. The only other customers were three odd-looking women sitting at a booth in the far corner. Paul took out his cell phone and took a picture.

"What are you doing?" Sylvia whispered, quickly dragging him toward the order counter. "You can't just take pictures of random strangers."

"Of course, you're right," Paul said, tucking the phone back into his sport coat pocket. "It's just that, the gorgon lady—"

"Who?" interrupted Sylvia.

"Mrs. Cadwell, resident PTA president and royal pain in the neck."

"You call Elizabeth Cadwell the gorgon lady?"

"Not just me. Pretty much everyone does."

"Continue."

"Anyway," Paul said, "I ran into her in the hallway on the way to see you, and she was at it again about witches—"

"Witches?" said Sylvia. "Not swords or those leaflets?"

Paul let out a sigh. "She didn't mention either. Perhaps Winston talked to her. Maybe she's calling the two sets of leaflets a draw."

"That doesn't explain the sword."

"I can only imagine that Lenny talked her down about the sword. If he's willing to say it was nothing, it will be difficult for his mother to claim otherwise. Anyway, she was complaining about the three witches in the cast."

"Four," said Sylvia. "Don't forget about Hecate."

"I don't think she realizes there are four. The gor—Mrs. Cadwell—said that she saw our three young witches at Value Village, shopping for witch costumes."

"Mrs. Cadwell shops at Value Village?" Sylvia's expression was priceless

"That's what I said." Paul couldn't stop himself from laughing. "Anyway, I told her that our witches aren't witches; they are hags and witch costumes are completely inappropriate."

Sylvia nodded. "I agree with you about the costumes. Pointy hats won't do. But they are witches."

Paul spoke in a hushed voice. "The gorgon lady doesn't need to know that."

"I see. I'll have the FlameThrower GrillBurger and a Diet Coke."

"What?" Then Paul noticed the wizened, older woman waiting patiently to take his order. "I'll have the same."

"And we'll both have chocolate-dipped cones on the way out," Sylvia added.

Paul paid and they found a table near the door to wait for their order.

"None of this explains you taking that picture," said Sylvia.

"Oh, right. Well, those women at the booth are more like what my students should be going for. See the shawls and the haystack hair and the frumpy hat the short woman is wearing."

"You're saying they look like hags?" said Sylvia.

"I bet they're wearing boots," Paul said. "Those short rubber ones. And baggy pants."

Scene 11: Let This Habit Make Thee Blush!

"WELL, OF COURSE we wear boots," Gertrude said. "We spend so much time on the heath."

"And our pants are baggy," Netty added. "Pants aren't comfortable unless they're baggy. I'd hardly call my hat frumpy, though. I think it has style."

"Of course is does," said Gertrude. "I'd wear a hat just like it if I could hold my head up straight."

"What does he mean we don't look like witches?" Agatha ground her teeth as she spoke. "We are witches. We're exactly what witches look like. Hags! Hags, he called us. I've half a mind to make him choke on his GrillBurger."

"Don't do that," cautioned Gertrude. "He's the director. They may cancel the play if something happens to him."

"You're right, of course," said Agatha. "Curses get no respect when they happen behind the scenes."

"His wife, then," suggested Netty. "Let's give her a blast of salmonella. See how she looks with fins!"

"Eh?" said Gertrude. "I don't think that means what you think it means."

Agatha slammed a gnarled hand on the table. "But the woman hasn't said an unkind word about us. What would you want to go curse her for?"

"The play itself is cursed," Gertrude said. "And who do you think is going to get all the blame? The director. Heh? Consider the man cursed and enjoy your Turtle Waffle Bowl."

"What? This?" Netty pointed at a chocolate-tipped waffle bowl half emptied of ice milk and caramel sauce. "There's not a single turtle in here. False advertising, that's what it is."

The three witches looked to where Netty pointed and saw a small green turtle pushing its flippers through the melting ice milk.

"Humph," said Netty. "That wasn't there a moment ago."

Suddenly a fourth hag was sitting with them in the booth, only this hag looked like she had just stepped off the cover of a Victoria's Secret magazine, wearing a skin-tight black outfit that revealed more than it hid and all but shouted cleavage.

"Tsk, tsk, tsk," said Hecate. "You should never mix turtles and ice cream. It's bad for the indigestion."

"You can't dress like that here," Agatha scolded, looking the senior witch up and down. "They'll think you're a hooker."

Hecate let out a delicate laugh. "My hooker outfit is much brassier than this. For hookers, you want sleaze. This is my bedroom-eyes look. I just dropped in on my way to a photo shoot to get a status report on your *Macbeth* project."

"A photo shoot?" Gertrude grinned. "Updating your résumé? Still seeking a change of employment, perhaps?"

"You wish." Hecate tossed her hair. "Why would I do that when I have the greatest job in the world?"

"Yes," said Netty. "Why would you?"

"What are you up to at this photo shoot?" Agatha asked. "You going to make it a real shoot and add guns?"

Hecate shook her head. "Bor-ring. Models are shot by ex-boyfriends all the time. No, the shoot is happening at a hotel swimming pool. I thought I'd work up a little gas line explosion on the tenth floor and rain broken windows down on our gaggle of supermodels. Nothing like a few nasty scars to ruin a young glamour girl's career. But I'm not here to talk about me. I hope you have better news for me today than yesterday?"

Agatha fondled her silver pendant. "We've been stirring up the natives."

Hecate stared at her. "Stirring up the natives? What's that supposed to mean?"

"Sowing discord," Gertrude said.

"Causing general unrest," added Agatha.

Hecate looked at Netty.

"Ooooh." Netty's eyes bounced in their sockets. "Uh, like they said. Stirring up a cauldron of discord and sowing the natives."

"I see," said Hecate. "In other words, nothing."

Netty's lips sputtered. "We have big plans for next week."

"Next week?" Hecate's beauty-queen face held an expression of horror. "What is wrong with right now? Why do you have to wait until next week?"

"Drama class is over for today," Agatha said. "School is out until Monday."

"We can't do anything until Monday second period," Gertrude added. "Heh. That's the downside of dealing with schools."

"Sounds fishy to me." Hecate's flawless face darkened. "I think you're all just a bit lazy. Sitting here all day, getting fat on ice cream while the world strolls merrily past the window."

"Then perhaps you'll invite us to help with your broken-window caper?" Agatha suggested. "It's been ages since I wore a bikini."

Netty chortled. "You've never worn a bikini. None of us have. Weren't popular in the eleventh century. They wouldn't know what to think of a woman in a bikini back then. Women wore more than that when they were in private, never mind public."

"I think they're getting ready to leave," Gertrude said.

"Who is?" asked Hecate.

Agatha pointed with her extensive chin. "The director and his wife. They've been having a spot of lunch over there."

Hecate rose up out of the booth and turned around to discover a forty-something couple collecting chocolate-dipped cones from the counter. The man nearly dropped his ice cream as his eyes bulged in their sockets. Hecate put on her best bedroom-eyes smile.

The man did a double take then pulled a cell phone out of a coat pocket and took a picture. His wife whispered something nasty to him, and he put the phone away, shaking his head and obviously trying to justify his actions. They left the Dairy Queen rather more quickly than was natural.

Hecate swept back her hair and sat down again.

"What'd you go and do that for?" Agatha demanded. "They're not supposed to be fighting. Not yet, anyway. You could have ruined our plan."

A light chuckle escaped Hecate's lips. "Just having a bit of fun. No harm done. Husbands and wives fight all the time. Now I'm off to have more than just a bit of fun." Her expression grew serious. "I expect next week that you'll be highly productive." Then she was gone.

"'I expect next week that you'll be highly productive,'" Agatha repeated in an unconvincing imitation of the senior witch.

"Speaking of next week." Gertrude looked pointedly at Netty. "Perhaps you'd like to share with your sisters these big plans you mentioned."

Netty shook and waggled her fingers in the air. "Big plans? Of course I haven't got any big plans. I couldn't very well tell her that we've no idea what to do next, now could I?"

"Well," said Agatha. "Looks like we've got the weekend to come up with something. In the meantime, I think I'll have an extra-large Cappuccino MooLatté. I could use a caffeine fix about now."

"Make it three," suggested Gertrude. "Heh. Time to storm some brains."

Scene 12: Is This a Dagger Which I See before Me?

PAUL DOWNLOADED THE photos from his phone to his Mac mini, and stared at them on his computer screen. No, he hadn't dreamed it. Three of the haggiest hags he had ever seen. Perfect looks for the play. He would show this photo to Gemma and his other witches. But the second photo? That one he wouldn't show to anyone. Who would believe it?

There was no way a beautiful woman wearing nothing but lingerie could have walked into Dairy Queen without his noticing. He and Sylvia were sitting right by the door! And why would such a woman go and sit with the hags? It wasn't because opposites attract. The woman hadn't ordered any food, not that they would have served her, dressed as she was. But the clincher, the real thing that made this so unreal, was the smile she had flashed at him. No woman had ever looked at Paul that way.

It had to be a joke. Someone had set him up. But who? This wasn't Winston's style. Or the gorgon lady's. Elizabeth Cadwell wouldn't even conceive of anything so . . . risqué.

The woman had to have been hiding in the washroom. She probably wore a long coat and only took it off when she stood up to cast him that smile. But why? What did it accomplish? If it was designed to help kill the play, he was lost as to how.

Unable to draw any conclusion, Paul closed the photo viewer and turned his attention to the prop box Gemma had brought to school, which he had brought home to inspect properly. Anything to get his mind off that photo.

Yorick's skull would be unusable, of course, except as a Halloween ornament. It was a standard plastic skull you could buy at any costume shop. The only label on it read, *Made In China*.

The crown was also cheap plastic from China. The aluminum one Lenny had brought was better. Perhaps Siward could wear this one. Earls didn't wear crowns, but it would help differentiate the British allies from the Scots supporters, especially as none of his actors would incorporate accents to help determine who was who.

The chalice would be perfect for the banquet scene, when Macbeth drinks himself stupid while seeing Banquo's ghost. It, too, was plastic but large and bright gold. It would catch the eye as Macbeth staggered about the stage, arguing about a ghost none of his guests could see.

The daggers must have been made for the play. They had rubber retracting blades, with one side painted silver to catch the stage lights and the other side silver stained with rusty red. Before murder and after murder. Paul couldn't see a manufacturer's mark, but initials had been scratched at the tip of each hilt: *S. R.*

The final prop was an ornamental lamp, aluminum painted bright silver, with plastic instead of glass so it weighed almost nothing. There was what looked like a Christmas bulb inside shaped like a flame and a place at the back for a AAA battery. Paul flicked the on/off switch and discovered that either the battery was dead or the bulb was burned out. After replacing the battery with one he found loose in his desk drawer, the lamp came on and he was delighted to see the bulb was the flickering kind meant to imitate a flame.

He turned the lamp off and examined the coat hanger wire that had been glued onto the back and bent so the lamp would hang off the top of a scenery flat. Ingenious. Paul would have to send a thank-you note back with Gemma to give to her dad.

He was about to put the props, all but the skull, back into the box, when he noticed a white slip of paper lying at the bottom. He picked it up and turned it over then gawked as he read the words typed on it in faded ink: *Property of Simon Riordan.*

How could that be? Simon Riordan was Paul's old drama teacher from back when Paul was in high school. What were the odds that this box would make its way through two decades and into Paul's hands?

He let the slip of paper flutter back to the bottom of the box and leaned back in his chair, memories flooding his thoughts of his old mentor, larger than life, swaggering across the stage like a human blimp, flourishing his arms and grinning like a madman. A grin crossed Paul's own lips as he shook his head. He remembered the first day he had seen Mr. Riordan. Six foot five, a lion's mane of hair on an oversized head, broad shoulders, a capacious gut, narrow hips and legs, and tiny feet. How the man walked without falling over was a miracle of science.

Drama had held no interest for Paul before that first day. Like many of his own students, Paul had taken the elective for what he hoped would be an easy pass. But Simon Riordan had changed all that, opening Paul's eyes to a whole new world where you could pretend to be another person and people would applaud you for it. The only limits were your imagination and, as Paul discovered when he began working as a teacher himself, the intolerance of the school and the parents.

He lost his grin as he remembered that third and final year, when Riordan failed to show up for class and a few days later was replaced by a phys ed teacher who showed zero interest in being there. No explanation was given except that Mr. Riordan had suddenly decided to retire from teaching. Overnight, drama lost its magic, and Paul had never pursued acting as a career.

Only later, when Paul earned his teaching degree with no specialty, had he decided to accept his first job teaching as a drama instructor. It was the only position available. It could as easily have been home economics. Paul discovered that he was good at teaching drama, though not as good as Simon Riordan, and never looked back.

Paul turned his gaze back to the box. He was certain he had never seen these props before. Simon Riordan had loved Shakespeare, and Paul remembered playing the part of Verges in Riordan's high school production of *Much Ado about Nothing*. But there had been no *Macbeth*. No *Hamlet* either.

Turning madly to his computer, Paul called up Google and entered *Macbeth* and *Simon Riordan*. Several hundred hits came up, many of them nothing to do with either search term. After scrolling through quite a few useless pages, he kicked himself for being so clumsy with computers. He tried again, adding the term *retired*.

Fewer hits came up, and the fourteenth was what he was looking for. It showed a photo of Simon Riordan and several other actors in full costume, posing in front of a marquee proclaiming *The Tragedy of Macbeth.*

Riordan was an actor? He'd never once mentioned it in class. Paul had always assumed that his mentor was much like himself, opting to teach rather than face the treadmill of auditions, learning parts, and suffering the abuse of prima donna directors as well as the criticism of an impossible-to-please public. But here he was proved wrong. Apparently when the school day was done, Simon Riordan had taken to the stage.

Paul began scanning the article for a date but stopped when he realized that the short write-up wasn't a review, but an article describing how the community theatre production had been cancelled due to the death of one of the actors during rehearsal. Scarlet Walker was rehearsing the role of Lady Macbeth when a box of tools that had been left on the scaffolding above the stage somehow fell, striking Scarlet on the head, killing her instantly.

Paul looked up to the page banner to see where this article came from and was dismayed to see that it was an entry in a blog discussing The Cursed Play, apparently listing examples of the curse. He continued reading the article and saw Simon Riordan's name and a statement where Riordan swore that the play was cursed and that he was retiring from acting as well as his teaching position. A little farther down was the date when this had happened. It was the same date that Simon Riordan had quit teaching Paul's class.

Riordan must have contributed the props for the play then abandoned them when he quit. A quarter century later, after being passed hand to hand, they had miraculously arrived in Paul's study. Recalling the photos on his computer, Paul counted that as two impossible things in one day.

-Act III-

Scene 1: The Greatest Error of All the Rest

ANOTHER MONDAY.

"Okay, class, today we are going to walk through the banquet scene."

Paul was sitting in his director's chair at centre stage just in front of the first row of theatre seats. With the help of Jerry the caretaker, he had retrieved the scenery flats from the art room and positioned the inside castle walls for the scene. In front of the walls stood four prop tables. From the theatre seats, they looked like large, eight-by-four-foot trestle tables but were in fact only a foot wide and made of foam. Regular folding chairs sat behind them, awaiting the banquet guests. On one of the scenery flats near the head table, Simon Riordan's ornamental lamp flickered like a castle candle sconce.

Adjusting his megaphone, Paul said, "This is the busiest scene in the play. The servants will come in from stage right, set dishes on the tables, and then stand near the castle walls. Macbeth, Lady Macbeth, the thanes, and attendants will all enter from stage left. Macbeth smiles at the audience and says his first line." Paul paused for a moment, trying to gauge the students' comprehension. When he was satisfied, he said, "Action!"

Paul watched without expression as the servants wandered onto the stage, looking like Christians who had been pushed into the arena, waiting for the lions. Eventually they decided where to set the dishes they carried then turned their backs to the audience, walked to the prop walls, and turned around.

Paul took no notes, nor did he stop the action, as these were all common and expected mistakes. He'd wait until an exceptional error happened before stopping the action.

The lords entered with more aplomb than their servants, and Lenny, with a new plastic sword wedged under his belt, did a passable job nodding hello at his followers before turning to the audience. "You know your own degrees; sit down: at first and last the hearty welcome."

"Thanks to your majesty," the lords mumbled in a discordant chorus.

The action continued with Lenny striding across the stage as the lords took their assigned seats. He introduced Lady Macbeth, and Susie offered her welcome with the zeal of a true queen. Paul couldn't be prouder. So proud, in fact, that he made his own error and did not look stage left, where Jordan Little was supposed to appear as the first assassin.

Lenny gave his next line then strode quickly to stage left to tell the murderer, "There's blood on thy face." But there was no assassin to receive the line.

Paul yelled through the megaphone. "Cut! Where's Jordan?"

Jordan Little poked a startled face through one of the side curtains.

Paul let out a calming breath. "You missed your cue."

"Oh," Jordan said. "Sorry. I'm still learning my lines. I haven't learned my cues yet."

"You still have your script?" Paul asked.

Jordan held up a ragged sheaf of papers.

"Then follow along when you're backstage."

"Right." Taking this command as a dismissal, Jordan ducked back behind the curtain.

Paul turned his face back to the stage. "Let's take it from the top. Servants, please set the tables as though you have done it a thousand times. Do you know why? Because you have done it a thousand times. And don't show your backs to the audience. Set the tables, and then fade slowly to the walls. Don't hit the walls; you'll knock them down. Lords, show some enthusiasm. You're at a party. Free food and drink. Act like you're having fun."

The scene opened better the second time. The assassin arrived on cue, and this time Jordan even had blood on his face—a splash of makeup. But the old problems were replaced with new. When the ghost of Banquo arrived, most of the lords watched him. William even moved aside so Banquo could pass and sit in Macbeth's chair. Lenny did a good job ignoring these errors, and the lords eventually remembered through Lenny's dialogue that they weren't supposed to be able to see the ghost.

Then Lenny busied himself drinking from the gold chalice while Lady Macbeth made excuses, and the ghost left with less attention than when he arrived.

The return of the ghost was a bit of a fiasco, however. The tables and lords all seemed to be in his way, so he wandered upstage and tried to get past the servants, who all ignored him. He must have tripped over someone's shoe as he pitched forward, knocking into one of the servants, who went flying into the castle wall, striking one of the scenery flats to the floor, the same flat that held Riordan's lamp.

"Cut! Cut!" Paul leaped out of his director's chair and strode across the stage. "Congratulations, you have just committed the gravest error stage actors can commit. You've knocked down the set. All we can do is draw the curtains, fix the set as best we can, and resume the scene. There is nothing more embarrassing."

Scene 2: And an Eternal Curse Fall on You!

HECATE, FOR ONCE, was dressed in normal clothes. Boots, baggy pants, oversized sweater. Even her hair was bedraggled.

"Taking the day off?" Agatha asked, looking up from a plate of chicken fingers and fries and eyeing the senior witch up and down.

"Taking the day off?" Netty echoed. "I can't remember the last time I had a day off. Might have been in the fifteenth century."

Hecate let out a loud sigh, obviously in a bad mood. "Just came from an assignment. Nothing I'd choose to do. I would have sent you three if you weren't already . . . busy."

"A dirty job, then," said Gertrude. "I don't mind dirty jobs. Heh. Done enough of them. What did you do?"

"Earthquake," Hecate said, spitting the word as though it were distasteful.

"No," said Agatha. "Not an earthquake. I'd give my right nostril to start an earthquake."

Hecate looked at the skinny witch out of one eye. "Would you, now? If you had finished this job, you could have had the opportunity. But apparently it takes you three weeks to do something as simple as curse a play."

"Well, of course we could curse and run," Gertrude said, "but that's been done. Countless times. Where's the finesse?"

"Finesse?" Hecate almost shouted the word. "What's the point of finesse? Just have Lady Macbeth choke on an olive so that your candidate misses his big chance to be a star. Set him up and cut him down. This is isn't rocket science!"

"We've done the olive," Netty said. "Twice."

"We've been cursing this play for four hundred years," Gertrude added.

"It's getting old," agreed Agatha.

Hecate shook her head. "The play hasn't gotten old. It gets produced countless times each year. Every few decades they make a new film version. Until the play gets old, cursing it can't get old."

"That's easy for you to say," Agatha said. "You're always doing something new and different."

Hecate let out a loud cackle, which looked oddly appropriate coming from a bedraggled supermodel; several heads at other tables turned to look at her.

The senior witch regained her composure and lowered her voice. "Look, sisters, if they are still putting on the play four hundred years from now or four thousand, cursing it will be your job. Got it? So what have you done for me lately?"

The three witches stared at her.

"Your big plans, remember? The ones you promised me on Friday."

"Oh, yes." Netty screeched out a laugh that felt like nails on a chalkboard. "We brought the house down."

Hecate raised an eyebrow. "You made the play a tremendous success?"

"She means literally," said Agatha. "We brought the castle walls tumbling down atop the ghost of Banquo."

"With the idea of making Banquo a real ghost," Gertrude concluded.

Hecate smiled. "That sounds delightful. I assume they immediately cancelled the play."

"Not . . . immediately, no." Netty glanced about for a distraction and stole a chicken finger from Agatha's plate.

"Turns out the accident wasn't fatal," Gertrude said, following Netty's cue.

"They could still cancel, of course," Agatha said. "That's three accidents in three weeks. Schools frown on accidents."

"I see." Hecate squeezed her eyes half shut. "Keep me apprised."

Then she was gone.

"Do you think we should have mentioned that the walls were canvas?" asked Netty.

"No!" shouted the other two witches.

"Hmm," said Netty, taking another morsel from Agatha's plate. "Who'd have thought chickens had such large fingers."

Scene 3: Methought I Heard a Voice Cry

PAUL STAYED BEHIND after the bell to see what he could do about Simon Riordan's prop lamp. Sylvia had a house to show, for a change, so he was on his own for the day. He was surprised how much he had come to count on his wife's help in just a week.

The scenery flat was undamaged. Canvas is pretty tough unless you poke it with something sharp or apply enough pressure to rip it away from the staples attaching it to the frame. They had set it back up right away and continued rehearsal. The lamp, however, had refused to come back to life and had sat on the wall, refusing to flicker light on the actors.

Shaking the lamp now, Paul could hear the broken filament rattling inside. Besides the filament, he thought he heard something else, something odd, like a voice whispering. He continued to shake and listen until he thought he heard words. They sounded like, "Let me out." He stopped shaking the lamp, and the whispering stopped.

Paul looked around the stage and auditorium to make sure he was alone then shook the lamp again. Almost immediately he heard it. "Let me out." Louder. It was a woman's voice.

He slammed the lamp down onto the prop table and backed away from it. Once more, the auditorium was silent.

A third time he picked up the lamp and shook it.

"Will you stop fooling around and let me out?"

Paul pulled the lamp away from his ear and stared at it.

Someone was screwing with him. Again. First the lingerie woman at Dairy Queen, and now a tiny speaker planted inside Simon Riordan's prop lamp. This was insane! Paul had no idea who would do something like this. Who *could* do something like this.

Placing the lamp back on the table, he reached in and unscrewed the broken bulb. All the while, he peered at various parts of the lamp, trying to see where the speaker could be. And where was the radio receiver? There simply wasn't enough lamp to hide those things. He moved his ear in close and listened but heard nothing.

Shaking his head, he strode out of the auditorium. He would have an early lunch in the teachers' lounge and head out to the Light House on Fifth Street and get a replacement bulb. He would test the new bulb before the fourth-period bell for first-year drama, and that would be the end of it. He refused to give in to this nonsense.

In the hallway, he almost immediately ran into the gorgon lady.

"Mrs. Cadwell," he said. "Do you teach here?"

"What?" said the gorgon. "Of course I don't."

"Then why," Paul asked, "can't I take ten steps outside the Ashcroft-Tate Auditorium without running into you?"

The gorgon's eyebrows rose against her forehead. "Mr. Samson, I have no idea what your problems are today, but I'll thank you not to take them out on me."

"Then you'd have no idea what I was talking about if I asked you if you happened to have a radio transmitter concealed about your person? Or if one of your PTA members has a thing for lingerie?"

Mrs. Cadwell stared at him. "No, I most certainly would not. But this sounds like something I should bring up with Mr.

Winston."

"You go ahead," Paul said. "The sooner I get an explanation, the better."

Then he stormed off before he stuck his foot any deeper into his mouth. As soon as he had spoken the words, Paul realized what they must sound like. And how would the gorgon sneak a tiny receiver and speaker into the lamp, anyway? James Bond would have difficulty pulling that off. Had she hired a spy? Or enlisted the services of the NSA? He'd be lucky if the gorgon only accused him of harassment, rather than of having lost his mind.

Sure enough, he hadn't made it to the teachers' lounge before Mrs. Kennedy was calling him on his cell phone. That, in itself, was unusual. Winston must have run out of runners in detention. The week was young, after all.

"I had a very interesting chat with Mrs. Cadwell just now," Winston mentioned casually once Paul had entered his office and taken position standing behind one of the visitor chairs. "She suggested that you were acting peculiar towards her in the hallway."

"Yes," Paul admitted. "It may have seemed that way. I'll have to apologize to her." How it galled him to say that. "Someone has been playing tricks on me. I ran into Mrs. Cadwell so quickly after the last one that I accused her without thinking things through."

"Tricks?" said Winston. "Students play tricks on their teachers all the time. Last week provided ample evidence of that. Why would you accuse the head of the PTA?"

Paul wasn't convinced that students had anything to do with the previous week's shenanigans but was just as happy that Winston appeared to be putting them behind him. "Like I said, I wasn't thinking. Of course Mrs. Cadwell isn't responsible. It just seems odd that she is always hanging around the school."

Winston nodded and Paul could see that this bothered the principal as well. Perhaps he'd found an ally. The administrator added, "Mrs. Cadwell takes her job perhaps too seriously. The woman has too much time on her hands and is always looking for trouble, even when there is none to be found. And sometimes she makes her own trouble."

Opening a drawer of his desk, Winston pulled out a framed picture and set it out so Paul could see. It was one of the leaflets with the cartoon gorgon lady. "Jerry Noonan is still finding these leaflets around the school."

"Still no word on who made them?" Paul asked.

Winston shook his head. "They've left Mrs. Cadwell on a hair trigger. I suggest you steer clear of her."

"Sage advice," Paul said. Winston really was in a good mood. Nothing earth shattering must have happened this week . . . yet.

"That is all," Winston said.

Paul slowly made his way to the door. It didn't feel like that was all. As his hand touched the doorknob, Winston coughed. "Oh, by the way, how's that play of yours coming?"

Winston didn't have to say which play. Paul had three classes, but he meant the senior class. *Macbeth.*

Paul turned and leaned back against the door. "It's coming along nicely. Some of the students are even surprising me. They've really taken to it."

Winston frowned. "Have they?"

"Oh, yes." Paul nodded.

The principal pursed his lips. "Kim Greyson will be back in class tomorrow."

"Good," Paul said.

Winston leaned back into his chair. "I understand that Kim has a full leg cast. And crutches. You'll see that you don't put too much strain on him, will you?"

"Of course," Paul said. And he fled the principal's office.

Scene 4: Come, You Spirits

DWELLING ON THE mystery of the lingerie lady and the voice in the lamp, Paul swallowed a lunch he didn't taste then went shopping, something he abhorred because he was so lousy at it. But what increasingly worried him was Winston's less-than-subtle instructions to leave Mrs. Cadwell alone while she quietly plotted the destruction of his play.

He may have told Winston what he wanted to hear, that the gorgon lady couldn't be responsible for any of the weird goings-on, things that could only get the play cancelled. But who else would bother? Mrs. Cadwell wasn't just his prime suspect; she was his only suspect. And now he couldn't even point a finger.

Winston was laughing at him. He could sit there behind his desk, wiping sweat from his face, and pretend he was on Paul's side. Meanwhile, he was stacking the deck in the gorgon's favour. When the play failed, Winston would shrug and tell Paul that he tried but that Cadwell was too much for the both of them.

By the time Paul returned to the school, he had decided to just focus on his students and ignore the gorgon lady and her tricks. Maybe whoever had retaliated for the leaflets would continue to deal with Mrs. Cadwell. Paul just had to keep his nose clean. Sometimes the best offense really was a good defense.

Ten minutes before the bell for his fourth-period class, Paul hovered over a table in the backstage storage area of the Ashcroft-Tate Auditorium. He screwed the new bulb into the lamp and turned it on. The lamp came to life, flickering like a burning candle. Then the bulb went pop and let out an acrid smell.

Which was why Paul hated shopping.

He unscrewed the new bulb and compared it to the old one. "It's the right bulb," he said aloud.

"Yes, it is," said a pleasant female voice. "That was me, I'm afraid. Sorry about that."

Paul lifted his head and looked around. Apart from boxes, tables, closets, and scenery flats, the storage area was empty. But the voice no longer sounded like it came from a tiny speaker in the lamp, a speaker he had never found. This voice was full and rich, as though its source were standing right in front of him.

Then it hit him. He wasn't being tricked. He was going insane.

In a strange way, he felt relief. The gorgon lady hadn't employed the services of secret agents or the NSA. Her attacks had simply driven him mad. Then he frowned as he wondered if insanity might be worse than the gorgon lady upping her game.

"I suppose I should explain," said the voice.

Paul was surprised that the voice didn't feel as if it were in his head. He was definitely hearing it though his ears. He didn't think insanity worked that way. The school library should have some books—

"You can hear me, can't you?" A note of fear touched the voice.

Paul turned his head, trying to focus his eyes instead of his ears on the source. Maybe there was a second speaker, in addition to the one he hadn't found in the lamp. The voice seemed to be coming from an empty space between two costume racks.

"Who are you?" he asked.

"Oh!" said the voice, excited this time. "You can hear me. It feels like forever since anyone has heard me."

"Who are you?" Paul repeated.

"How rude of me. I'm Scarlet. And you're Paul Samson. I've overheard your wife and the students call you that. Oh. That's rude too. Overhearing, I mean. I had no control over that. Though that's all I've pretty much been able to do for years. Of course, I've spent most of my time in a basement, under the stairs, I think, and there wasn't much to hear. I thought I'd go mad. What year is it, anyway? I miss having a watch."

The words had come as a torrent, and it took Paul a moment to realize they included a question. "What year is it?"

"It's not important, I suppose," said the voice. Scarlet. "But I am curious."

Paul didn't see anything wrong with telling her. "Twenty-fifteen."

"Oh," Scarlet said. "I thought it would be later. I guess time moves more slowly when you don't sleep."

"Could you answer one of my questions?" Paul asked.

"Of course!"

"Who are you?"

"I'm Scarlet. I thought I mentioned that. Scarlet Walker."

Paul had the odd feeling he should know that name. It was at the tip of his thoughts. "Okay, Scarlet. Perhaps you could tell me where you are."

"But you're looking right— Oh, you can't see me, can you? Let me try something."

As Paul watched, a twenty-something Lady Macbeth, decked out in a flowing crimson dress with Celtic-patterned trim and long, black, braided hair, materialized into view. Paul recognized her instantly. "You're the actress who died!"

"Oh!" said Scarlet, her expression brightening. "Am I famous?"

Paul wasn't sure how to answer that. Fame held deeper meaning for actors than for other people. Then he realized what he had just said.

"You're dead! How can you be talking to me?"

Scarlet turned her head slightly as she thought about that.

"I'm pretty sure that I'm a ghost. I remember dying and everyone gathered 'round, crying and wringing their hands. It was touching, really. Bill was a little over the top, but he always did overdo things. Then I remember paramedics arriving and shaking their heads and carrying my body away. Oh, and Simon! Simon looked devastated. He kept saying that it was his fault. I stayed near Simon, trying to calm him down and getting exactly nowhere. He was weeping as he packed up his box of props. And then, when he turned off his wall lamp, I found myself inside it. I remember thinking it was like a genie in a bottle. But I knew I wasn't a genie. I was a ghost. I think that my breaking the replacement bulb let me out."

Throughout this explanation, Paul's mind ran a mile a minute. There were two possible explanations here, three if you included insanity. Either ghosts were real, and everything Scarlet was saying was true. Or the gorgon's convoluted, secret agent plot to cancel *Macbeth* had attained a completely new level of complication.

Paul could only think of one way to find out. "Do you think you died because the play is cursed?"

"Cursed?" Scarlet's eyes widened. "I never believed in those stories. I wouldn't have tried out for the part if I had." She touched the folds of her long, red dress with delicate fingers. "Of course, I never believed in ghosts either. So I don't know if the play is cursed. I do think that, knowing what I know now, I wouldn't disbelieve in curses."

Paul rubbed his eyes. Could her answer be more vague?

Scarlet wasn't finished, however. "I don't think that you should disbelieve in curses either. As much as *Macbeth* is my favourite Shakespeare play, it may not be worth the risk of continuing."

Paul gave no warning as he lunged forward to touch Scarlet's arm. The woman's jaw dropped even as she let out a loud gasp and took an involuntary couple of steps backward. Paul succeeded in merely brushing his fingers through an intangible sleeve. Not that he had expected to touch a flesh-and-blood person.

"What are you doing?" Scarlet shrieked. She backed even farther away.

Rather than try to touch her again, Paul dashed to one side, running as much of a circle around the young woman as the costume racks would allow. Scarlet spun in place, watching him with a mix of fear and curiosity. At no time did her image falter due to Paul's passing in front of a projector.

Paul was no technical whiz, but he had watched enough television to know about 3-D projection systems and the possibilities of holographic representations. When he failed to disrupt Scarlet's image, he looked up toward the ceiling, the perfect place for such a system. But the only lights he saw were the normal backstage lighting.

"A gentleman," Scarlet said, her voice frosty, "would have asked to touch me. I would have agreed."

Paul let out a pent-up breath. "I don't believe in ghosts. This is a trick. You're just helping the gorgon lady to cancel the play."

Scarlet stared at him. "You don't believe in ghosts, but you believe in gorgons?"

Paul was about to answer when the fourth-period bell rang. His first-year students would be arriving.

Scarlet cocked an ear and began fading away.

"Wait!" Paul cried. But she was gone.

Scene 5: Rest, Rest, Perturbed Spirit!

PAUL, SYLVIA, AND Susie sat at the supper table, enjoying a pot roast, carrots, potatoes, and gravy. Everything was perfect, and Paul was loath to destroy it all by bringing up the subject of ghosts. But he had been agonizing about it all afternoon and was at his wit's end.

If he was being tricked, he had been unable to reveal the trick or even identify the trickster. While he wouldn't put it past Mrs. Cadwell to go to any extreme to get her way, enlisting the NSA or some other black ops agency with the know-how to pull this off, it just wasn't her style. And why would such people help her? It was a high school play, not some plot for world domination.

And if the ghost was real, perhaps so was the curse.

He couldn't decide which explanation scared him more.

"I encountered a ghost today," he said then waited for the

laughter.

"Someone from your past?" asked Sylvia. She was smiling but not laughing. Susie was texting on her phone and probably hadn't even heard him.

"Ah," Paul said. "Not my past. Simon Riordan's."

"Who?"

"My high school drama teacher."

"Of course," said Sylvia. "You haven't mentioned him in years. You saw Mr. Riordan?"

"Not Riordan, no." Paul realized he was messing this up. "A friend of his. They both performed in a community theatre production of *Macbeth*."

Sylvia frowned. "I thought you said Mr. Riordan was just a teacher. Like you. Did he act before becoming a high school teacher?"

The phrase *just a teacher* grated on Paul's nerves. He knew Sylvia didn't mean anything by it, but it grated just the same. "That's what I thought. Apparently he was leading a double life and performing in plays after school."

"Mr. Riordan's friend told you this?" Sylvia asked.

Paul realized he needed to set the conversation back on course. "If only it was that simple. When I said I saw a ghost, I meant a real ghost."

Sylvia smiled again. "As in walking through walls and rattling chains?"

Susie had put down her phone and was now paying attention. She, too, allowed a smile to bend her lips.

"No rattling," Paul said. "But she did talk a lot. I suppose it's because she'd had no one to talk to in twenty years."

A short "Ha!" escaped Susie's mouth.

"She?" Sylvia's expression said the rest.

"Twenty-something," Paul said, creating some distance. "Dressed as Lady Macbeth. She died. It was Simon Riordan's last play. He quit acting and teaching when it happened."

"Lady Macbeth!" said Susie.

"And where," asked Sylvia, "did you meet this ghost?"

"She was trapped inside a prop." Paul looked at Susie. "That lamp that broke today. It belonged to Riordan and was part of the set when Scarlet died."

"So your ghost has a name?" said Sylvia.

"Everyone has a name, Mother," Susie said. She looked at Paul. "Scarlet was playing the part of Lady Macbeth when she died? That's my part."

"Surely there are no such things as ghosts," said Sylvia. "Who is this woman?"

"That's just it." Paul sagged in his chair. "Of course I don't believe in ghosts. But she appeared and disappeared, just like a ghost. And my hand went right through her."

"You touched this woman?" asked Sylvia.

"Let it go," Susie said, looking sharply at her mother. "Jealousy doesn't become you."

"I'm not jealous," Sylvia said, perhaps a bit too loudly. "I'm just concerned that your father is being played."

"As am I," Paul said. "All the evidence says that this woman is a ghost, which is impossible. And if she is not a ghost, why is she pretending to be one?"

"What does she want?" Susie asked.

Paul thought for a moment. Scarlet hadn't asked for anything, except for him to believe her. But that wasn't quite true. "She suggested that *Macbeth* may really be cursed and that I might want to cancel the play."

"Not that lame curse." Paul's daughter rolled her eyes.

"You know about the curse?" Paul asked.

"Well, duh!" said Susie. "Who doesn't?"

"There you have it," said Sylvia. "Mrs. Cadwell put her up to it. Did you know that since her leaflet stunt failed, she's passing around a petition to cancel the play?"

"What!" said Susie, echoing Paul's unspoken reaction. "That bitch!"

Sylvia slapped her hand on the table. "Language, young lady."

Susie glared at her mother, unrepentant. "It's a heartfelt response. No gratuitousness included."

Sylvia glared back. "We all know what Mrs. Cadwell is. It doesn't bear repeating."

"Ladies," said Paul, a little surprised that his wife and daughter had stronger feelings regarding the gorgon lady than he did. "You're not helping my dilemma. What should I do about the ghost?"

"Well, you're not going to cancel the play," said Susie. "It's the most fun I've had at school since . . . ever."

"Susie's right," Sylvia said. "You don't know this woman. And she's certainly no ghost."

"But what should I do?"

"Play along," said Sylvia. "She'll slip up. I'll be in class again tomorrow, and the three of us can keep an eye out."

Scene 6: Here Comes the Good Macduff

PAUL SAT IN his study, wondering if waiting and watching were enough. If the curse was real, every minute's delay put the students at risk, put Susie at risk. Scarlet had been playing Lady Macbeth when she was killed. If something happened to Susie, he would never forgive himself. And Kim Greyson had broken his leg. The curse?

But Paul didn't believe in curses. Or ghosts. How could any of this be real? Turning on his Mac mini, Paul opened his Web browser, did a search for *ghosts*, and got forty-two million hits. He added *Macbeth*, and got one million hits, the first few pages apparent references to Banquo. He tried various other combinations of words, but not really knowing what he was looking for, he failed to find anything. About the only thing he did know for certain was that Simon Riordan had suddenly quit teaching back when Paul was in high school. And Riordan had known Scarlet.

Paul called up the article from his browser history and stared at the cast photo. It was a high-quality image, undoubtedly the promotional photo for the play. He didn't recognize the man posing as Macbeth next to Lady Macbeth, but there was no doubt in his mind that the lady and the ghost were one and the same. The face, the smile, the clothes. The same person. Yet the photo was decades old. Simon Riordan, dressed as Macduff, could be no older than forty-something. Today he would be in his sixties. Today.

Of course! Riordan could tell him. Was Scarlet really Scarlet? For all Paul knew, the Internet article was a fake, placed there by the gorgon lady's high-tech minions for Paul to find. Which was, of course, absurd. But the alternative was that Scarlet was a ghost. Even more absurd.

He was always hearing stories in the teachers' lounge about fake news on the Internet. Anyone could post anything; it was the perfect medium for propaganda and deceit. Yet people flocked to the Internet for their daily news fix. Not Paul, of course. He had no interest in news. The world continued to turn whether he paid attention or not. A good novel was Paul's fix. Or a good play.

But Riordan could shed light on things. Did he really quit drama because The Bard's Play was cursed? What evidence did he have that the curse was real? And would he be willing to meet with Scarlet Walker's ghost?

It took forever to find Simon Riordan. The name was more common than Paul would have thought. And if Riordan had moved to another part of the country, Paul would have never found him. After random Web searches failed, he asked Susie to look on Facebook. No joy there. Then Susie suggested online phone books and gave him a Web address to try. There was exactly one *Riordan, S.* in the book.

Paul punched the number into his cell phone and prayed.

"Spring Hills Convalescent Home," said a female voice.

"Uh," said Paul. "I'm calling for Simon Riordan. Is he at this address?"

"I'm not allowed to give out that information. Are you a family member?"

"Well, no. But this is important."

"I'm sure it is. But I still can't give out any information."

"Can I give you my name and number?" Paul asked. "Will you ask him to call me?"

"I can take your information, but I can't guarantee anything."

"Fine." Paul gave her the information, thanked her for her time, and hung up. "Bureaucracies!"

But what was Simon Riordan doing in a convalescent home? He's not that old. Was Riordan ill? Did he work there? Was Paul's one hope of making sense of things an empty hope?

Scene 7: Out, Damned Spot! Out, I Say!

ON TUESDAY MORNING, Paul watched with rapt attention as Susie walked slowly across the stage holding an unlit candle with an outstretched arm.

On the other side of the stage, Grace Potter batted Brian MacKay on the arm three times. "Lo you, here she comes! This is her very guise; and, upon my life, fast asleep. Observe her; stand close."

Brian, dressed in white clothes approximating a modern doctor's garb and nothing like what a medieval doctor would wear, scrunched his eyes. "How came she by that light?"

"Why, it stood by her," said Grace. "She has light by her continually; 'tis her command."

Brian nodded. "You see, her eyes are open."

"Ay," said Grace. "But their sense is shut."

"What is it she does now?" Brian asked. He leaned his head forward. "Look, how she rubs her hands."

"It is an accustomed action with her," said Grace, "to seem thus washing her hands: I have known her continue in this a quarter of an hour."

There was a pregnant silence; then Susie spoke. "Yet here's a spot."

"Hark!" said Brian with much too little surprise. "She speaks." He pulled a notebook and pencil, also anachronistic, from his lab coat pocket. "I will set down what comes from her, to satisfy my remembrance the more strongly."

Susie turned to face the audience and rubbed her hands as though they offended her. "Out, damned spot! Out, I say!"

It was with enormous difficulty that Paul kept a smile from his face. He had never been more proud of Susie than right now as she stood centre stage, wracked with guilt for having committed murder. The students all understood that she was brilliant. Even Gemma, who had wanted the part. But that didn't stop them from feeling petty jealousy or claiming favouritism from the director. Paul had to be on his best behaviour to weather the storm.

He frowned as one of the students walked onto the stage and kept pace with Susie, at times almost stepping underfoot as she gave close observation to Susie's performance. He would have yelled, "Cut!" and asked the student if she was out of her mind but stopped himself when he realized that it wasn't a student at all, but Scarlet Walker, wearing the same costume as yesterday. Susie continued with her lines, undaunted by Scarlet's interference, and none of the students seemed to notice. Even, Sylvia, who sported the same wide grin that Paul was forced to suppress, paid no attention to the ghost. Like Macbeth's vision of Banquo's ghost, Paul was the only one who could see her.

The scene ended with Susie and Scarlet having left the stage, the doctor's brief soliloquy delivered, and Grace's parting words. "Good night, good doctor."

"Well done," Paul said. "Brian, Sylvia will speak with you about your costume. Let's continue with Act V, Scene 2. The country near Dunsinane. Anna? Your crew should already be bringing the forest scenery flats on stage."

"Well," said Scarlet. Though the ghost had come around to stand by his left ear, Paul kept his eyes on the students bustling about the stage. "Given your limited praise for such a grand rehearsal, that must be your daughter. She's much better than the other students. Did you know that Simon is also a drama teacher? How he makes time for school in addition to the theatre is beyond me. It takes me forever to learn my lines. I suppose he can do it because he's single. No family life to balance. Of course, I'm single too, but I have a busy social life. *Had* a busy social life. Did you know it takes almost as much time to get ready for a date as it does to go out on one? I don't think Simon dates much. Of course . . . neither do I, now that I'm dead."

Scarlet ceased speaking and Paul detected a loss of exuberance in her final words. He allowed his gaze to swing in her direction.

Scarlet noticed him looking, and her face turned, well, scarlet. "You'd think I would have cried myself out by now. I've had forever to accept that I'm dead and to count my regrets. But I've never been able to tell anyone. It's like losing everything all over again. Still, I'm thankful that you helped me escape that lamp. To tell you the truth, if I had to stay in there any longer, I think I'd lose my mind."

Paul whispered so Sylvia wouldn't hear him. "Like I'm losing mine."

Scarlet stopped talking, her eyes wide with astonishment.

The conclusion was obvious. Since no one else could see Scarlet, Paul really was losing his mind. Unlike Macbeth, he hadn't murdered a king and a friend to earn insanity. He must have done something, however. Not eaten right? Allowed his family to grow too far apart. Chosen *Macbeth* for a high school play? Was insanity a curse?

Paul's inquisition into his own demise was interrupted by the buzzing of his cell phone.

"Continue with this scene," he said to Sylvia.

Then he left his director's chair and answered the phone after taking a few steps into the audience seating area. "Paul Samson."

He listened as he walked up the centre aisle to the back of the auditorium, Scarlet at his heels.

"You tried to call me?" The voice on the other end was recognizable across the years. A joyous baritone with a hint of a British lilt, the words crisply enunciated.

Paul could hardly speak. "Mr. Riordan? I can't tell you how happy I am to hear your voice."

A pause on the phone. "Your note says you were one of my students. I'm sorry but I had a lot of students. And it was a long time ago. I'm not really sure . . ."

Paul's heart fell. The one teacher he'd had in high school who had made a difference didn't remember him. How could that be? "You cast me as Verges. In *Much Ado about Nothing*."

"Um," said Riordan.

"Is that Simon?" Scarlet was now in front of Paul, leaning in to try to hear the phone.

Paul turned away and said into the phone, "That's not important. I need your help."

"Help?" said Riordan. His tone was lower and carried less joy. "I'm not sure I know what you mean."

"I'm a drama teacher now," Paul said. "And I've gotten into a bind."

Riordan's voice went flat, any trace of an accent gone. "I gave up drama years ago. I'm sorry. I can't help you."

Afraid that Riordan would hang up, Paul said quickly, "Just one question. One only you can answer."

Silence. Then, "Go ahead."

"Is the curse real?"

Paul waited for his mentor's reply. His sanity—and the safety of his students—hung on the answer. Even Scarlet knew to stop interrupting while he waited for Simon Riordan to confirm or deny what had happened to him twenty years ago.

Paul waited.

And waited.

Then he looked at his phone: disconnected.

"I'd interpret that as a yes," said Scarlet.

Scene 8: Lay on, Macduff

"WHO WAS THAT, dear?" Sylvia had joined Paul in the seating area, concern written on her face.

"Simon Riordan."

"Really?" Sylvia sounded impressed. "What did he say when you told him about Scarlet? Does he think she could be a real ghost?"

"Of course I'm a real ghost," Scarlet said. "I should know. I've been a ghost for what feels like forever."

Paul observed that Sylvia neither heard nor saw Scarlet.

"I didn't get that far," he said. "Mr. Riordan hung up when I asked him about the curse."

"Why would you ask him that?" asked Sylvia. "He's no better at distinguishing between bad luck and a curse than you are. And speaking of bad luck, that boy with the broken leg just arrived."

Paul returned down the aisle toward the stage. The thanes had finished the scene. It was short, after all, fewer than twenty lines. The armed boys now surrounded a wheelchair. Many of the others students had also come out on stage.

Kim Greyson was not a happy camper. This surprised Paul. Usually when high school kids were injured, they wore their bandages like badges of honour. Kim should return the conquering hero, the centre of attention, all the girls wanting to sign his cast. Instead, he sat in the wheelchair, his blond hair unkempt and his face wearing a heavy sulk. The other students stood back a ways, staring at him.

"Do they believe he's cursed?" Paul whispered under his

breath.

"What?" asked Sylvia, who walked beside him. The aisle was wide enough for two with room to spare.

"How did he break his leg?" Scarlet asked. She walked at his other side, stepping through the cloth and steel of the audience seating. There wasn't room for three.

"Do they believe he fell down the stairs because of the curse?" Paul said to Sylvia, trying not to look like an insane monarch talking to himself.

Sylvia shrugged.

Scarlet, however, nodded. "That explains it, then. Too embarrassing an injury. If he'd broken his leg playing football or climbing a building, he'd be a hero. For falling down some stairs, he's just a klutz."

Of course. A klutz instead of a hero. Maybe being insane and hearing voices had its advantages. Voices could tell you things.

By now they had returned to the stage. Paul put on his best smile. "Welcome back, Kim! I hope your stint in the hospital wasn't too . . . inconvenient." Paul had no idea what to say.

Kim did. "They told me I'm not Macbeth anymore. I won that part, fair and square."

"Um," said Paul. He glanced around and saw no sign of Lenny. "I'm sorry Kim, but Macbeth is in almost every scene and does a lot of . . . walking, fighting, and winning his fights. A soldier in a wheelchair or on crutches isn't going to win a swordfight. You're going to have to be Thane Angus, an older general wounded in battle."

"Isn't that Thane Angus?" Kim was looking at Jocelynn, who had played Angus in the last scene.

"Jocelynn is your understudy," Paul said. "It's her job to cover for you when you're absent. We'll run the scene again so you can get familiar with your lines."

Kim tried and failed to rise from his chair. "But that's not fair!"

Sylvia stepped in. "No, Kim, it isn't. But life is rarely fair. The best you can do is to roll with the punches. With that broken leg, I'm afraid that you've been punched good and hard. Sorry."

Paul stared at Sylvia. Why couldn't he say things like that? He'd just tell the boy to buck up, and what good would that do?

Kim also stared at her. "Um, are you another teacher? I haven't seen you around."

"I'm Susie's mom," Sylvia replied, sticking out her hand.

"Mr. Samson's wife?" Kim said, taking her hand automatically and shaking it but looking at Paul.

"Yes, dear," Sylvia said with a smile and stepped back again.

Kim actually shook himself, getting back his train of thought. "But I'm supposed to be the lead," he said. "I've never been the lead before."

"Instead you'll be a wounded general," said Sylvia. "The best wounded general this stage has ever seen."

Kim's expression gave a hint of appearing mollified.

Bruce Filman stepped up to Kim's wheelchair. "I'm a thane too. We'll both be the best thanes ever."

"Me too," said Mike Mitchell. "The three thanes. We'll steal the show."

"Hey," said Susan Williams, who played Thane Caithness because there were more male roles than male students. "I'm a thane too."

"You can be d'Artagnan," Kim said.

The three boys and one faux boy cheered and yelled, "All for one and one for all!"

It was a line from a different play, but Paul couldn't keep the grin off his face. Perhaps the day wasn't turning out so bad after all.

Scarlet sighed into his ear. "I love the theatre."

Right. Paul had forgotten about the ghost. Then his phone rang again.

Paul stepped away. "Paul Samson."

"Why would you ask that?" The voice was low and serious.

"Mr. Riordan, thank you for calling back. I'm sorry, but I'm directing *Macb*—The Bard's Play, and some strange things are going on." Paul had barely remembered that the curse was supposed to be brought on by referring to the play as *Macbeth* instead of as The Bard's Play or The Cursed Play.

"Stop!" said Riordan, his voice unnaturally loud on the speaker.

"What?"

"Don't do it."

"What? The play?"

"Has anyone died?"

"Died? No, a student broke his leg. But that isn't the problem."

"Thank God," said Riordan. "But you have to stop the play."

"I need to tell you the problem," Paul said.

A pause. "All right. What's the problem?"

"I think I'm going insane," Paul whispered.

A longer pause. "That's a new one."

"A new what?"

"Why do you think you're going insane?"

Paul lowered his voice. "I'm seeing ghosts."

"Ghosts!" Riordan's voice was loud on the phone.

"Well, just one ghost. Someone you know."

The voice grew louder. "Someone I know?"

"Scarlet Walker."

Silence.

Paul looked at his phone again: disconnected.

Scene 9: Ask Me What Question Thou Canst

THE BELL RANG and the students departed, Kim Greyson smiling and being cajoled by the others. His cast even sported several signatures. Sylvia left as well, off to go shopping or show a house or something. Paul hadn't paid attention. He had only one thing on his mind: a ghost.

Paul sat in his director's chair as Scarlet Walker danced across the empty stage, the folds of her long, red dress twirling as she spun. It took him a moment to realize he was mesmerized. The ghost pranced and flew through the air with the grace of a ballerina. Finally she stopped and laughed and shook out her waist-length hair, tucking the cloth it had been tied with into a hidden pocket in her sleeve.

"Dancing is so much easier when you don't weigh anything," she said. "I feel so free on the stage. There's no room to even move inside the lamp. It's like being bound and gagged. I hate having to go back in there."

Paul started. "I thought you were free now. Why would you have to go back?"

Scarlet gazed at the lamp where it still hung on a castle wall, despite having a broken bulb. "Well, I'm haunting it, of course.

103

It's not much but it's mine."

"You're haunting a prop lamp?"

Scarlet let out a deep breath. "Don't ask me how it works. Being a ghost doesn't come with an instruction manual. All I know is that I can only come out when you're nearby and producing *Macbeth*. It kinda sucks."

"When I'm producing *Macbeth*?"

Scarlet spun on her heels. "I can hear you working with other students sometimes, but I can't leave the lamp."

"That would be my other two classes," Paul said. "But you suggested that I stop *Macbeth*. Won't that mean that you'll be stuck back in the lamp permanently?"

Scarlet stopped spinning. "Better that than endangering your students. Like I said, it kinda sucks."

Paul walked over to the lamp and looked at it. It was just a cheap lamp. "So when I go to lunch, you go back in the lamp? Like a genie?"

Scarlet laughed. "Sorry. If you're looking for three wishes, you're out of luck. All you get is what you see." The young woman sobered. "I guess ghosts aren't worth much."

"No," Paul said. "You're terrific. Really. I might be going insane, but if insanity means having you around, I'll take it." It was a cheesy thing to say, and Paul wasn't even sure he meant it, but he couldn't deny how his words lit up the young woman's face.

Just then his phone rang. Paul looked at the display then hit the answer button. "Hello! Mr. Riordan!"

"Scarlet Walker?"

"I'm speaking with her right now."

A pause. "Put her on."

It was Paul's turn to pause. "I don't think that will work. I'm the only one who can see and hear her."

He looked at the phone: disconnected.

"Are you tormenting Simon?" Scarlet asked.

Paul shook his head. "Unless you can speak with him on the phone, I don't know what else to do."

Scarlet bit her lip in thought then shook her head.

The phone rang again.

"You're having me on," said Simon Riordan. "Who are you? You're not one of my students."

"I am," Paul said. "Was. Ask me a question only Scarlet could answer."

"You're kidding."

"No. Really. Any question."

"What role was I originally cast for in *Macb*—The Bard's Play?"

"Just a minute," Paul said.

Scarlet must have heard the question. "Banquo. But then Mrs. Ascott had to shuffle some parts when John and Elizabeth Moore dropped out the third week of rehearsal."

Paul repeated the answer to Riordan.

"Did you just look that up somewhere?" Riordan sounded angry. "Do you have Ascott's notes?"

"Ask me something else," Paul suggested. "Something Mrs. Ascott wouldn't have written down."

A pause. "What line did I totally mess up in rehearsal?"

"That sounds a little vague," Paul said, but Scarlet had an answer.

"'Scotland hath foisons to fill up your will.' Scarlet says you said 'poisons' instead of 'foisons.'"

"A slip of the tongue," Riordan muttered. A longer pause. "We need to meet."

Paul knew just the place. "The Dairy Queen across from Ashcroft Senior High School?"

"What about me?" Scarlet demanded. "I can't go there!"

Paul cast the ghost an uncomfortable glance. "The way he keeps hanging up the phone, I think I need to set him at ease first. We'll come back here when he's ready to meet you."

"What was that?" asked Riordan.

"Just speaking with Scarlet," Paul said.

"You'd better be straight with this," said Riordan. "If you're putting me on, I'll have you arrested. Dairy Queen, you say? I'll get a day pass and meet you in an hour."

Then Riordan hung up.

"Day pass?" Paul said aloud.

"Oh, dear," said Scarlet. "Poor Simon."

Scene 10: Let Us Call Thee Devil

THERE WAS NO sign of Simon Riordan when Paul stepped inside the Dairy Queen, but that didn't surprise him; hardly thirty minutes had passed since their last conversation. Apart from the three hags in the far corner booth, the exact same booth where he and Sylvia had seen them last week, the place was deserted. Paul knew that would change when the bell ending third period rang.

He chose a booth by the door and sat so he could keep an eye on the hags. Not that he expected them to cause trouble. He could think of worse places where three lonely, old women could spend their time. Paul rubbed his face, wondering where he would be in thirty years. Retired, bored, possibly idling away the hours at Dairy Queen, recounting the good old days with a couple of other gaffers. He shook his head. Denny's was more his style.

Paul wondered if he should order some lunch or wait for Mr. Riordan. He had no idea if Riordan was interested in eating. The man was getting a day pass. Like he never left the convalescent home. They must feed him there. Three meals a day. Like in a hospital. Or a prison. Had Mr. Riordan been institutionalized?

He noticed that the staff behind the counter were giving him dirty looks, so he ordered a soda.

Kids began flying in through the doors, ordering burgers and shakes and filling up the other tables. Paul glanced at his watch. It was the right time, but there was still no sign of Riordan.

Paul kept his eyes glued to the space just inside door and stood when a grey-haired skeleton of a man crept inside and glanced about uncertainly. The man looked nothing like Simon Riordan, but Paul recognized him anyway. Riordan's once broad back and shoulders curved forward in a slouch that took inches off his formerly impressive height. His gut was gone, but not in a good way. He still had narrow hips and legs and tiny feet. Paul felt sure that a stiff breeze would blow him away. Simon Riordan was ill. If Paul were a doctor, he would have never authorized a day pass.

"Mr. Riordan!" Paul waved and the walking skeleton navigated his way through some students and fell onto the bench seat across from him.

"You're Paul Samson?" The British accent was back.

"I am," Paul said. "I can't express how glad I am that you agreed to meet me."

"You're old," said Riordan.

"What?"

"You said you were one of my students. You're as old as I was when I taught."

Paul's mouth hung open for a moment. "Right. It's been twenty years. I'm a teacher now. I mentioned that on the phone."

The older man glared at him. "Of course you did. I'm not an idiot. I never see my old students. You took me by surprise. Students never grow up. They just get replaced."

Paul nodded and offered a nervous smile. "Sometimes it seems that way." Was the man ill mentally as well as physically? He wondered if he should ask. Would it be too brash?

"You said—" Riordan faltered. He took a breath and lowered his voice. "You said that you saw Scarlet."

Paul nodded again. "She's across the street at the school. Apparently she's haunting the lamp from your prop box."

"Lamp?"

"The one with the flickering bulb made to look like a sconce. I found it in a box of props one of the students brought in. A note in the box said property of Simon Riordan."

Riordan blinked and turned his head slightly as the cackling of the hags on the far side of the seating area penetrated the mass of noisy students to reach their table. Riordan shook himself and waved his hand. "That's not important. You're sure it's Scarlet?"

Paul nodded a third time.

"How—?" Riordan paused and took a slow, trembling breath. "How is she?"

Another round of cackles was followed by a loud *shhh*, but the old man seemed not to hear.

Paul pushed the distraction from his mind. How to answer Riordan's question? She's fine. She's dead. She's a freaking ghost. How should I know? I've only just met her. But Paul could see that the question was important. Simon Riordan, sick as he obviously was, had left his hospital bed to come across town and ask Paul this question. Paul's answer had better be worth it.

"She's in good spirits," Paul said. "She'd talk my ear off if I let her. And just this morning she was dancing." Paul couldn't help but smile as he spoke.

Riordan also smiled. And a tear began to work its way down one cheek.

"I'll take you to see her," Paul said. "Well, so she can see you, anyway." Paul felt himself growing almost giddy with excitement. Riordan could prove if Scarlet was a real ghost or just a delusion brought on by insanity. "I'm happy to act as a go-between," Paul said. "Or a medium. I never thought I'd hear myself say that."

He stopped speaking as he saw that Riordan was no longer smiling. His old mentor shook his head. "No. I don't want her to see me."

"Oh," Paul said. "But she was so looking forward—"

"She was?" The old man shook his head again. "No. I can't. It would be too painful."

"But then why did you come here?"

Again, Riordan lowered his voice, so low that Paul could barely hear him. "The curse."

"What?"

Riordan leaned forward and whispered. "It wasn't you, was it?"

"Me what?"

"Who struck the bargain?"

"What bargain?"

Riordan abruptly straightened. "Then it must have been someone else."

"Someone else what?"

The old man, who looked far older than his years, pinched the bridge of his nose. "Gods. It must be one of the students."

"Um," said Paul. "I'm not quite sure what you're saying."

"Look," said Riordan. "Curses don't just happen. Someone has to strike a deal. Who among your students is doing better than expected?"

It was a simple question. And Paul realized it had a simple answer. There was only one student who had surprised him: Susie. What Riordan was suggesting, however, was anything but simple.

"There is," Paul said slowly, "a student who comes to mind. But tell me, strike a deal with who?"

Riordan grimaced. "With Hell, that's who. This student of yours has struck a deal with the Devil!"

More cackling from the hags, but this time Paul scarcely heard it. His heart had stopped in his chest. Susie? Made a deal with the Devil? So that she could play the part of Lady Macbeth in her father's drama class? A month ago Paul would have laughed out loud. Any deal Susie made would have been to avoid such a fate. But today? Susie had never been happier. Did he know his own daughter that badly?

"That is," said Riordan, "if you really have a curse."

Paul remembered to breathe. "How do I tell?"

Riordan shrugged his thin shoulders. "You could ask your students if any of them have made such a deal. Ha! Like they'd ever admit it. Or you can wait until someone falls off a ladder and breaks their neck. Or until the school burns to the ground."

"But—"

Paul lurched back against the bench seat as Riordan stabbed at him with a bony finger. "The deal's a lie. Hell promises something the supplicant already has, and in return, the play gets cursed, usually to the point where the supplicant loses what they asked for." The old man lowered his voice. "And then some. Tell that to your students."

Suddenly Riordan was on his feet. Paul also stood and grabbed the old man's arm. "But what should I do?"

Riordan stared at Paul's clutching fingers until he let go. "Don't be an idiot. Cancel the damn play. Continuing is not worth the risk."

Again, the hags burst out in a chorus of loud cackling, so shrill that even the students at other tables paused in their lively chatter. Paul watched, stunned, as Simon Riordan spun around and nearly injured himself, caught as he was in the tight confines between the bench seat and the table. Then Paul looked past his old mentor's contorted form to the booth where the three hags sat. Or had sat, for the booth was now empty.

Riordan turned around, his blanched face three shades paler and his greying hair perhaps that much whiter. "I must go now," he whispered. And Simon Riordan extricated himself from the booth and shambled out the door.

Scene 11: Give the Devil His Due

"OH, LOOK," SAID Agatha. "Here comes our brash director."

"Perhaps he'll join us," suggested Gertrude. "Might be nice to enjoy some male conversation."

Agatha stared down her boney nose at the misshapen witch. "Really? What would we discuss? Sports? Cars? Argue about which brand of beer is the best?" The tall witch turned her head to eye the slight, balding drama teacher. "I don't think he'll have much to offer on any of those topics."

"He's sitting by himself," Netty mumbled around a mouthful of fries. "Do you suppose that wife of his will be joining him?"

"We haven't done anything to spoil their relationship yet," Gertrude said. "Perhaps this will be our chance."

Agatha curled one lip. "Perhaps you could make her jealous by smiling at him wearing nothing but your skivvies. Oh, wait. Hecate already did that. And you saw how well that worked."

Gertrude smirked. "Perhaps Hecate was just the wrong witch. You haven't seen me in skivvies."

All three witches burst out laughing.

"Look," said Gertrude. "He's got himself a drink. Perhaps he is going solo. I had no idea this was a pick-up diner."

"We've been here for days," said Netty. "No one's tried to pick us up."

"Just as well," said Agatha. "I can't stand dating. All the primping and preening, and remembering to smile. The awkward conversation. And at the end of it all, will he or won't he? It's just not worth it."

The other two witches stared at her.

"You've been on a date?" asked Netty.

"Well, of course," Agatha said.

Gertrude peered up at Agatha through beady eyes. "Truly?"

"Yes," said Agatha. "I mean, no. Of course not. I've thought about it, though. Gives me the willies."

"Dating is for ponces," Gertrude agreed.

"Damn straight," said Netty. A pause. "Do you really think this is a pick-up diner?"

"Now he's got a guest," said Agatha.

"Male or female?" asked Netty. The rotund witch had left off the fries and was chewing on a Crispy Chicken Sandwich, no mayo. "I'm not turning around and craning my neck unless you tell me it's worth the trouble."

Agatha's eyes went wide. "It's well worth the trouble, dearie."

Netty put down the sandwich and craned her neck, several vertebrae grinding loudly in the process. "Oh! It's Simple Simon."

Gertrude tsked. "It hasn't been that many years since we last saw Simon. What's happened to the poor fellow? He's but a shadow of himself."

"Less than a shadow, I'd say," said Agatha. "The man's aged fifty years if he's aged a day."

"Cadaverous," Netty said. "That's the word I'd use. There's nothing left but skin and bones . . . and regrets."

"Yes," Gertrude agreed then chuckled. "It's a sight to warm the heart."

"Where is Hecate when you need her?" Agatha asked. "I'd love to rub that pompous crone's pert, upturned nose in this shining example of our handiwork. Twenty years later and the man's still a ruin. Curses don't get much better than that."

"Oh, my," said Gertrude. "Did you hear that? They're talking about that Scarlet Walker woman."

"The one who died?" asked Netty. "After all these years, he still feels responsible?"

"He is responsible," said Agatha. Then she cackled, the other two joining in.

"Such a promising career," Gertrude mused. "I actually admired the woman. She lived life to the fullest, that one."

Netty nodded, her cheeks flapping. "Which is why she was the one who had to die!"

Again, the witches cackled, louder this time. Then Gertrude pressed a finger to her lips. "Shhh! Let's not ruin it for them. There's some serious man talk going on over there."

"Sports, cars, or beer," said Agatha. "I missed the big one. Women. Men do love to talk about women."

"Twenty years dead," said Gertrude, "and they're still talking about Scarlet Walker. I guess I'm not the only one who admired her."

"What are they saying about her?" asked Netty. "I'm having a bad case of earwax today. All I hear is students spewing nonsense."

Agatha snorted. "There's no such thing as a case of earwax. And the students are spewing nonsense. There's nothing wrong with your ears."

"I bought a case of earwax once," Gertrude said. "Never found a use for it. The box is still sitting in my attic. All eight pounds."

"Have you tried candles?" suggested Agatha. "I hear earwax burns tolerably well."

"Sisters!" said Netty. "The conversation. Please. And my ears are full of wax, thank you very much."

"Oh, my," said Gertrude. "Now they're talking about the curse."

"Not comparing notes, I hope." Agatha wrinkled her already contorted nose. "I detest cheaters."

"The nerve," said Gertrude, suddenly angry. "Simple Simon is suggesting that one of Samson's students has made a deal with the Devil."

"He didn't!" cried Netty. "I mean, he didn't. He made a deal with us. The Dark One wouldn't be caught dead wasting his time on anything as paltry as a cursed play."

Again the witches cackled.

"But why?" asked Agatha. "Why is Simple Simon giving the Devil our due?"

"He hasn't told him," Netty suggested.

"Of course he hasn't," Gertrude agreed. "Simon can't talk about us. Samson would ask him how he knows. And then he'd be outed."

"This is rich!" Agatha said, her thin lips spreading in a horrific grin. "Samson manages to somehow find Simon to learn about the curse, and Simon won't tell him!"

"If only Hecate were here to witness," said Netty. "Then she'd know we aren't just sitting on our behinds, eating fries and guzzling sodas."

Gertrude cocked an eye at the mess of fries, burgers, and soda cups cluttering the table and shrugged her misshapen shoulders.

"Hecate wouldn't see it," Agatha said. "It's too sophisticated. The irony would be lost on her."

"When you're right, you're right," said Gertrude.

"Oh," said Agatha. "Simple Simon is leaving. But Samson's stopping him. He's demanding that Simon tell him what to do.

Simon's telling him to cancel the play."

"The suspense is killing me," Netty said.

"Oh, the humanity," Gertrude added.

Again, the three hags burst into cackling glee and at once ducked beneath the table, banging their knobby knees into each other's elbows.

After two minutes, Agatha poked her head up to see if the coast was clear, only to find someone sitting in the space next to Netty's generous backside.

"I assume," said Hecate, "that you have an excellent explanation for why you are all hiding under the table."

Scene 12: Or Have We Eaten on the Insane Root

PAUL SAT AT his desk in his study, contemplating suicide. Not literally. But he couldn't see how asking Susie if she had made a deal with the Devil was any different. She would judge him insane, unworthy of being her father, and would never speak to him again. Sylvia would have no choice but to side with their daughter. And it wouldn't be long before the entire school knew. The gorgon lady would be in her glory, adding deals with the Devil to her list of reasons to cancel the play. And Winston would save face by firing him. Paul would likely never work again, his reputation following him wherever he went as the teacher who accused his students of devil worship.

And that was the *good* scenario.

The bad scenario was if Susie said yes, she had made a bargain with Hell. Paul had no idea how you undid a deal with the Devil. Would the Devil own his daughter's soul?

Through the wall, he could hear Susie listening to music in her room. It didn't sound like devil music. It was more a bubbly dance number. Paul let out a silent groan. Who was he kidding? He had no idea what devil music sounded like. Or if there even was devil music. Perhaps he should consult a priest.

After meeting with Simon Riordan, Paul had sleepwalked through the remainder of the day. Scarlet would be furious with him for not bringing Riordan back to the school, and he had no idea what he would tell her in the morning when she demanded to know why Riordan wouldn't see her. Should he tell her that Mr. Riordan was ill? Or would that only upset her more? He shook his head. Riordan and Scarlet were the least of Paul's worries.

He had skipped supper with Sylvia and Susie. Besides having no appetite, despite having only a soda for lunch, he didn't know how he could have sat at the table with Susie and not stared at her like an idiot. Had his beautiful daughter made a deal with the Devil?

Sylvia had cornered him in the living room and asked about Mr. Riordan's calling during rehearsal. Paul told her about their meeting after class. He described Riordan's reluctance to see Scarlet and purposefully left out any mention of deals with the Devil. Paul still had no idea if Scarlet was the real thing or just a tool of that other devil, Mrs. Cadwell. If only Riordan had been able to confirm that Scarlet was a real ghost. Then maybe Paul would know what to do. Or at least where to start.

Had Susie made a deal with the Devil?

Paul turned on his computer and entered *Devil*. Google returned more than three hundred million results. He added *deal*, which reduced the count to one hundred million. His fingers shook as he added *curse*. Google's responses plunged to seventeen million hits, enough to keep Paul busy for the rest of his life. He added *Macbeth* and hit Enter. Zero results.

Zero? How was that possible? Riordan had been adamant.

Paul shut off his computer and stared at his overflowing bookshelves.

Was he betting too heavily on Simon Riordan? The man was, after all, ill. Perhaps even delusional. He had quit acting and teaching and disappeared for twenty years. Paul had found him in a hospital.

He turned his computer back on and entered *Spring Hills Convalescent Home*. The first hit was the company Web site. Paul read through the politically correct description that danced around what the place really was, a home for the mentally unstable.

Paul couldn't help but laugh. For the past week, he'd been thinking himself insane, and he had turned for help to the one person who was no better off than he was. Perhaps worse off, given Riordan's physical state. Simon Riordan's demons, his devil, were eating him alive. Could the man even be trusted?

There was a tapping sound, and Paul looked down to find his hands trembling, his wedding ring striking a tattoo against his desk. He stilled his fingers. He had come so close to confronting his daughter.

Even cancelling the play, as Mr. Riordan had suggested, would be an error. Two weeks ago, the students would have rejoiced at Shakespeare being cancelled. But now they were genuinely into it. Paul had never seen students work harder at learning their lines and understanding their roles. And the costumes they were assembling! Everyone had looked at Lenny's costume and tried to outdo him or at least keep up. Even the witches had put away their broomsticks and their warts and had gone with gothic gypsy.

Witches. Paul turned back to his computer and printed off the photo of the three hags he had taken on his phone at the Dairy Queen. He must have done something wrong, however, as both photos printed. He shook his head at the lingerie model who had stood near the hags' table and smiled at him. He went to crumple up the printout but folded it into his pocket instead. He couldn't bring himself to destroy it. No one had ever smiled at him like that.

Again Paul laughed. It was all too much. Curses. Ghosts. Devils. Enigmatic women. He had to be losing his mind. And there was sweet nothing he could do about it.

Scene 13: I Pray You, Deliver Him This Petition

HALF A WEEK later, it was Friday, and Paul was no closer to recovering his sanity. Fortunately he could take refuge in his work.

Paul sat on his director's chair, enjoying the march of Birnam Wood as Malcolm's army approached Dunsinane. The students' lines were coming along. They even had most of the stage blocking down. He had never been more proud. Even the ushers and stagehands had created bit parts for themselves to get a few moments on stage, even if those parts wouldn't be part of the final performance.

Several members of the class had asked Sylvia if they could paint additional scenery flats to allow the set to fill more of the stage. *Macbeth* would be the best performance in Ashcroft High history!

Paul had to admit that his decision Tuesday night to ignore the curse had been the correct one. Wednesday and Thursday had proceeded without incident, and Friday, so far, had been perfect. For the first time in days, Paul had slept soundly. To be honest, the only problems the so-called curse had caused were in his own head. He could kick himself for having gotten so worked up about it. There had been nothing to worry about.

"Not bad for high school kids," said Scarlet, who stood next to his chair, also watching the Birnam Wood scene.

Well, there was the ghost.

Paul had yet to decide if Scarlet was a real ghost, a spy for the gorgon, or just a figment of his own imagination, perhaps brought on by his fixation with the curse. Was that what had happened to Simon Riordan? Had he so convinced himself that *The Tragedy of Macbeth* was cursed that he had lost his mind?

Even Scarlet wasn't convinced about the curse, and she was the one who had died. Neither was she happy with Paul's explanation that Simon wasn't yet ready to see her. A day didn't go by without her asking him, repeatedly, when Simon would be coming back.

"I think you could use some additional leaves on the papier-mâché branches," Scarlet said. "Some in the audience won't know the story and may think Malcolm's army is attacking with clubs."

Paul passed this advice on to Sylvia, who sat in a second director's chair on his other side. "Good idea," his wife said and jotted it down.

Sylvia occasionally remembered to ask if Scarlet was still haunting him, and each time Paul had shrugged it off, saying that he was doing as she had suggested and was keeping an eye out. So far, nothing had happened to tip Scarlet's hand. Until Paul made up his own mind, he didn't see how adding to Sylvia's confusion would help.

"Five weeks to show time?" Sylvia asked.

Paul nodded.

"The play will be more than ready," Scarlet said. The ghost clapped her hands as the scene ended with Macduff's cry: "Make all our trumpets speak; give them all breath, those clamorous harbingers of blood and death."

"Mr. Samson?"

A girl who was not one of Paul's students approached and handed him a slip of paper. There were two words on it: *Principal's Office*. Now what? The past few days had been so quiet. Paul couldn't imagine why Winston would want to see him.

He turned to Sylvia. "Run the class through scenes five and six again. The scenery flats need to change quicker. And ask Malcolm and his soldiers to cross the stage more slowly. The army was at the gates before Macbeth finished his speech. I have to go see Winston."

Sylvia frowned but knew better than to ask what it might be about. Winston wasn't one to give warning.

Scarlet, however, swept in front of Paul, her expression serious. "Take your daughter with you."

Paul almost asked her why but held his tongue. He couldn't afford to be seen talking to himself, and not doing so was an increasing challenge. No wonder insane people ended up in institutions.

"Susie?" Paul called. "Come with me for a moment?"

Act V, Scene 5 was where Lady Macbeth dies, but as Susie had already plaintively pointed out, it happens offstage, so she wasn't in the scene.

"What's up?" Susie asked.

"Winston's summoned me to his office. I may need reinforcements."

To Paul's surprise, Susie simply nodded rather than attempting to bow out.

When they reached the principal's office, Mrs. Kennedy appeared scandalized when Paul insisted that Susie go in with him.

"You can't take a student with you," the school secretary insisted.

"I'm not," Paul said. "I'm taking my daughter with me." He opened Winston's door and ushered Susie inside before Mrs. Kennedy could respond.

"Samson, I—oh, hello, Susie." The principal frowned then

narrowed his eyes at Paul. "You can't bring a student in here. I asked you here alone."

Paul shrugged. "She's not here as a student. She's here as my daughter. Susie was helping me with some errands when your page handed me your message."

The school administrator raised his brows. "My what?"

Paul let out a sigh. "Your page? Messenger? Good grief, Winston. Even Susie knows what a page is. You're supposed to be the principal."

The red in the heavy man's face told Paul that he had crossed a line. Oh, well. Conversations with Winston were never pleasant anyway.

"I know what a page is," Winston bellowed. "I just didn't expect to hear it in the context of summoning one of my teachers to my office. My education is in administration, not dead languages! And good luck, young lady, finding a job with *I know what* page *meant twelve hundred years ago* written on your résumé. Why we even teach liberal arts anymore is beyond me. There's not a job to be had within a thousand miles."

Winston clamped his mouth shut, perhaps realizing that he, too, had crossed a line.

Paul opted to eschew defending the liberal arts—again—and call it a draw. "You summoned me to your office?"

"We're just waiting on Mrs. Cadwell." Winston began shuffling some papers on his desk.

"Cadwell? You told me to stay away from her and I have. I haven't seen her in days." Another reason the week had been so quiet. "What can Cadwell possibly have to complain about now?"

Paul had begun to believe that the gorgon lady had given up her crusade against the play. Her own son was the lead, after all. And her attempts at intimidation had failed, especially the leaflet fiasco. She'd been scarce and Paul had counted it a blessing. None of that meant that she had given up her crusade against him personally. They had crossed swords too often for her to simply walk away.

There was a tap at the door, and Mrs. Kennedy peeked in. "Mrs. Cadwell is here."

Then the door swung all the way open, and Mrs. Cadwell strode in as if she owned the place. "Thank you, Mrs. Kennedy," the gorgon said without once looking at the woman.

The PTA president lost her grin when she saw Susie. "Oh? I thought this would be a private meeting."

"And I thought I'd even up the odds," Paul said. "Two against two."

"No one is against anyone," said Winston. "Something has come to Mrs. Cadwell's attention, and we've agreed to bring it to yours."

Susie was doing the smart thing and had kept quiet all this time. Paul decided to follow her lead. "Okay. Let's hear it."

The gorgon lady resumed smiling as she pulled a sheaf of papers from her purse. "Apparently there's been a petition going around."

Paul had forgotten about the petition Sylvia had mentioned on Monday. He also had forgotten deciding just moments earlier his resolve to keep quiet. "Going around? I was led to believe that this was your petition."

"My name does appear near the top," Mrs. Cadwell said, skirting the question. "There are three hundred and fifty names on this petition."

"Really?" said Paul. "Congratulations! You've expanded your reach beyond the PTA. I'll give you an *A* for effort."

"Sadly," said Mrs. Cadwell, her expression inadequately conveying said sadness, "not all of Ashcroft Senior High's parents take a proper interest in their children's education."

"Or more accurately," Paul said, "not all of the parents agree with your rather narrow view of their children's education."

"You—!" began the gorgon lady.

Winston rose from his desk and waved his hands. "Enough! We're here to talk about the petition. I'm not going to referee your differences of opinion."

"But that's exactly what you are going to do," Paul said. "That's all that petition is. Mrs. Cadwell's opinion. Sure, she's gone and brainwashed and browbeat other parents into agreeing with her. But it's still just an opinion. There is no law against *Macbeth* in high schools. On the contrary, *Macbeth* is the law. It's been read in practically every high school in the world. And schools with drama departments have been producing it for decades. *Macbeth* is a classic even among classics. A bunch of names on a piece of paper doesn't change that."

"It's more than a bunch," said Mrs. Cadwell. "It is three

hundred and fifty parents who feel that *Macbeth* has no place in this school."

"She has a point," said Winston. The heavyset man was sitting again. "I told you there'd be trouble when you first picked this play. You wouldn't listen to me. Now I have to answer to three hundred and fifty parents. What do you want me to tell them? That their concerns don't count?"

Paul had no response for that. He stood there, silent. She had won. The gorgon lady had won. And she knew it too. There she stood, sheaf of papers in her fist, a gleaming smile covering half her face. And her eyes, her eyes were mocking him.

"Excuse me," said Susie. "But I have six hundred names."

The gorgon lady waved her hand. "Thank you, dear. But we don't need any more names. I think we all know what has to happen now."

"Susie?" Paul said. "You have names?"

Susie pulled a notebook out of her backpack and began flipping through the pages. "Almost six hundred. I've only had three days to collect them. I can get more."

"Your daughter's an angel," the gorgon lady said. "You see? No one wants *Macbeth* in this school."

Susie walked over to Mrs. Cadwell and glared at her, eye to eye. "My list is a petition for keeping the play."

"What?" Winston choked on the word, and his face turned red. Perspiration broke out on his forehead.

"Let me see that list!" Mrs. Cadwell ripped the notebook from Susie's hands and began flipping through it. "But . . . these are students' names."

"Mostly students," said Susie. "We were afraid the parents would let you know what we were up to, so we didn't ask many."

"But . . . but . . ." Mrs. Cadwell continued to flip through the pages. "Students don't count."

"Students don't count!" Paul felt heat flow out from his stomach into his face, his hands, his feet, and everywhere in between. He was a volcano about to erupt. His tongue felt thick like a sponge, and he wasn't even sure he could speak coherently. But speak he did. "Students don't count! Of course they count! Mrs. Cadwell, as much as you want to believe that this school exists for the parents, that view is flawed. This school exists for the students. Without the students, the doors would be closed and barred. Principal Winston, myself, and all of the other teachers at this school are here to serve the students. The parents only get in the way. Just as you, right this moment, are getting in the way. I should be in class right now, teaching my students. Instead I'm here, debating William bloody Shakespeare with one of the parents. You have some nerve. The students don't count!"

"I didn't mean . . ." the gorgon lady whined. "Of course the school is for the students. Don't be absurd. I simply meant that the students' opinions don't count when it comes to determining what is good for them. They don't get a vote. This petition"—she thrust the notebook back into Susie's hands—"is worthless."

Paul sputtered, trying to speak, but his tongue kept getting in the way. He felt a hand touch his arm, and he turned to see the principal's pudgy fingers. The stocky man was shaking his head. Winston then let go of Paul's arm and pulled a handkerchief from his pocket. He wiped his face and looked at the gorgon lady.

"No," he said. "The petition is not worthless."

"What?" Mrs. Cadwell looked ready to explode.

Winston glowered at her. "Mrs. Cadwell, you assured me that no one wanted this play. Not the parents and not the students. Susie Samson here has proven that assurance to be false."

"But students hate Shakespeare!" The gorgon lady snatched the notebook back from Susie and flipped a few pages. "Here. Look. The girls' soccer team. Jocks don't read Shakespeare. And they certainly don't go to see Shakespeare plays. This list is just an agenda. No one even knew what they were signing."

"The same—" began Paul, finally able to speak again, at the same time Susie said, "But—"

"I'll take this," said Winston, cutting them both off. "The same can be said about your list, Mrs. Cadwell. Most parents don't really care what the play is, especially those who don't have kids in drama class."

The gorgon lady ground her teeth. "The fact remains that I have more parents on my petition than this student has on hers."

Winston's eyes went wide. "Are we reduced to that, now? My dad is bigger than your dad?"

"The will of the parents—" Mrs. Cadwell began.

"Is in question," said Winston.

The gorgon lady actually pouted. "Are you going to ignore my petition?"

Winston sighed. "I have two petitions. What they tell me is that opinion is split. So what else is new?"

"What shall I tell the PTA?"

Winston wiped his face again. "Tell the PTA that I appreciate their concern but that there is significant opposition to their petition."

"But—"

"Tell them that other parents and what appears to be the majority of the students disagree."

"But—"

"And tell them that I would appreciate it if they would expend their considerable energy on something more constructive than demonizing classic literature."

"But—"

"And if I see another damn leaflet, I'm going to kill somebody."

"But—"

"That is all."

"But—"

"I said, that is all."

On her way out, Mrs. Cadwell slammed the door.

"And wipe that smile from your face, Samson."

Paul tried his best but knew the smile was still there. Susie sported the same smile, so it was unclear which Samson Winston was speaking to. Perhaps both. "I had no idea you were on my side," he said.

The principal harrumphed. "I don't take sides. Today I just happen to like Cadwell less than I like you. The only one who has impressed me in all this is you, Ms. Samson." A smile spread across the beefy principal's face. "You showed real initiative collecting your own petition. That kind of forethought and effort should be rewarded, don't you think?"

"I just thought that Mrs. Cadwell should be stopped," Susie said. "Who is she to tell everyone else what to do?"

Winston laughed. "Who indeed. That's my job. Damned if I'm going to let a parent tell me how to run my school. Now back to class, the both you."

Scene 14: Consort with Me in Loud and Dear Petition

"I NEVER PUT much stock in petitions," said Agatha. "More often than not, they just encourage the other position."

Gertrude nodded. "I remember the Olive Branch Petition of 1775. King George summarily disregarded the quite valid concerns in the petition and declared war on the colonies instead. Served him right that he lost."

"Which George was that?" asked Netty. "The mental one? I can never keep my kings straight."

"King George III," Gertrude said. "And yes, the mental one. Heh. Not that any of them had enough sense to fill a thimble."

"Don't forget the Hawaiian Patriotic League," said Agatha. "They petitioned Congress to block a perfectly legitimate treaty from President Benjamin Harrison to make Hawaii the fiftieth state."

Gertrude frowned. "Didn't the Hawaiian Patriotic League win that petition?"

"That's one way of looking at it," Agatha admitted.

"What's the other way?" Gertrude asked.

Agatha smiled. "A few months later, Congress used the Spanish-American War as an excuse to annex Hawaii anyway, making the petition moot. Even a winning petition can lose."

"But some petitions are worthwhile," Netty argued while poking a finger at a piece of popcorn shrimp stuck in her teeth. "Look at the 1674 Women's Petition against Coffee."

The two witches stared at their sister.

Netty gave them her best gap-toothed smile. "To this day England remains a tea-drinking nation."

Gertrude wagged her misshapen head. "That petition wasn't about coffee. It was about coffee*houses*. The petitioners wanted their husbands to drink coffee at home."

Netty lost her smile. "Are you sure? I don't much like coffee."

"The nerve of that woman, anyway," said Agatha, bringing the discussion back on track. "Trying to cancel our play."

"That would put us right out of a job, wouldn't it?" Gertrude said.

"No one puts a stop to the play but us," said Netty. "That's the way it's always been."

"You could have told us." Gertrude gave Netty a cold eye.

"Told you what?" asked Netty.

"About the girl's counterpetition. If you hadn't made her run around collecting names for half the week, this could have ended badly. For us, I mean."

"It wasn't me." Netty's head rolled fiercely on her shoulders. "I thought it was Agatha."

Agatha nearly choked on her GrillBurger. "I didn't do it. I was waiting for Netty to come up with more of those big plans she was so proud of last Friday. And here it is, Friday again."

"I never had any plans," Netty said. "You know that was just to get Hecate off our backs. It's your turn to come up with the plans."

"Oh, so were taking turns now, are we?" said Agatha. "I thought we were supposed to be a team. Three heads are better than one and all that."

"Sisters!" said Gertrude. "Even with three heads, none of us saw this petition thing coming. I'm beginning to think that Hecate is right and that we are being just a little bit lazy this time around."

"Lazy?" asked Agatha. "I'll have you know that I won an award for being the busiest witch. Mind you, that was back in eleven hundred and something. But I haven't slowed down— What?"

Both of the other witches were chortling.

"What are you two on about?" the tall witch demanded.

"You never read that certificate, did you?" asked Gertrude.

"Of course I read it," said Agatha. "Well, I looked at it. Couldn't find any reading glasses to see the fine print."

"Blind as a—" began Gertrude.

"It didn't say *busy*," Netty said. "It said *busybody*."

"That's what I said," snapped Agatha. "The busiest witch."

"Busybody doesn't mean busy," Gertrude said. "It means sticking your nose into other people's business."

"Your nose got an award," said Netty. "And believe me, it deserves one."

"Well." Agatha sniffed. "I'm a witch. I'm supposed know what's going on."

"Not when it involves other witches," Gertrude said. "We're private people, we witches are. Keep ourselves to ourselves.

Intruding noses are not welcome."

"Who's not welcome?" Hecate asked. She was sitting on a section of bench beside Netty that a moment before had been unoccupied.

Gertrude didn't drop a beat. "The gorgon over at the school. She almost succeeded in stopping the play."

Hecate's eyes brightened with interest. "The school has a gorgon? Why am I only hearing this now?"

"Not a real gorgon," said Agatha. "Just a parent who acts like one. She collected a petition to cancel the play."

"We stopped her, though." Netty's grin widened with pride. "We arranged for one of the students to collect a counterpetition." The rotund witch tapped her head. "Part of our big plan."

"I see," said Hecate. "Perhaps you should have let that parent's petition stand. Seems to me that this gorgon is doing a better job of cursing the play than you are."

Agatha coughed around the last bite of her GrillBurger. "A petition isn't even in the same country as a curse."

Hecate rolled her eyes. "This big plan of yours is taking too long. It's been three weeks and all you have to show for it is a broken leg and some collapsed canvas. Oh, yes. I know the castle wall was canvas."

"That's not all we have to show," said Agatha. "Our drama teacher is questioning his sanity. We have him believing that his own daughter has struck a deal with the Devil."

"We do?" asked Gertrude. "Heh. I mean, we do."

"Hmm," said Hecate. "Insanity is a slow and tedious process. I'm not sure I have the patience for it."

"We still have five weeks until the public performance," Netty said.

"One way or another," said Agatha, "the show will not go on. If our teacher hasn't cracked by then, we'll take more direct action."

Hecate stared at them each in turn. "You want five more weeks? That's two months! Two months to curse a simple play? I'm in and out with my curses. Right now I'm off to Washington, where I'll curse a Tea Party petition so that the tea baggers get exactly what they don't want, and I'll be back in Hell before the kettle even begins whistling. And you want two months!"

Gertrude stared back, just as hard. "We are talking about the production of plays here. You can't just kill a play in day one. There's been no investment. Everyone would just shrug and do something else. There's no stakes."

"Gertie is right," said Netty. "No one eats steak until all the hard work is done and the show is ready to go on."

Hecate blinked her eyes in incomprehension.

"What Netty means," said Agatha, "is that the more blood, sweat, and tears that are invested, the greater the loss when it all comes crashing down."

"I see," said Hecate. "Then you'd better give me buckets of blood, rivers of sweat, and enough tears to drown an elephant, or you'll learn what loss really is." And she was gone.

"Someone's in a foul mood," Netty said.

"If you want to see a real foul mood," Gertrude told her, "just call me Gertie one more time. You'll learn what foul really is."

Then they all burst out laughing.

-Act IV-

Scene 1: Wicked Dreams Abuse the Curtain'd Sleep

ANOTHER WEEKEND WENT by, giving Paul an inadequate two restful days to recover from five hectic days of school. As he often did on Monday mornings, Paul wondered what it would be like if it were the other way around, with five-day weekends and the school week lasting two days.

This was a common discussion in the teachers' lounge, with most teachers arguing that students would learn more with two solid days of classroom instruction and five days of homework. Paul sat on the fence of the issue, and when he spoke, it was usually just to say that Winston and the school board would never try it, even as a test. Bureaucrats lived in fear of change, and Paul couldn't think of any change larger. Still, it would be a grand experiment.

"No, no, no!" Paul shouted into the megaphone. "Lennox can't stab Macbeth. How is Macbeth going to have his argument with Macduff, concluded by Macduff taking his life? Macbeth is unbeatable! He defeats everyone in battle, until Macduff."

"But he's just standing there!" Bruce Filman waved his plastic sword in the air. "How am I supposed to *not* stab Macbeth?"

Lenny took no part in the conversation. He just stood with his arms folded across his chest and a look of staunch disinterest on his face.

"How?" Paul asked. "By stabbing someone else, anyone else.

In this part of the scene, Macbeth stands alone at centre stage while the battle whirls around him. He can't be killed by any man of woman born, so he knows no fear. Lennox senses that confidence and looks for easier prey."

"But there's only ten of us on stage," Bruce said. "Not much of a whirling battle."

Paul had to give him points for that.

"Put the girls in the battle," said Scarlet.

"What?" Paul said, forgetting himself and responding to the ghost's suggestion.

"Especially," said the boy, misinterpreting Paul's response, "if none of us are allowed to fight Macbeth. It's the most boring battle ever."

"He's right," Sylvia said. "I'm barely able to stay awake during this battle. It's just a lot of standing around with the occasional clack of swords. Ooh! I know. We could let the girls fill out the numbers."

"But the women never fought," Paul said, stubborn even in the face of both his female advisers independently making the same suggestion. "Men fought from the age of six on, but girls and women stayed home and kept the hearth. That's how Scotland was back then."

"Then dress them up as soldiers," Sylvia suggested. "Turn them into men."

"Make them English soldiers," said Scarlet. "The boys can be the Scots."

Paul rubbed his jaw. "I suppose the girls can be English soldiers," he said.

"Good idea." Sylvia jotted down some notes. "We won't have to get carried away with costumes. Jeans, dark shirts, and baseball caps. The Scots don't respect the English anyway. Let's give them something to not respect."

"We'll need to find more swords," Paul said.

"Who's that man sitting in the back row?" Scarlet asked.

Paul turned and saw a shadowed figure sitting in the dark at the back of the auditorium. "I can barely make him out."

"Who, dear?" asked Sylvia.

"There's someone sitting at the back of the auditorium. Don't you see him?" Paul prayed that it wasn't another ghost, making it two people no one but he could see.

"Of course I see him," Sylvia said. "But I don't recognize him." The man stood and a rich, British baritone boomed across the auditorium. "I didn't mean to scare you."

"Simon!" Scarlet cried. The ghost leaped off the stage, flew up the aisle, and came to a skidding halt in front of her old friend.

Simon Riordan didn't notice the ghost. He stepped through her into the aisle and hobbled slowly past the rows of theatre seats toward the stage. If anything, he looked worse than he had a week earlier. His face was drawn; his hair a nest; and, impossible though it seemed, he looked even more skeletal.

"I'm sorry," the old man said, "but I couldn't stay away." His drooping eyes searched the stage as he approached Paul's and Sylvia's director chairs.

Paul jumped down out of his chair. "Sylvia, this is Simon Riordan, my drama teacher from when I was in high school. I've told you about him."

Sylvia stretched out her hand and smiled. "Of course. Pleased to meet you."

"Simon, this is my wife, Sylvia."

Riordan took Sylvia's hand in a loose grip and leaned forward for a brief peck on the back of her wrist. "Pleased to meet you, my lady."

Then he looked at Paul. "I was hoping you would . . . make that introduction we discussed." His eyes left Paul's face to roam about the stage.

The students, having finished the final battle scene, were milling around, many of them watching Simon Riordan with curious looks.

"An introduction?" asked Sylvia. "With one of the students?" Her expression was one of puzzlement and concern.

Paul didn't know what to say. How could he explain Riordan's interest in any of the students? In Winston, maybe. But even that was a stretch. He shook his head. Sylvia would never buy it. Gemma? Riordan's props had wound up in her parents' basement. But Paul had no idea how. Then it hit him.

"Susie, could you come here for a minute."

Susie put down the plastic sword she had been swinging, apparently having overheard the decision to enlist the girls in the English army, and walked to the edge of the stage.

Riordan stared at her as though she were from another planet.

"This is our daughter," Paul said, speaking slowly. "An overnight convert to drama, just like I was, although I can't credit her teacher. While it was you who turned me on to drama, Susie came to it on her own."

Riordan must have taken the hint. He smiled and nodded. "A pleasure to meet you, my dear. I am only saddened that I didn't get to see you perform this morning. Your father has spoken nothing but praise in that regard. Perhaps another time."

Susie smiled in return, but Paul could also see a hint of unease. Through no fault of his own, Riordan had just embarrassed her in front of the entire class and fed the deep-seated feelings of favouritism that Susie had worked so hard to extinguish.

Paul searched for a way to rescue the moment and was saved by the bell, literally. The students hustled to put away their props and stack the scenery flats in the backstage storage area, no one moving faster than Susie.

"I have a home to show," Sylvia said. "You boys should go have an early lunch."

In less than two minutes, the auditorium was empty save for Paul, Simon Riordan, and a ghost.

"What's wrong with him?" Scarlet demanded, apprising Riordan up and down.

"I am truly sorry to intrude," Riordan said, "but since we spoke last week, I haven't been able to eat or sleep." He lowered his voice. "I told you that I didn't want to meet with Scarlet . . . and I don't. But how else am I to know if she is real or just some delusion that you're suffering from? I—I have to know."

Riordan's accusation took Paul by surprise. It was one thing for him to question his own sanity, but for someone else to suggest he was delusional? Especially someone who'd spent the past twenty years inside a thinly disguised insane asylum.

Paul spoke through a clenched jaw. "You're familiar with delusions, are you?"

Riordan blinked. "What are you asking?"

"That home you live in," Paul said, "the one that gives you day passes. Some of your neighbours have delusions?"

"Some." Riordan shrugged. "All kinds of people check themselves in. Some have drug problems. Others just need encouragement. No one believes they are Elvis if that's what you're asking."

Paul didn't know what he was asking. Riordan was a voluntary patient? No one had committed him and locked him in a padded room? Paul almost asked why Riordan was there but lost his nerve.

"I guess I'm asking how you would know if I was delusional or really seeing the ghost of your dead friend."

Riordan nodded. "A fair question. And one I can't answer. I'm no expert. And from what I've seen, even the experts can't tell a delusion from a dream. To be honest with you, I'm not here for your peace of mind. I'm only trying to ease mine. I'm hoping that seeing Scarlet, even if it is just through you, will help me in some small way."

Paul was stunned. The Simon Riordan he had known was the most giving person in the world. Mr. Riordan had spent more one-on-one time with his students than any teacher Paul had ever met, including himself.

Now that he thought about it, Paul couldn't remember the last time he had helped any student who needed extra time. He hated to admit it, but he was probably more like the Simon Riordan standing in front of him now than the Mr. Riordan he had idolized in high school. Was that his path? To become the sorry, skeleton of a man who stood before him?

Paul refused to accept it. He had turned to drama then to teaching because this man had shown him that it could be an honourable, enjoyable profession. That Riordan had turned his back on that was on him. Paul would have no part of it. No. Paul Samson would be the better man. If Riordan wanted a conversation with Scarlet for the sole purpose of easing his own mind and not give a damn about Paul's problems, so be it.

He looked around for Scarlet, eager to get this over with, and discovered she was nowhere in sight. He realized that he hadn't seen or heard her since shortly after the students had left.

"Is she here?" Riordan asked.

Paul let out a breath. "No. She left when you said you didn't want to meet with her."

Scene 2: Ghosts Will Haunt Me Still

"DIDN'T SIMPLE SIMON used to be bigger?" asked Agatha.

"Bigger?" Gertrude grinned wickedly. "Have you been sticking your nose where it doesn't belong?"

"Of shoulder," Agatha said, her face darkening to the colour and texture of rhubarb. "The man used to be a turnip: broad of shoulder, narrow of waist, tiny of feet."

"I think you mean he was a carrot," Netty said. "Turnips have broad waists as well as shoulders."

"You're both wrong," Gertrude said. "Carrots are tall and thin. Heh. The man was a squash."

Silence ensued while the witches considered Gertrude's metaphor.

"But," said Agatha, "squash comes in all shapes and sizes."

"Round like a pumpkin," suggested Netty, who was herself round like a pumpkin.

"Tubular like zucchini," said Agatha

"Pear-shaped like a gourd," Netty added.

"And everything in between," said Agatha. "I once saw a squash shaped like the Louvre."

The other two witches stared at her.

"You know," said Agatha. "The squash-shaped façade at the south end."

"Not the Louvre," said Gertrude. "You must be thinking of the Guggenheim. East side. Definitely squash shaped."

"Am I hearing this correctly?" asked Netty. "The two of you are arguing over buildings that resemble squash?"

"I'm not arguing," said Agatha. "I don't even like squash. I'll take a turnip over a squash any day."

"But many buildings do resemble squash," Gertrude insisted. "The Appledore House in Wotton-under-Edge for example. Architects often borrow from nature. Why not borrow squash?"

"That's—" Agatha began. "No, you'll not get me talking about squash. I've had it up to here with your rambling about squash, and earwax, and what men like to talk about. You should win an award for inane conversation."

"I did win an award," Gertrude admitted. "Not for inane

conversation. Heh. For thinking *outside the box*."

"No such thing," said Agatha. "Outside the box is a recent turn of phrase. Hadn't been invented when they were giving out awards."

Gertrude grinned. "They called it the Unconventional Witch award, for doing things differently."

The two witches laughed.

"What?" asked Gertrude. "I earned my award fair and square."

"That's not an award," said Netty. "It's a reprimand."

Agatha chortled like an ailing coffee pot. "Witches aren't supposed to be unconventional."

"How?" Netty demanded. "Would anyone know that we're witches if we kept changing up the way we do things?"

"Tradition is the key," said Agatha. "Bubbling cauldrons."

"Curses," said Netty.

Agatha nodded. "Cackling."

"Gingerbread houses," suggested Gertrude.

The other two looked at her.

"That was you with the gingerbread house?" Agatha's eyes were agog.

Gertrude grinned. "Just before I got my award."

"No wonder you were reprimanded," Netty said. "Witches don't do gingerbread."

"It took me a whole month to bake it." Gertrude said. "And sugar didn't grow on Dilly Bars like it does today."

Agatha nodded. "Then the first two children who came along trapped you inside your own oven. You were the talk of the coven."

"Seemed like a good idea at the time." Gertrude sighed. "I've always had a fondness for children."

"Simon was an upside-down pear," said Agatha.

"What?" asked Netty.

Agatha twitched her nose. "We were talking about what shape Simple Simon used to be. He was an upside-down pear."

"An upside-down gourd," said Gertrude. "Pears have stems. Why are we talking about Simon, anyway?"

"Because he's over there having lunch with our drama teacher," said Agatha.

"You call that lunch?" Netty asked. "The smallest burger on the menu and a cup of water. Not even any fries. No wonder he's a scarecrow."

"Skeleton," said Agatha. "He's not lively enough for a scarecrow."

Netty wiggled a loose tooth with a grubby finger. "Whatever."

"What are they talking about?" Gertrude asked. "Maybe we can use it in our next curse."

"Ghosts," said Agatha.

"Ghosts?" Gertrude suppressed a cackle. "That's an odd lunch topic. Are you sure they're not discussing the play. Banquo's ghost?"

"Might be Banquo's ghost. But that's not important." Agatha rubbed her hands together. "Our drama teacher is telling Simon that he's seeing a real live ghost—"

"A live ghost?" said Netty. "I don't like those."

"A real ghost, then," Agatha corrected.

"Don't like those either," said Netty. "I almost had a spot of bother once, trying to boil tea in a haunted house."

"Sounds harmless enough to me," said Gertrude. "Ghosts don't usually object to tea."

"This house didn't have a stove," Netty admitted.

"Oh, my," said Gertrude.

"The Order of Witches didn't take too kindly to me trying to burn down a haunted house," Netty said. "Goes against article six hundred forty-seven in our agreement with the Ghosting Union."

Gertrude nodded. "Hallowed ground so far as witches are concerned. Safest just to give haunted houses a pass."

"If you two are quite finished," Agatha said, "Simon seems angry. Says there's no such thing as ghosts. He's demanding that our teacher prove it."

Gertrude let out a loud cackle, and the three witches ducked below the table as the two men glanced their way.

"Where's the chatter of unruly students when you need it?" Gertrude asked.

"Still in school," said Agatha. "The lunch bell hasn't rung yet."

"Is it you?" Netty asked Gertrude once they were sitting upright again.

"Me what?" asked Gertrude.

"Making our teacher see ghosts?"

"Of course not."

"That would be too traditional," said Agatha. "I thought it was you, Netty, expanding on the insanity angle. First deals with the Devil and now ghosts. How could a mere mortal not go insane?"

"Simple Simon is doing our job for us," Netty said. "And he's not even part of this curse. Is that good or bad?"

"Is what good or bad?" asked Hecate. The senior witch stood next to their booth, wearing a server outfit. She held a tray with both hands, upon which sat a basket of chicken and fries and a big, frosted mug wafting the aroma of cough syrup.

"Smells delicious," Netty said. "And it's almost lunchtime. Are you going to share?"

Hecate smiled through an application of too much makeup. "I should let you eat this. It's loaded with Ebola. I'm off to San Francisco to kick off a hemorrhagic fever epidemic."

"Oh," said Agatha. "I love a good plague." She pinched her lips. "Can't remember the last time I caused one."

Hecate wagged her head. "If you were done here, I'd invite you along. I assume there is no progress, as usual."

"Our teacher's insanity is coming along nicely," Netty said. "Now he's seeing ghosts."

Hecate's eyes widened with interest. "Banquo's ghost?"

"Yes," said Netty.

Hecate's eyes narrowed and she peered at the round witch. "Not your idea, surely. Turning your teacher into his own Macbeth is . . . brilliant."

"I can be brilliant," Netty said.

"No," said Hecate. "You can't. You're the dullest witch I've ever had the displeasure of knowing."

Netty sputtered. "Wha—?"

But Hecate was already gone, sashaying along the tables until she came to the booth at the other end of the seating area, where the drama teacher and Simple Simon were just getting up. The drama teacher did a double take at seeing her, and Hecate gave him a shameless, bedroom-eyes smile.

The teacher let out a suppressed gasp and fumbled in his pocket for his cell phone.

Hecate continued to smile as she posed with her tray of Ebola and he took her photo. Then she turned and swaggered out the door into the street.

"That was cruel," said Agatha.

"Tormenting our teacher?" asked Gertrude.

"No, tormenting our Netty. Calling her a dull witch."

"I am dull." Netty's round head drooped, and her hat slipped to one side. "I'd never have thought of making our teacher see Banquo's ghost."

"Neither would I," Gertrude said, "and I've got an award for thinking outside the box."

Agatha puckered her wrinkled lips and let out a raspberry. "Faux hauntings are a traditional curse. Hardly unconventional." A pause. "But I didn't think of it either."

"Neither did Hecate," Gertrude said. "Not really. It thought of itself. Heh. Hecate was more surprised than we were."

"You told her it was Banquo's ghost," Agatha said to Netty, frowning.

Netty lifted her head and let out a halfhearted cackle. "If it wasn't, it will be. We're committed now."

"I can work with Banquo's ghost," Gertrude said. "I even remember where he's buried."

Agatha stared at her. "The real Banquo? From Scottish history?"

Gertrude nodded. "We had tea once. It was an enlightening conversation. You wouldn't believe how much delight he took in murder. He was completely open about it. Claimed each and every death was justified. He liked to taunt his victims before disembowelling them."

"Tea?" asked Agatha.

"Don't look at me like that." Gertrude grinned. "The tea was poisoned. One of Banquo's victims had a son who struck a bargain. He couldn't go after Banquo himself. Said Banquo would eat his liver if he went after him with a sword. Apparently Banquo was quite the swordsman."

"A bargain." Agatha waggled her brows. "And how fared this victim's son?"

Gertrude fixed her crooked expression in a wide grin. "I ate his liver. Heh. He didn't see that coming."

"Speaking of eating," said Agatha, "I'm hungry." She glanced at Netty, who was still sulking over Hecate's remarks. "GrillBurgers are on me," the tall witch said. "And extra fries."

That brought a smile to Netty's lips.

Scene 3: Perilous Stuff Which Weighs upon the Heart

"LINGERIE?"

Simon Riordan ran his hands through his unkempt hair. "The world has changed since I turned my back on it. A woman would be arrested if she'd done that twenty years ago."

Paul remembered some of the stunts he had taken part in during high school and decided that the world had changed less than Riordan suggested.

"Are you sure it's the same woman?" Riordan asked.

Paul took a quick glance around the school parking lot and, seeing no one near them, pulled from his coat pocket the photo he had printed by accident.

Riordan gawked at it then whistled.

Paul quickly put it away. "What do you suppose it means?" he asked.

"Means?" said Riordan. "It doesn't mean anything. The woman just gets off on yanking people's chains. Half the patients at Spring Hills are like that. Crying out for attention. Trying to feel anything but insignificant." He stopped and stared hard at Paul. "Most things don't mean anything. Maybe that's your problem. Looking for meaning where there isn't any will drive anyone mad."

"So you still think I'm just seeing things?" Paul asked. "Even though Scarlet has told me things I didn't know or wouldn't have thought of on my own?"

"You're not the first person to have an invisible friend," Riordan suggested.

Paul wasn't going to beat that dead horse again. He'd taken Riordan to lunch hoping to convince him that Scarlet was real, an impossible task without Scarlet to back him up. Having failed, he'd won a smaller victory by talking Riordan into coming back to the auditorium with him. It was his hope that Scarlet had cooled off after being insulted by the old man's dismissal.

The lunch bell rang just as he opened the school's main doors, and the two men had to fight upstream through a river of students before arriving at the empty auditorium.

There was no sign of Scarlet, of course.

"Is she here?" Riordan asked.

"Perhaps you could apologize," Paul suggested.

The skeletal old man showed his teeth. "It's your job to convince me. I'm not going to look the fool just to feed your delusion."

Paul shook his head. If he were Scarlet, he, too, would want nothing to do with this Simon Riordan. "She lives inside your lamp when she's not out and about."

Riordan grunted and walked over to the row of scenery flats that leaned against each other near the prop cupboard in the backstage storage area. The lamp was hanging on the first flat. Riordan lifted it down and shook it. "Sounds like the bulb is broken."

"That's how she got out," Paul said. "One of the students knocked down the flat and the bulb broke. More or less."

Riordan looked at him. "Cardinal sin."

Paul grinned. "That's what I told the boy."

Riordan turned back to the lamp and almost spoke. Then his fingers began trembling, and he hooked the lamp back up onto the flat. He took two steps back. "Any sign of her?"

"There's a slight hitch," Paul said. "She can only come out when we're rehearsing *Macbeth*."

"Fine," said Riordan. "Let's rehearse." And he immediately jumped into Macduff's taunting of Macbeth. "Despair thy charm; And let the angel whom thou still hast served tell thee, Macduff was from his mother's womb untimely ripp'd."

Paul glanced around but saw no sign of Scarlet. So he began speaking to the lamp, talking over Macduff's call to yield.

"Simon doesn't believe you're real," Paul said to the lamp. "That's why he said he didn't want to see you. He doesn't believe in ghosts. He says you died twenty years ago. How can he possibly see you now?"

Still no sign of Scarlet.

Paul took a chance. "Simon does miss you, however. That's why he's here, even though he doesn't believe. All I had to do was mention your name, and he came."

There was a choking sound, and Paul turned to see Riordan wiping his eyes with a handkerchief. He had broken off from Macduff's speech. "You bastard," he said to Paul. "You have no idea."

"What's wrong with him?"

Paul turned and there was Scarlet. She was staring at Simon Riordan, squinting as though she were trying to find the lively man she had known beneath the bitter carcass that stood before her now.

"It's been twenty years," Paul said. "People change."

"What?" asked Riordan.

"She's here," Paul said. "She wants to know what happened to you."

"What happened to me?" Riordan laughed. "*Macbeth*. That's what happened. Everything was fine until *Macbeth*. And then Scarlet died."

Paul was taken aback by the man's sudden outpouring of emotion. "You and Scarlet weren't . . ."

"No!" said Scarlet.

"An item?" Riordan asked. "No, of course not. The girl was young enough to be my daughter. Too young to die. It should have been me that died."

"How can you say that?" Scarlet asked him, though of course he couldn't hear her.

"Scarlet wants to know why you would say such a thing," Paul said.

Riordan clamped shut his teeth. His eyes flicked around the storage area then out onto the stage. "The play was cursed." He nodded at Paul. "You're wondering if your production is cursed. I know for a fact that mine was. I—I should have known better. It's my fault Scarlet died. I could have stopped it. She died because of me."

Then Simon Riordan walked quickly across the stage, through a side door, and was gone.

Paul moved to follow, but Scarlet was suddenly in front of him. "No. Let him go. Harassing him won't help."

"I'm not going to harass him," Paul said, but he knew what she meant. Riordan was too caught up in his own anguish to abide company. "What does he mean that you died because of him?"

Scarlet shrugged. "Survivor's guilt?"

Paul shook his head. "The article I read said a box of tools left in the rafters fell on you. I sincerely doubt that Riordan misplaced a box of tools up there. It would have to have been someone in building maintenance."

"Oh!" said Scarlet. "That's where those tools came from. I always wondered why my corpse was surrounded by rusted hammers and saws and other things I didn't recognize."

"You never knew how you died?" Paul asked.

"Dead is dead," said Scarlet. "It never seemed important."

"I think I'd want to know, especially if someone was behind it."

"I always assumed it was an accident," Scarlet said. "After all, who'd want to hurt me?"

"Who indeed," Paul said. "Maybe that's why Riordan is so distraught. Maybe someone else was supposed to be the victim?"

"Someone else?" asked Scarlet. "We were just a band of actors."

"Riordan said it should have been him." It occurred to Paul then that he might be looking at the whole thing the wrong way 'round. Riordan's odd comments. His failing health. His guilt. His locking himself up in an insane asylum. Had Scarlet's death been a botched suicide attempt? Had Riordan positioned those tools to fall on himself?

Scene 4: Banquo's Buried; He Cannot Come out on's Grave

PAUL HAD NEVER felt more exhausted. And it was only Tuesday morning. He'd spent half the night staring at the ceiling, racking his memories of those last few weeks of drama class back in high school for signs of advanced depression in Mr. Riordan's actions.

Back then, Paul hadn't known what depression was. At the time, the nation had been hooked on Valium, and high school kids, like himself, saw it simply as some form of legalized LSD. It wasn't until doctors had stopped overprescribing the drug and alternative treatments were sought that chronic depression became an everyday phrase.

But even knowing what he knew now, Paul couldn't recall a single sign. Mr. Riordan had been one of the most life-loving people Paul had ever met. Smiles and jokes came to his lips as easily as breath. It was one of the reasons Paul had looked up to him.

"What scene shall we run through now?" Sylvia asked.

Paul shook himself and realized that the students, having finished the Banquo murder scene, were looking at him. "The banquet scene is next," Paul said. "We still don't have the blocking down. And the guests still just stand around, looking at each other, rather than making small talk."

The students assigned as stagehands immediately began moving the castle wall flats into place, while Banquo and the three murderers helped to move the scenery flats depicting Scotland's forested countryside out of the way. The murder actually took place in a park outside the castle, but using the rougher forest setting worked just as well.

Fleance joined the banquet cast, pulling a white tunic on over his woodsman costume. He would double as one of the servants.

When the set was ready, Paul lifted his megaphone. "Curtain rises."

The servants hustled out onto the stage, looking much more organized than they had in past run-throughs. In no time, they were standing against the castle walls as the guests arrived. Macbeth and Lady Macbeth smiled and laughed politely as they greeted them.

Then Macbeth turned to the audience and spread wide his hands. "You know your own degrees; sit down: at first and last the hearty welcome."

The guests began finding seats while the First Murderer appeared at the edge of the stage and Macbeth quietly joined him. A few lines later, "Most royal sir, Fleance is 'scaped."

Dismissing the murderer, Macbeth exchanged words with his wife, Lennox, and Ross. Then Lenny proceeded to give perhaps the best performance of his life when he glanced at his supposedly empty seat. Macbeth stared then did a double take.

"What is't that moves your highness?" Lennox asked.

Macbeth looked out over the guests and said, "Where the hell is Banquo?"

"Cut! Cut! Cut!" Paul almost threw down his megaphone in despair. "You have the sentiment correct, Lenny, but your line is: *Which of you have done this?*"

Lenny lifted his hands. "But there's no Banquo. John was supposed to ghost his way through the guests and sit in my chair. He didn't."

Paul was at a loss. Banquo was sitting right where he should be. Paul had watched his entrance and stumble-free passage across the crowded stage. It wasn't John Freedman's best effort in the scene, but it was passable.

Lenny and the other students were looking about the stage, as if trying to find the missing student. If it was a joke on their teacher, Paul failed to see the humour. John was still sitting in Banquo's chair, and Scarlet was talking to him. John was talking back.

Paul felt the megaphone slip through numb fingers and clatter against the hardwood floor. Almost before he could wonder how John could talk back to Scarlet, Paul saw that Banquo wasn't John Freedman at all but a smallish man with dark hair tending to silver. His chin showed several days' growth, and his costume was . . . the only way Paul could describe it was that the man's costume was more authentic than the tunic, workpants, and boots John Freedman had assembled.

"I found him!" one of the students yelled from backstage.

Paul forced himself to ignore Scarlet and the mystery Banquo and follow his wife and the other students to the farthest corner of backstage, where John Freedman lay curled up in a ball, snoring away.

"Should we call the nurse?" asked Gemma.

Paul couldn't tell if she was worried or stifling a laugh.

"Let's wake him up and ask," Paul said.

One poke and the boy jumped awake. "What? What? What happened?" John looked around at everyone watching him then climbed quickly to his feet.

"Are you okay?" Paul asked. "We found you sleeping back here instead of haunting the banquet scene."

"I'm fine," John said. "Fine. I don't know what came over me. One moment I was watching for my cue, and the next I was dead tired." His face reddened. "Sorry if I ruined the scene."

"That's not important," Paul said. "As long as you're okay."

The bell rang, ending class.

Sylvia stopped John as the students began stowing their costumes. "If you feel tired or in any way odd, go see the nurse.

There's a cot in the room beside her office where you can catch a nap if you need one."

"I'm not tired," John insisted. "I don't know why I fell asleep." He left with the rest of the students, appearing just fine, if a bit shaken.

"Feel like an early lunch?" Sylvia asked Paul.

But Paul hadn't forgotten the false Banquo. "I have a lot of things to do before my first-year class," he lied. "Rain check?"

Sylvia smiled. "Sure. I'll let you get to it."

By the time the auditorium was empty and Paul had returned to the stage, the odd little man was gone and Scarlet was sitting in Macbeth's chair, frowning.

Scene 5: Round about the Cauldron Go

"YOU'LL NEVER GUESS who that was," Scarlet said when Paul approached.

"Probably not, so I won't even try."

Scarlet let out a short, high-pitched laugh. "That was Banquo's ghost."

"Well, obviously," Paul began.

"No, I mean the real Banquo."

Paul dropped into one of the other banquet chairs. "There was a real Banquo? *Macbeth* is just a play."

"Based on real history," Scarlet said. "Apparently Shakespeare took a lot of liberties with it. Banquo said that he was forced to read the play before making his appearance and that he was rather appalled by the whole thing."

Paul grinned. "Too much ruthless bloodshed?"

"No," said Scarlet. "Not enough. But that wasn't what rankled him. It was the ghosts and witches. He says there's no such thing."

"But he's a ghost himself, isn't he?"

Scarlet rose up from the chair and stepped along the trestle table. "He is now. But he says he never even met Macbeth, never mind haunted his banquet. He also thought it amusing that Shakespeare drove Macbeth insane with guilt for murdering Duncan, when Macbeth was only defending himself from

Duncan's ambition. He said that Macbeth went on to have a relatively long, peaceful, and prosperous reign."

"That's all very interesting," Paul said, and it was, "but where did this ghost come from?"

"You're not going to like that part." Scarlet paused a moment. "He said that a witch summoned him from his grave to haunt the play."

Paul swallowed. "A witch?"

Scarlet nodded.

"A real witch?"

"Apparently it was the same witch who killed him almost a thousand years ago."

Paul wasn't sure yet if he himself believed in ghosts, never mind witches. He could certainly feel where Banquo was coming from. "Yet he said he doesn't believe in ghosts or witches."

Scarlet let out a small laugh. "That's why he was rankled. He didn't know that the decrepit old woman who had poisoned him was a witch until this morning, when she summoned him out of a cauldron."

"A cauldron?"

Scarlet shrugged. "I'm just the messenger."

"Well, why wouldn't a witch use a cauldron? Where is he now?"

"He said he's only allowed to appear during the banquet scene to take your Banquo's place." Scarlet put up a hand. "No. *Allowed* is the wrong word. He is forced to appear."

"That's inconvenient," Paul said. "Did he say why?"

"I started to ask him that when he faded away. From what little he said, I gather he's supposed to frighten you into insanity."

Paul flexed his hands. "He may annoy me to death, but I've sort of gotten comfortable with ghosts."

"But you should be frightened," Scarlet said. "According to him, a witch is trying to curse the play."

"Oh, I will be frightened," Paul said, knowing that he was right back to where he was a week ago. "As soon as all this sinks in, I'll be so frightened that I won't be able to leave my house." *A witch is trying to curse the play.*

As Scarlet's ghost faded away, Paul still didn't know if he could believe any of it, but he did know one thing: he could no longer ignore it.

Scene 6: Macbeth Does Murder Sleep

IT WAS ALMOST midnight, and Paul still hadn't woken up from the nightmare he'd been living since second-period class. He lay awake with Sylvia snoring beside him, oblivious to the news that a witch was cursing his high school production of *Macbeth*.

There was no such thing as witches.

Paul had made some allowance for ghosts. He could almost believe that the play was haunted by not one but two ghosts. He had seen them with his own two eyes. He had spoken with one. And she had spoken with the other. They seemed harmless. He could almost even ignore them and life would go on.

But the second ghost had been sent by a witch . . . to drive Paul insane. Paul couldn't imagine what he had done to deserve such attention.

"Are you still awake?"

Paul hadn't noticed when Sylvia had stopped snoring. "Restless," he said.

Sylvia slid herself up against the headboard and adjusted her pillow. "It's more than that. You've been sleeping badly on and off since the school term started. Something's troubling you. It's not the gorgon lady, is it? What's she up to now? Since Susie put the kibosh on her petition, I know she must be planning something. People like Cadwell don't lose graciously."

"No doubt," Paul said. "But I have no idea what she's up to. Winston has demanded that I keep my distance."

"Not too much distance, I hope," said Sylvia. "There's a PTA meeting tomorrow night. Perhaps we should go."

Paul sputtered as he attempted to talk. "Attend a PTA meeting? They'd skin us alive."

"But we're parents!" said Sylvia.

"We're not Cadwell's brand of parents. We'd be as welcome as a bad rash."

"I supposed you're right," Sylvia said. "But we do need to place a spy in their ranks. Maybe one of Susie's friends' parents."

"A spy?" In all Paul's years of teaching, he had never once thought of spying on the PTA. "That's . . . brilliant! We can be two steps ahead of Cadwell instead of two steps behind."

Sylvia reached over and squeezed Paul's shoulder. "Maybe now you can get some sleep."

Paul placed one of his hands over one of Sylvia's. Planned or not, Sylvia was his partner in this play, and he had been keeping her in the dark. "The gorgon is the least of my worries," he admitted.

There. He had opened the door. He knew Sylvia well enough to know that she wouldn't let him close it again or pretend that it wasn't open. He had as good as told her everything already.

Sylvia remained silent, and Paul decided to keep talking rather than wait for her to prod. "You must think I'm nuts since I told you I was seeing Scarlet Walker's ghost," he said.

"I've chosen to keep an open mind," Sylvia said. "Stranger things have happened. Like Susie enjoying drama." His wife chuckled.

"Then you'd better keep that mind open a little longer."

"Go on."

Paul took a deep breath. "Yesterday I introduced Scarlet to Mr. Riordan."

"I see," said Sylvia. "How did that go?"

"Of course he couldn't see her," Paul said, "but Scarlet was happy to see him. I sort of translated their conversation."

"Mr. Riordan believed you?"

"To be honest," Paul said, "I'm not really sure. It freaked him out and he left."

Sylvia was silent for a moment. "So you still have no real evidence that this ghost is real?"

Paul could almost hear his wife's next words. *Have you seen a doctor?*

But that isn't what she said. "You're going to have to get proof."

"Proof? Why? It's not like I have to convince anyone. Scarlet is harmless."

Sylvia moved her hand from beneath his and punched him in the shoulder. "So you can convince yourself, silly. So that you can sleep."

Paul took a deep breath. "That's not what's keeping me awake. A second ghost showed up today."

"A second ghost?" For the first time, Paul heard disbelief creep into his wife's voice.

"Yeah. The weird part is that this ghost claims to be Banquo. The real Banquo. From history."

"There was a real Banquo?"

Paul shrugged. "So the ghost claims."

"The ghost told you this?"

"He told Scarlet while we were making sure John Freedman was okay."

Sylvia's hand tightened on his arm. "The ghosts were there today? Both of them? I didn't see either."

"I told you. Only I can see them. And they can see each other."

Sylvia was silent for a moment, thinking. "So you're saying that this ghost of Banquo took John's place in the rehearsal?"

"Yes!" Paul said, perhaps a little too excitedly. Did Sylvia actually believe him? "That's why I didn't stop the scene when John didn't show up. I was watching the real ghost of Banquo in his place."

His wife nodded, causing her pillow to shift against the headboard. "It's not actually proof, but it's a start."

"It is?"

"Of course it is. That boy didn't just spontaneously catnap in the middle of rehearsal. He was put to sleep."

"By the ghost? But Scarlet said that she couldn't interfere with real life. She can only observe."

"Has she tried?" Sylvia asked. "I don't know much about ghosts. But can't they move objects and make people see things?"

"In the movies," Paul said. "But that's just stories."

"All stories have a basis in fact. You just told me there was once a real Banquo."

"Nothing like Shakespeare's Banquo."

Sylvia harrumphed. "Even so, this Banquo's ghost put one of your students to sleep. No wonder you're worried."

"Actually," Paul said, "that's not what's worrying me."

"There's more?"

"Banquo said that he was sent by a witch to drive me insane."

Stunned silence. Then Sylvia said, "That ghost is out of his mind. There's no such thing as witches."

Scene 7: Our Fears in Banquo Stick Deep

PAUL WAS BOTH exhausted and invigorated as he and Sylvia entered the empty auditorium on Wednesday morning just before class. The exhaustion was from getting little sleep two nights in a row. The invigoration was because he was no longer alone in his potential insanity. Sylvia not only knew about both ghosts but also seemed more inclined than he was to believe they were real. And today they were on a mission: to find out more about this so-called witch behind Banquo's ghost.

"Is she here?" Sylvia asked.

"Standing right in front of us," Paul said. "Scarlet, this is my wife, Sylvia. Sylvia, this is Scarlet. She's an actress who performed with Mr. Riordan."

Scarlet frowned. "I know who Sylvia is. She's been here almost every day. And I never performed with Simon. We shared several weeks of rehearsals before I died." Then she smiled. "Pleased to meet you."

"Scarlet says she's pleased to meet you," Paul said to Sylvia.

Sylvia spoke to the ghost's left shoulder. "Have you tried to make other people see you? Ghosts in the movies can do it."

"I'm not in a movie," Scarlet said. "And of course I've tried. I've tried until I'm blue in the face. Not literally, of course. And I've tried moving things. With my hands and with my mind. The only thing I've been able to accomplish is to not fall through the floor."

"Scarlet says she's tried," Paul said. "And she can't move objects either."

Sylvia shook her head. "But the other ghost can make Paul see him. And he put that boy to sleep."

Scarlet waved a dismissive hand. "I've been thinking about that. It must have been the witch who did those things."

Paul conveyed Scarlet's words then added, "We have to find out more about this witch. We're going to run through the banquet scene again today, and Scarlet, I need you to find out from Banquo as much as you can."

"Promise him anything," Sylvia said. "But make him agree to not tell the witch that we're on to her."

"What if the witch is here watching? Invisible?" Scarlet asked.

Paul let out a deep breath and repeated the ghost's question to Sylvia.

Sylvia shook her head. "Then we're pretty much screwed no matter what we do. But we can't do nothing. If Scarlet has a better idea, we'd love to hear it."

Scarlet didn't. And by the time Paul and Sylvia had set the stage and the students began arriving, none of them had come up with a better plan.

Paul sat in his director's chair and toyed with his megaphone while his actors assembled. The second chair was empty. Sylvia had gone backstage and concealed herself behind the forest scenery flats. Paul had no idea if she could hide from a ghost or if she would see anything, but it was worth a shot.

"Okay, students," Paul said. "We're going to pick up from where we left off yesterday: the banquet scene. Go get your costumes and get ready for the curtain to go up." When they were ready, Paul said, "Curtain."

Like the previous day, the servants hustled out onto the stage, once again looking like real servants. They placed their burdens on the trestle tables and faded backward to stand against the castle walls. The guests entered merrily from stage left and mingled in front of the tables, Macbeth and Lady Macbeth greeting them.

Macbeth then spoke the cue for the guests to sit. "You know your own degrees; sit down: at first and last the hearty welcome."

The First Murderer appeared and reported to Macbeth. "My lord, his throat is cut; that I did for him."

Macbeth dismissed the murderer and hobnobbed with Lady Macbeth and some of the thanes. He then went to his seat, looked out at his guests, and went horribly off script. "Banquo's missing again."

"Pretend he's there!" Paul shouted into his megaphone. He waved back at the empty theatre seats. "The audience is watching. Unless the director lowers the curtain, you continue the scene. Adlib if necessary. You can't just stop. The show must go on!"

Lenny shrugged and made a halfhearted effort at his lines, pretending to see the ghost taking up his empty seat. "Prithee, see there! Behold! Look! Lo! How say you?"

Paul didn't care what Lenny or the other students did, so long as the scene continued. What was important was that Paul could see the ghost sulking in Macbeth's seat, then vanish, then return after Macbeth's toast to the absent Banquo. All the while, Scarlet hounded him, talking fast and waving her hands, coaxing words out of the reluctant ghost until Macbeth's final importuned banishment sent him away for good.

The scene ended two minutes later, and Paul called, "Curtain."

The students immediately rushed backstage, Paul chasing after them, and found John Freedman fast asleep with Sylvia standing over him.

"Unbelievable!" said Lenny. "Is John trying to ruin my performance?"

"This isn't about you," said Gemma. "John must have mono or something."

Paul hadn't heard anyone mention mono since he was in high school. He wasn't even sure it was a real illness. A kissing disease that made you sleepy? There were just too many connotations you could hang on that.

"Gemma," said Sylvia, "you and some of your friends please take John to the nurse's office and ask her to check him out."

"The rest of you," Paul said, "go find a spot up in the theatre seats and practice your lines until the bell. Some of you aren't completely off book yet."

John looked sheepish when Sylvia woke him up but knew better than to argue. There was no argument for falling asleep twice in two days.

Once they were alone backstage, Sylvia said, "John just sat down and fell asleep. One moment he was awake, and the next, he was visiting dreamland."

"It happened the moment Banquo appeared," Scarlet said. "Banquo didn't do anything. He just appeared from thin air, and the boy dropped off."

"What did he say?" Paul asked. "Banquo didn't look very cooperative from where I was sitting."

Scarlet shook her head. "It was confusing. I think he was scared. He said the last thing he remembered was talking to me yesterday. The next moment, he was here again. It's like he didn't exist during the time in between."

"That's not what it's like for you?" Sylvia asked when Paul

relayed Scarlet's words.

Scarlet nodded. "I've been awake every moment since I died. No sleep. No lost time."

"Did he agree to help us?" Paul asked.

Scarlet shrugged. "He said he hasn't seen the witch since she woke him up and ordered him to read Shakespeare's play. After that, he's been with us twice, with no memory of anything in between. He doesn't think there is anything he can do. He sounded pretty fatalistic." Scarlet shuddered. "I'm glad I'm not him."

"So we still know nothing about this witch," Sylvia said. "What she can do. Why she's doing it. What we can do about it."

"Maybe she's cursing the play," said Scarlet.

"Should we cancel the play?" Paul asked.

"But the kids," said Sylvia. "They're working so hard. And Susie has never been happier."

"I know," Paul said. There was a heavy lump in his stomach. "But I'm out of ideas."

Scene 8: I Dreamt Last Night of the Three Weird Sisters

"I'M RELUCTANT TO admit this," said Agatha. "But I'm growing tired of GrillBurgers and fries."

"Try one with cheese," Gertrude suggested. "And order poutine instead of fries."

"I can't abide poutine," said Netty. "Or anything else French. Quiche. Crepes. Baguettes. You call that food? How the French can stomach any of it is beyond me."

"Poutine originated in Canada," said Agatha, "not France."

"You like the French fries well enough," Gertrude said. "Heh. You've eaten enough fries to sink an iceberg."

"You're mixing your metaphones again," said Netty. "They might call the fries French, but they're from Belgium, along with Trappist Beer, Godiva chocolate, the Smurfs, and Jean-Claude

Van Damme."

Gertrude's eyes went shiny. "Jean-Claude Van Damme."

"I'm going to send out for pizza," Agatha said. "Who's with me?"

"No anchovies, please," said Netty. "It was the French who put anchovies on pizza."

"No it wasn't," said Agatha.

"From that little place downtown?" asked Gertrude. "Where they weave a rope of cheese through the crust?"

Agatha nodded.

"Then count me in." Gertrude licked her disfigured lips. "I don't care what's on it. I'm just going to eat the crust."

"That's no proper way to eat pizza," Netty said. She looked at Agatha. "What's that you've got?"

The tall witch's face reddened. "A cell phone. How else am I going to order pizza?"

"You?" Gertrude asked. "A cell phone? Heh. You're the one who still takes carriages rather than a taxi."

Agatha harrumphed. "Have you seen taxi fares lately? Five dollars. And that's before you've even left the driveway." She pressed the number three on the phone and held the device to her ear.

"You've got the pizza place on speed dial!" Netty crowed.

"Sometimes," Agatha sniffed, "you need to give a nod to change. Yes, it's Agatha. I'd like the usual. Times three. On my tab, yes."

"You've got a tab?" Netty let out an uncomfortable cackle.

"Deliver it to the Dairy Queen next to Ashcroft Senior High. Yes, the Dairy Queen." Then she hung up and buried the phone somewhere in her layers of shawls. "We've got twenty minutes. Perhaps we should see how our ghost is doing."

Gertrude smiled like a Cheshire cat. "You just don't want us to heckle you about your cell phone."

"Heckle all you like," invited Agatha. "No phone, no pizza. Oh, look! We have company."

Where moments earlier the bench seat next to Netty had been vacant, it was now occupied by a diminutive man with scraggly, greying hair and three days' growth on his chin. He sported a scar beneath his left eye, was missing half his teeth, and wore a grey tunic that had seen better days. His eyes were very wide, with a yellow tinge where there should have been white. Those eyes were currently shifting among the witches' faces.

"There are three of you!" he said.

"Oh my," said Gertrude. "The boy can count. Who knew?"

"You brought him here?" Netty cried. "To the Dairy Queen? What will the staff think?"

Agatha let out a cackle. "They'll think that we haven't moved from this spot in three weeks and that Hecate has dropped in every day or three wearing some outrageous outfit. In other words, they won't think anything. It's business as usual."

"What do you want?" Banquo mewled in a trembling voice.

"The boy's got cojones too," said Gertrude.

"He's ill?" asked Netty. "I didn't think ghosts could get ill."

Gertrude rolled her eyes at Netty. "Christmas is coming. I'll get you a dictionary."

"Please," Banquo whimpered. "Just let me go to my rest."

"Of course," said Agatha. "When the job's done. Tell us, how goes our drama teacher's sanity?"

"Who?" asked Banquo.

"The man in charge of the play," Gertrude said, "the one who can see you."

"Oh," said Banquo. "The fellow shouting through the horn. What a magnificent device. I could have used that on the field of battle. If I—"

"His sanity!" Agatha repeated just a tad more forcefully.

Banquo looked at her and at the other two witches with large eyes.

"He's thinking something," Netty said. "I don't like ghosts who think."

"Stop thinking!" Agatha ordered.

Banquo shrank back against the bench seat. "I—I'm just trying to decide how to answer. I've only observed him for perhaps ten minutes in total. And all that time he was sitting a distance away from me in a tall chair, watching. When he wasn't shouting 'Curtain' or 'Cut' into that horn of his, whatever that means."

Gertrude frowned. "He didn't jump out of his chair and cry out with fright that he was seeing a dead man while no one else around him could?"

Banquo stared at her. "Um, no, the boy in the black outfit did that. Which is odd because he also claimed that he should be able to see me but couldn't. Is confusion adequate? I don't know if anyone was insane, but there was much confusion in the room."

Then Banquo was gone.

"It's too soon," Gertrude said.

"What's too soon?" asked Hecate. "And who was that fellow warming my seat for me?" The senior witch wore a fluffy white dress with puffy sleeves and had a piece of white cloth woven through her hair. Her makeup was modest, and she looked a decade younger than usual.

"That was Banquo's ghost," Netty said. "He was reporting in."

Hecate grimaced. "I don't like ghosts. They're always uppity and protective of their haunts."

"Banquo is a summoned ghost," said Gertrude, "not a haunting ghost. We wouldn't dream of meddling with a haunting ghost. Nothing good can come of it."

"What are you supposed to be now?" Agatha asked. "Snow White?"

"Don't be ridiculous," said Hecate. "Well, actually, yes, I am. But it's a complicated story, so I'm not getting into it." Princess Hecate sniffed. "I was thinking about our last conversation, and I've changed my mind. Using Banquo's ghost to turn the director into his own Macbeth isn't brilliant. I finally got around to reading the play and—"

"Yhaaaah!" Agatha let out an ear-rending howl. "You've never read the play?"

Hecate continued as if nothing had happened. "—the ghost played a much more minor role than I had been led to believe. He was barely on stage for five minutes."

"You've never read the play!" repeated Agatha.

"And he had no lines," Hecate finished. "Using him as a curse is like slapping a soldier in the face with a duck."

Silence.

"A what?" asked Gertrude.

"A minor inconvenience," suggested Hecate. "No wonder it is taking you weeks to curse the play. If all you're using as ammunition is wilburys from a gaudy Anglo-Saxon skit—"

"Skit!" Actual thunderclouds formed over Netty's head. "This 'skit' has been our livelihood for over four hundred years. We have slept, eaten, and breathed this 'skit' until we are red in the face."

"Blue," suggested Gertrude. "Blue in the face. Not red."

"Blue, then," said Netty. "And we have been doing this on your orders!"

Hecate let a cold smile creep across her young, flawless lips. "Well, what did you expect? Ineptitude is punished, not rewarded. And four hundred years is just the beginning of your punishment."

Gertrude turned to Agatha. "What is this silly young girl on about?"

"She's on my nerves," said Agatha. "Apart from that, I have no idea."

Hecate's girlish face grew suddenly long and horselike, the carefully styled hair fought against the white bow, and the heads of snakes emerged and bobbed about as though dancing to a soundless tune. If a thundercloud had formed over Netty's head, the rest of the storm had found refuge above Hecate.

Hecate grinned though overlarge teeth. "You didn't think your reprimands were the end of it, did you?"

A weathered document appeared on the table in front of Agatha. Parchment that was once the pale white of human skin was now almost black with age, yet the words could still be read. *A Weirding*, it said. *For Sister Agatha, for sticking her nose where it doesn't belong.*

A similar document appeared in front of Gertrude. *A Weirding for Sister Gertrude, for behaviour unbecoming of a witch.*

A third document appeared in front of Netty. *A Weirding for Sister Anjennette, for failing to show the merest smidgen of witchlike zeal.*

Gertrude stared at Netty. "You got an award too? You never said."

Netty's thick lips curled into a frown. "Didn't seem worth mentioning."

"Award!" shrieked Hecate. "You have you no idea what *Weirding* means, do you? You three have the distinction of being the only witches in history to be so disappointing, so vexatious, so utterly useless as witches as to earn the Weirding title!"

"Are we?" asked Agatha. Hecate's visage and demeanour were enough to frighten bark off a tree, but Agatha was having none of it. She tapped a bony finger on the table in front of the senior witch. "If we're such pariahs, what did you do to earn the privilege of being our boss?"

Hecate glared at each of them in turn then vanished.

"Uhrm," said a voice.

Standing next to the table was a skinny, freckle-faced kid with long hair and bad breath. He held three pizza boxes in his trembling hands. "Did someone order delivery?"

Scene 9: Aroint Thee, Witch!

PAUL SPENT THE remainder of the day, when he wasn't in class, in the school library. He flipped the pages of countless books and searched the Internet until his eyes were sore. If he had thought the World Wide Web held too much inconsistent and frivolous information on ghosts, ghosts had nothing on witches.

They ranged from housewives experimenting with herbal remedies to candle-lighting sorority girls, to baby-eating daughters of the Devil. And he found all that in the first five minutes.

Eventually he focused his efforts on the Weird Sisters from Macbeth, who were arguably not witches at all. If the three hags hadn't been focused on Macbeth's destiny, they might be hedge witches or village wise women. The more he searched, the more he confirmed his original thought, that the Weird Sisters were just Shakespeare's literary device to push Macbeth down the road he was already traveling, but at a quicker pace. They weren't key to the story at all.

When his sixth-period class ended at four o'clock, Paul received a summons to Winston's office.

"You had some trouble in class this morning," the heavyset man said from behind his desk.

"Trouble?" Paul asked. There were a dozen things Winston could be referring to. None of which would be good for him to know.

Winston tapped a sheet of paper on his desk. "You sent John Freedman to the nurse's office."

Paul let out an involuntary breath. This was nothing he

couldn't handle. "John fell asleep in class."

"Kids fall asleep in class all the time."

Paul smiled. "Two days in a row. I was concerned he might be ill."

Winston frowned at the paper. "Nurse couldn't find anything."

"That's good news," Paul said.

"Is it?" Winston's eyes narrowed. "Freedman is in your senior class, isn't he? Your *Macbeth* class?"

"The play is coming along nicely," Paul said, grinning. "I've never seen students more excited."

Winston echoed Paul's grin, adding a hint of mockery. "So excited they're falling asleep."

"Which is why I was understandably concerned."

Winston stared at him.

"I'm glad John was just tired and not sick," Paul said.

The principal dropped his faux grin. "You are aware that there is a PTA meeting tonight?"

"I don't pay attention to PTA meetings," Paul said.

Winston suppressed a chuckle. "Perhaps you should. Your play is sure to be on the agenda."

"I'm not going to let Mrs. Cadwell's agenda run my life."

"I hear you." Winston waved a hand in the air. "You can be sure her petition last week wasn't the end of it." The principal leaned forward over his desk. "Next time I may have to decide in her favour. Cadwell may be a bigger thorn in my side than you are, but I can't ignore half the school's parents."

"I'm just trying to do my job," Paul said.

"As am I," said Winston, leaning back in his chair. "You can go now."

Paul left the principal's office kicking himself. He had forgotten all about the PTA meeting.

Scene 10: Friends, Romans, Countrymen

"WELCOME," SAID MRS. Cadwell, "to Ashcroft Senior High's second PTA meeting of the school year. I am overjoyed to see that so many of you made the time to come out tonight."

"I don't see what all the fuss is about," Agatha said from where she and her sisters sat in the back row of chairs. About three hundred chairs had been set up in the school's smaller gymnasium.

"Bunch of people in a room listening to a prig," Gertrude agreed.

"I gave up listening to prigs centuries ago," Netty said. "Why are we here?"

"To see this woman talk," said Agatha.

"She's been doing a better job of cursing the play than we have," added Gertrude.

Netty grumbled. "Says Hecate. You're not putting any stock into what she says, are you?"

"Says me," said Agatha. "Hecate can go disembowel herself."

Gertrude erupted with laughter. "I'd like to see that."

"Shhh!" said a man with psoriasis and a bad toupee who was sitting in front of them.

"As you know," said Mrs. Cadwell, "our petition to halt the *Macbeth* play didn't go as planned. Apparently Mr. Samson made his students round up a counterpetition."

"Can a teacher do that?" someone asked.

"Oh, poo," Netty spit in a whisper. "Samson didn't even know about the petition. Either petition."

"You can't be a prig without lying to your constituents," Agatha said.

"Should we let the people know she's lying?" Netty asked. "I can't abide a liar. Well, when it's not me doing the lying."

"Because calling a prig a liar has worked so well before?" suggested Gertrude. "She's only telling them what they want to hear. Prigs have been doing that for longer than there have been witches."

"And so," said Mrs. Cadwell, "we'll move on to plan B."

A hand went up. "Ah, Mrs. Cadwell. Wasn't the petition plan B. I thought plan A was the meeting in the auditorium where your son stabbed us in the back."

The entire gymnasium sucked in its breath.

"Demonstrating," said Mrs. Cadwell through clenched teeth, "what a terrible influence Mr. Samson, with his outlandish methods, is on our children."

The air in the enclosed room actually stirred when its

occupants resumed breathing.

"Moving on to plan C," said Mrs. Cadwell.

"Did you hear that?" said Agatha. "Our Mr. Samson has outlandish ways."

"Man after my own heart, then, he is," Gertrude said.

"Shhh!" repeated the man in front of them.

"Monday morning," said Mrs. Cadwell, "we'll blockade the main entrance to the school. We'll have picket signs with appropriate slogans, like *No Macbeth Here* and *No Witches in Our School.*"

"How about *Macbeth Must Die!*" a woman with multicoloured hair shouted, followed by laughter.

"Or *Shakespeare Is for Pussies,*" shouted someone else. More laughter.

"But I have to be at work Monday," an angry male voice grumbled. "Can't we do this on Saturday?"

"Please, everyone," said Mrs. Cadwell. "This is serious. If our slogans are a joke, we'll be a joke as well. And no, Mr. Stewart, we can't do this on the weekend. The school is empty on weekends. No one will see us."

"We can call in the newspapers and television," someone suggested.

Mrs. Cadwell nodded. "Yes, we'll do that anyway. But it will be for eight-thirty Monday morning, when the teachers and students are trying to get into the school."

"What about the other doors?" someone asked. It was the woman with the multicoloured hair again. "Shouldn't we block those as well?"

Mrs. Cadwell tapped her microphone for order. "We can't block all the doors. We'd be spread too thin. And if no one can get into the school, Principal Winston will have no choice but to call the police. Our goal isn't to get arrested, but to inconvenience everyone and to let the world outside the school know that there is a problem." A rictus grin marred the gorgon's face. "If Winston won't listen to the parents, let's see how well he listens when the community at large speaks up."

"Oh, she's good," said Agatha.

Gertrude nodded. "Clever. Doesn't lose control. Has an answer for everything. Heh. She'd make a good witch."

"So," said Netty. "You admire the woman now?"

"She reminds me of Hecate," said Agatha.

Netty pursed her lips. "I'll take that as a no."

"She's a grade-A shit disturber," Gertrude said.

Agatha nodded. "But it's our shit she's disturbing."

"Shhh!" the toupee'd man said a third time. He turned completely around in his seat to glare at them.

Agatha glared right back, glowering down her long, crooked nose.

The man dropped his gaze and turned back around.

"It's settled, then," said Mrs. Cadwell. "We'll meet in the Dairy Queen parking lot at eight a.m. Monday. Keep your signs in the trunks of your cars until I give the signal. Then we'll cross the street to the school and form up in front of the main entrance. I'll let the press know to be there at eight-thirty sharp. Any last questions? No? Then let's adjourn for punch and cookies."

"There's cookies?" crowed Netty. "Then this evening wasn't a complete waste of time."

Scene 11: All Goes Worse than I Have Power to Tell

AFTER A THIRD night with little sleep, Paul arrived at the school Thursday morning well before his second-period class started.

"I wish I knew what went on at the PTA meeting last night," Sylvia said.

Paul's wife looked as tired as he felt. She had asked a few friends with kids at the school to attend and let her know what Cadwell was up to, but they unanimously declined, saying they wouldn't be caught dead at one of the gorgon's meetings. All of them had called her the gorgon lady. Seems the moniker was ubiquitous.

"Nothing good went on," Paul said. "Count on it. Cadwell's PTA is the worst thing that ever happened to this school."

The PTA meeting was half the reason Paul had slept poorly. The question of the witch was the other half.

Even though class hadn't started yet, Scarlet greeted them as soon as they stepped through the Ashcroft-Tate Auditorium's east entrance. The ghost knew they would be rehearsing before the students arrived, and that seemed sufficient to let her leave the confines of the lamp. "Do you really think this will work?" Scarlet asked.

"If it doesn't," Paul said, "then Banquo isn't much good to us."

"What?" Sylvia said. "Oh, she's here, isn't she? Hello, Scarlet."

Paul and Sylvia busied themselves arranging the set for the banquet scene while Scarlet paced nervously across the stage. Paul knew they couldn't keep rehearsing the same scene over and over again, especially with John Freedman falling asleep each time. Paul wouldn't be surprised if John stayed home sick today.

When the set was ready, Paul and Sylvia stood near Macbeth's chair and began reading the scene, Paul delivering Macbeth's lines while Sylvia delivered all the others. Scarlet stood at Paul's elbow, waiting to let him know when, or if, Banquo's ghost arrived.

Paul didn't know the lines well enough to go off book, but whenever Macbeth wasn't speaking, he looked up, hoping to see the ghost.

"He's here," Scarlet said even as Paul saw the diminutive once-man enter from stage right.

As much as Paul wanted to interrogate the ghost directly, he knew that Banquo would vanish once the scene stopped. So he continued reading as Scarlet played her part and paced the ghost, asking him questions.

When the ghost reached Macbeth's empty chair, Scarlet gave Paul a thumbs-up. He immediately set down the script.

The small man cast Paul a roguish grin and said, "Thank you." Then he promptly vanished.

"It's worse than we thought," Scarlet said.

Those weren't the words Paul wanted to hear.

"Banquo says there are three witches."

"Three?" said Paul.

"And they expect his haunting the play to drive you insane."

"Me?"

"Paul, dear," said Sylvia. "Could you be a little more coherent? I'd like to know what's going on."

Paul relayed what Scarlet had told him.

"Anything else?" he asked the young ghost.

Scarlet shook her head. "He only spoke with the witches for a moment. But he's agreed to help us. He said he doesn't much like the witches."

"So I guess they aren't good witches," Paul said.

"What?" asked Scarlet. "How could they be? They've summoned a ghost to drive you insane."

Paul laughed. "I wish them luck. If Cadwell and Winston haven't succeeded, why would a silent ghost?"

"Three witches and Banquo's ghost," said Sylvia. "That's straight out of the play."

"Not straight," Paul said. "You yourself reminded me that there are four witches in the play. Though Hecate only speaks twice, she seems to be the stronger, more dangerous witch. And Macbeth is already mostly insane from guilt. As is Lady Macbeth. Murdering Duncan had already done the job. Banquo's murder merely hastens Macbeth's fall."

"And you're not Macbeth," said Scarlet. "Lenny Cadwell is."

"I'm the director," Paul agreed, frowning. "Yet I'm the one who can see the ghost, not Lenny."

Paul hadn't forgotten Simon Riordan's suggestion that his daughter, Susie, might have made a deal with the Devil. Perhaps Riordan had it wrong. Was it a deal with the witches? Just as Macbeth had communed with the witches? But in Shakespeare's tale, no actual deal had been struck. The witches merely told Macbeth his destiny, and Macbeth hastened to follow it.

Then he reminded himself that, despite the similarities, he was not reliving the tragedy of Macbeth. It was more of a mash-up, a term he had heard his students use. Elements of Shakespeare's story were intersecting his production of the play, creating something different from both.

Banquo had been instructed to drive Paul insane. Did Susie somehow hate him? Was that the deal she had made? But he didn't believe it. Like most teenagers, Susie had struck out on her own, seeking independence, in a sense, rebelling against her parents, but more for self-discovery than for anything he and Sylvia may have done or not done. His daughter's sudden appreciation for drama was a surprise, but Paul preferred to see it as a step in finding herself rather than a convoluted plot to get back at a parent she had been ignoring for the past two years.

"What are you thinking?" Sylvia asked.

Paul hadn't shared with Sylvia Riordan's comments or his

own concerns about the Devil, and he wasn't about to now. So he said, "I'm thinking it's time to have another talk with Simon Riordan."

Scene 12: Our Fears Do Make Us Traitors

THE STUDENTS ARRIVED and rehearsals went smoothly. Paul started at the top, Act I, Scene 1, making notes of places that needed more work. The bell sounded before they reached the banquet scene, and Paul sleepwalked through the rest of Thursday, his thoughts distracted by Banquo's ghost, witches, and the prospect that his daughter had made a deal with the Devil. Never mind that the apparent purpose behind all three was to drive Paul insane.

On Friday they resumed rehearsal, beginning at Act III, Scene 3. They quickly reached the banquet scene, and the students, especially John Freedman, grew suddenly apprehensive.

Paul continued anyway, making as though nothing were amiss. Sylvia, however, went backstage and, shortly after Banquo's ghost began making his slow way among the seated guests, John stumbled out from behind the curtain and staggered his way through the scene. Paul noted ruffled clothing from where Sylvia had shaken him awake, and he worried that John would fall back asleep the moment he sat down in Macbeth's chair. As it was, when he did sit down, directly in the lap of Banquo's ghost, the ghost disappeared and John was suddenly wide awake.

For a moment, Paul feared the ghost might have possessed the boy. With everything else that had happened, why not? But John was obviously himself, and he left the stage with greater haste than when he had arrived.

Paul hated to put anyone, never mind one of his students, through that experience but saw no way to avoid it. Skipping the scene would have raised questions. Questions that no doubt would have made their way to the gorgon lady, who would have used them in ways Paul couldn't even begin to contemplate. Surviving the scene accomplished the opposite. The students were reassured, and no ammunition was provided to Mrs. Cadwell.

The rehearsal ended with the close of Act V, Scene 8, just minutes before the bell.

"That was great, class," Paul said. He looked down at his many pages of scribbled notes. "There are still a number of things we need to work on, but four weeks is plenty of time. Most of our scene changes are still too slow, but you're all off book now and more or less know your lines. The fewer mistakes, the better, so keep running them through your heads. Class dismissed."

Fifteen minutes later, Paul was seated at a booth in the Dairy Queen across from a foul-tempered Simon Riordan.

Riordan had returned his call late the previous evening. He hadn't wanted to talk and was about to hang up when Paul said, "There have been some developments."

"So," said Riordan, cradling a plastic cup of DQ water in his hands. "What are these developments?"

Paul had no idea where to begin. "For one thing, we have a second ghost."

"A second . . . ?" The skeletal man made a face as if he had eaten sour grapes. "Who?"

"Banquo," Paul said.

"Banquo? From the play?"

"No," Paul said. "From real life. Or so he says. He claims he lived a thousand years ago in the days of the real Macbeth."

Riordan waved a hand. "Ridiculous. Someone is putting you on."

"But that's not the interesting part," Paul said. "Banquo said he was sent to haunt the play by three witches."

At this, Riordan's face paled.

"He said he's supposed to drive me insane. How's that for developments?"

Riordan raised his cup of water to his lips and drained all six ounces. Then he put the cup down.

"Cancel the play," Riordan said. "Walk away and don't look back. Forget you ever heard of William bloody Shakespeare and don't even think about ghosts or witches."

"I'm not worried about Banquo," Paul said. "He's actually a pretty nice guy."

Riordan slammed his fist on the table. "Forget Banquo. He's

not your problem!"

"What do you know?" Paul asked.

"You don't want to know what I know."

"Yes, I do. I can't fight this thing if I don't know what I'm dealing with."

"Fight? You can't fight. You can't win. All you can do is run. And hope they don't give chase."

"They?" Paul asked.

Riordan glared at him.

"They?" Paul repeated.

"The witches! All right? There. I said it. The witches, damn you." Riordan picked up his cup, saw it was empty, and threw it across the seating area. The cup bounced off an empty table, hit the floor, and rolled to a stop against a wall.

"What do you know about the witches?" Paul asked.

"What do I need to know?" Riordan said. He clenched and unclenched his hands. "They're witches. That should be enough."

"So there is no Devil?" Paul said, remembering his first meeting with Riordan.

"I'm sure there must be a Devil," the old man said, "but what I saw were witches."

"You saw them?"

Riordan twisted his head back and rubbed his face with his hands. "I made a deal with them, damn you! Is that what you wanted to hear?"

Paul sat stunned. Mr. Riordan—his Mr. Riordan, from back when he was in high school—had made a deal with witches. Paul couldn't imagine it. "What kind of deal?"

One of the restaurant staff, an older woman with a net shrouding poufy hair, set a new cup of water on the table. Dairy Queen didn't wait tables, but Paul guessed that the staff had noticed when Riordan threw his cup. They also noticed that he was old, ill, and having some kind of fit. Paul supposed it was a blessing that they brought him water rather than call the paramedics. Or the police.

Riordan thanked the woman and took a small sip. "What kind of deal?" The skeleton snorted. "No deal at all." He shook his head. "I suppose it's about time I told someone. My doctors tell me I don't have much time left. And someone should know. It may as well be you." He took a deep breath, and life seemed to flow into him. Colour came to his cheeks, and he looked somehow more firm that he had a moment before.

"It was a dream come true," Riordan said. "Getting acting roles was difficult while working full time as a teacher. Even community theatre doesn't give you much time to learn your part. Twelve weeks. A couple of hours' rehearsal on two or three weeknights. A weekend if the space is available. You spend the first few performances tuning your part so that by closing night, you can put on a perfect show.

"Then a Hinton Valley community theatre group announced auditions for *The Tragedy of Macbeth*. All my life I had wanted to play Macduff—"

"Not Macbeth?" Paul asked.

"Macduff is the true hero of the play," Riordan said. "A tragic hero. He's not only true to proper rule but loses his family in the pursuit. He's also the one who kills Macbeth in the final battle, even though the crown falls to Malcolm.

"Anyway, the audition went smoothly, but it also went well for other actors trying out for the part. My stomach was roiling with worry that I would be passed over, that the part would go to someone else. I needed to get out of the city.

"I drove. No idea where I was going. And found myself parked at a rest area, watching the most fantastic sunset I had ever seen. I realized, as the sun lowered itself over a grassy plain, that what I was seeing was a heath, straight out of Macbeth. I know the countryside is more rugged in northern Scotland, but even so, I let my imagination run wild. The soldiers of Cawdor clashed against the swords of Macbeth and Banquo. Blood flowed across the fields. And as the sun vanished below the horizon and a gibbous moon dominated the sky, three women trudged up the road."

"The Weird Sisters," Paul said.

Riordan nodded. "I didn't know that at first, but that's the role I cast them in. Imagine my surprise when they stopped and one said, 'Hail, Macduff.' Then the second cackled and said, 'You misspeak, sister, for he is not yet Macduff.' The third said, 'Time is an illusion, lunchtime doubly so.' It got confusing after that. One of the sisters said something about giving Douglas Adams a rest, and they got into some kind of argument. Anyway, they went on to say that it was my destiny to play the role of Thane Macduff and that I should be of good cheer.

"The Weird Sisters moved on down the road, and I drove back home. The next day I received a callback."

"To play Macduff," Paul said.

Riordan shook his head. "No, the director said someone else would play Macduff, but that I so impressed her with my audition that she'd like me to try out for the role of Banquo. I did and I got the part.

"First chance I got, I drove back out to the heath. And there I found the Weird Sisters waiting for me. They had another argument and then told me that I was impatient. My destiny awaited me and could not be changed.

"I was too caught up in achieving my dream to consider that the witches were frauds, that someone was yanking my chain. I had little time to think about it anyway.

"At our next rehearsal, I learned that the actor playing Macduff had dropped out along with his wife, who was playing one of the witches. We were already three weeks into rehearsal, and there wasn't enough time for more auditions and casting, so the director elevated one of the murderers into Banquo's role and crowned me the new Macduff. She wrote Hecate out of the script and made the woman playing her the third witch.

"I literally didn't sleep for three days in an effort to learn my new lines and blocking. I got caught up with the new part, and two days before opening night, the director had nothing but praise. It was to be the role of a lifetime.

"And then it happened. Lady Macbeth—Scarlet—was walking the stage, rubbing her hands, calling, *Out, damned spot! out, I say!* when something fell from the rafters, striking her on the head. I rushed onto the stage, as did the director and the other actors. There was hardly any blood. Just a spot on her sleeve. But Scarlet was dead.

"The show was cancelled, of course. The troupe disbanded. I sat in my apartment, the lights turned on day and night. I called the school and told them I was done. I didn't think I could ever face a stage again. I haven't. Until last week when I visited your school. Eventually I went out to the heath. But there was no sign of the witches. Their task was done. They'd told me my damned destiny. And indeed, I had played Macduff, through all of nine weeks of rehearsals. But I never had an audience."

Paul sat stunned by what he had heard. It was like listening to someone read a fairy tale from a book. But with everything that had happened to him since the start of school, he had no trouble believing Riordan's tale.

"That's a grim story," Paul said. "But I don't understand. What was the deal you struck? Usually a deal involves a mutually beneficial exchange."

Riordan took a second sip of water. "I've been pondering that question for twenty years. Here's the best I've come up with. The witches offer you a destiny that happens to be your heart's desire. You believe them. I suspect that if you don't believe them, that they will then have no power over you. It may still come true, but the witches will have no involvement. But if you believe them, you have accepted their deal and they will meddle to ensure that your destiny technically happens but not in the way you want. And there is a cost. In my case, the cost was Scarlet's life."

"The witches killed Scarlet?"

Riordan nodded. "As good as. They caused her death. I'm sure they also created some tragedy that caused the original Macduff actor and his wife to drop out of the production."

Paul sipped cola through a straw, the first time he touched his drink since he sat down. "What do the witches get out of it?"

"The witches?" Riordan pushed a heavy breath out through his nose. "I have no idea."

Scene 13: And Question This Most Bloody Piece of Work

"ARE WE GOING to eat that pizza yet?" Netty asked. "It's been sitting there for two days."

"We'll eat pizza when I say we eat pizza," Agatha said.

Gertrude harrumphed. "Who died and made you Hecate?"

Agatha glared at her. "Don't you dare mention that harpy's name. She called The Bard's Play a 'skit'."

"That's not what's got your bloomers tied in a knot," Gertrude said. "You're upset because Hecate called us vexatious and said that cursing the play is a punishment."

"I always thought," Agatha admitted, "that being the Weird Sisters was an honour. And now, hundreds of years later, I learn that we're just a joke. A laughingstock. Assigned make-work projects to keep us out of the way of respectable witches."

Gertrude snorted. "Hecate never said any of that."

Agatha shook her head. "But she implied all of it."

"Oh, look!" said Netty. "Our Samson has made an appearance."

"I'm not in the mood," Agatha said.

"And Simple Simon is with him again."

"Still not in the mood."

"What are they discussing this time?" asked Netty.

"Oh, my," said Gertrude. "Our Banquo has been indiscreet. Seems he's been chatting up the enemy."

"I never trusted that little bugger," said Netty.

Gertrude's face turned dark. "He told them about us! I'm going to kill that pathetic little Scotsman."

"You already killed him," Netty said.

"Still not in the mood," said Agatha.

"Simon's telling our Samson to run and hide."

"No place in Earth, Heaven, or Hell he can hide!" Netty said. "Though a chase could be amusing."

"I'm not chasing anybody over a 'skit'," said Agatha.

"Oh, my," Gertrude said again. "Now Simple Simon has admitted that he's met with us."

"What was that noise?" asked Netty, the bulbous witch's eyes going round like plates, albeit filthy plates.

"Heh," said Gertrude. "He's thrown his water cup."

"Oh," said Netty. "That's sort of anticlimactic."

"Has this ever happened before?" Agatha asked. "A current curse getting a heads-up from a past curse?"

"I thought you weren't in the mood," said Gertrude.

"I have a short inattention span," Agatha admitted.

"I can't think of any time this has happened," said Netty. "People say it's a small world but it isn't. Especially if you're walking."

Gertrude nodded her crooked head. "Times were simpler when we confined ourselves to the British Isles."

"I had fewer corns in those days," Netty agreed.

The other two witches sighed.

Then Agatha made a rude noise in her throat. "As much as I enjoy hearing about your corns, Netty, I'd rather hear about what Samson and Simon are discussing."

Gertrude let out a lengthy yawn. "Oh, Simon's just reliving his glory days when he played the role of Macduff. He's at the part where he first met us out on the heath. His memory isn't very good, however. He says the three of us were arguing."

"We never argue!" Netty said. "We have enthusiastic conversations."

"In that case," said Gertrude, "his memory is spot on. He even remembers Douglas Adams."

"Who?" asked Agatha.

"You know, that marvellous London writer whose line Netty stole for that first meeting."

Netty grinned a gap-toothed smile. "Douglas Adams. His books are classics in the making."

"He's been dead for years," Gertrude said. "So now his books *are* classics. I understand he left his last book unfinished. Heh. Heard it was about salmon fishing."

Netty frowned. "I didn't know he wrote those kinds of books. Now I've lost all respect."

"As much as I'm amused by the concept of frivolous comedy being deemed as classic," said Agatha, "I'd still like to know what else Simon is saying."

"No," said Gertrude, "you don't."

"And why, pray tell, not?"

"Because," Gertrude said, "he's claiming we cheated him. Telling him what he wanted to hear and then pulling the prize out from under him."

Agatha scowled. "He's calling us prigs?"

"Not in so few words, no."

"I'll prig him," said Agatha. "Then he'll know what a prig is."

"I don't think you can use *prig* as a verb," Netty said.

"I'll use *prig* however I please, thank you very much."

Gertrude tsked. "Now he's claiming that we killed Scarlet."

"Who?" Netty asked.

"Lady Macbeth."

"Which one?" asked Agatha, calmer now that the conversation

was back in familiar territory. "There have been so many. I lose track."

"The one from when he was Macduff," said Gertrude. "Where that toolbox fell from the rafters and clocked her a good one."

"Ah, yes," said Agatha. "The toolbox. Funny how it suddenly slipped down from the rafters after resting there undisturbed for three years."

"I have no idea why everyone always blames us," Netty said. "Perhaps there was an earthquake."

"An earthquake?" asked Gertrude.

"Just a small one," suggested Netty. "Not so anyone would notice, but enough to dislodge a lost toolbox."

The other two witches stared at her.

"What?" asked Netty.

Agatha shrugged her narrow shoulders. "That's the first good idea you've had in the four hundred years since I've known you."

"It is?" A rosy smile spread like a disease across Netty's creased face.

Gertrude, however, was frowning.

"What?" asked Agatha.

"Our Samson just asked Simple Simon a telling question."

"What question?" asked Netty.

"He asked Simon what we get out of all the cursing we do."

"I'm curious as to Simon's answer," said Agatha.

"He says he hasn't a clue," Gertrude said.

Agatha harrumphed. "So Simple Simon isn't as smart as he pretends to be."

"Well, what *do* we get out of it?" Netty asked. "We've been cursing *Macbeth* for four hundred years, and I still haven't figured that one out."

"It's obvious," said Agatha.

"It is?" asked Netty.

"You tell her," Agatha told Gertrude.

"It isn't obvious to me," Gertrude said, "so you'd better tell us."

"Well." Agatha fiddled with the corner of a pizza box. "It gets Hecate off our backs."

"Not very well," said Gertrude.

"She's always riding us," added Netty.

"And it's what witches do," said Agatha. She nodded her pointed chin, implying that was the final word.

"Is it?" asked Netty, ignoring the implication. "It's what we do. But I've never heard of other witches cursing plays. Sure, the occasional opera or heavy metal concert gets cursed, but we've been cursing the same damned play for four hundred years."

"Netty has a point," Gertrude said.

Netty crowed with delight. "That's two good ideas in the space of ten minutes!"

Agatha glared at her. "Don't get cocky."

"I think Agatha already told us what we get out of it," Gertrude said.

"I have?" asked Agatha. "I mean, of course I have. When?"

"Just before Samson and Simon arrived. You said that Hecate was keeping us out of the way of respectable witches."

"I don't see how that gets us anything," said Agatha.

"It doesn't," agreed Gertrude. "Hecate has us cursing The Bard's Play for the sole purpose of benefiting other witches."

"We're the Weird Sisters!" Netty cried. "The unwanted stepsisters. Too ugly to be seen in certain company. Kept locked in the cellar, and made to shovel coal into the furnace."

"Heh," said Gertrude. "The imagery gets a *D*, but the sentiment is *A* material.

"I'm tired of shovelling coal," said Agatha.

Netty grinned. "Agatha likes my imagery."

"I think it's time," Gertrude said, "that Weirding was a reward rather than a reprimand. So what if we're different? Different is good."

"But not too different," said Agatha. "We're still witches."

"Yes," said Gertrude, "but we should be witches on our own terms."

"Let's cut Hecate's puppet strings!" Netty said.

"Um," said Agatha. She reached for her silver pendant and rubbed it with restless fingers. "Okay."

"It's settled, then," Gertrude said. "From now on, we do what we like, when we like, and how we like. And Hecate can go curse herself."

"Exactly!" crowed Netty. The rotund witch rubbed her pudgy hands together as a broad, gap-toothed smile crept across her face. "So what do we like right now?"

"I," said Agatha, letting go of her pendant, "would like some pizza." And with that, she ripped the lid off a two-day old box.

The cheese-laden ingredients inside stared up at them, looking indecipherable.

"Are those bat's ears?" asked Netty.

"I have dibs on the crust," said Gertrude.

-Act V-

Scene 1: Confusion Now Hath Made His Masterpiece!

"THE VULTURES BEGIN to gather," Agatha rasped. It was early Monday morning, and the tall witch was gazing out the booth window into the Dairy Queen parking lot. The Dairy Queen wasn't open for business yet, but when had that ever stopped a witch?

Gertrude set down a pizza crust she had been nibbling. "You mean the hyenas begin to gather. You defame vultures."

"Point to you," said Agatha.

"Do you see that Cadwell woman yet?" Netty asked.

"First to arrive." Agatha pushed a towering stack of pizza boxes across the table until they reached the end and crashed onto the floor.

"Hey!" Gertrude wore her most indignant face. "I was still eating that."

"Would you prefer to eat or be able to see outside?"

"Since you put it that way," Gertrude said. "Oh, my, doesn't the gorgon look smug this morning."

Netty flexed her fingers. "I'm tempted to turn the gorgon lady into a real gorgon. See how she likes that."

Agatha cackled. "She probably would like it. Make it that much easier for her to get her claws into things."

"No need," Gertrude said. "What we've already planned for her is much better."

179

"Oh, look at the lovely sign!" said Netty. "I thought the gorgon told her minions to keep them out of sight until she gave the word."

"What does the sign say?" asked Gertrude. "I can't see it from here."

"Something boring," Netty said. "There, I've fixed it. Now it says, *Shakespeare Is for Pussies*. I don't know what the gorgon has against cats, but she didn't like the slogan, so I do."

All three witches cackled, and Agatha said, "We should leave the signs alone for now. We don't want to stop the show before it begins. Oh, and there's the signal."

"Not very flattering to witches," Gertrude said as parents hauled signs out of backseats and trunks of their cars and marched across the street. "But I like that one. *Witches are the Devil's Playmates*. Makes me want to sign up. What I wouldn't give to be some Devil's playmate."

"*Witches Eat Babies!*" Netty almost leaped off the bench and ran outside. "I wouldn't touch a baby! They're all gamy and taste like squid!"

Agatha stared down her long nose at the shorter witch.

"Or so I'm told," Netty said. "Never had the inclination myself."

Gertrude remained conspicuously silent. The other two witches looked at her.

"What?" said Gertrude. "That was before I discovered pizza. And children taste nothing like babies."

"Oh! Are we going to order more pizza?" Netty looked pointedly at Agatha. "You pushed Gertrude's breakfast onto the floor."

Agatha took in a nostril full of air and returned her gaze to the window. "After the show. Isn't that our Samson's car coming down the street?"

"And there's a TV van!" Netty crowed. "Right on time. Do we do it now?"

"Let's wait until the news van stops," said Agatha. "Timing is everything." A pause. "Or perhaps it isn't. Now's as good a time as any."

MONDAY MORNING ARRIVED after a weekend spent wondering what to do and no conclusions reached. Paul had told Sylvia

everything he had learned about the witches from Riordan, and
they both admitted that the play should be cancelled but were
concerned that cancelling wouldn't solve anything. If someone
had made a deal with the Weird Sisters, as Riordan had, then
cancelling the play wouldn't necessarily end the witches'
meddling. It could even make things worse.

Paul hadn't mentioned his worry that the dealmaker might be
Susie. And Sylvia had suggested that all of the students had taken
to the play like children to crayons. Any of them could have made
the bargain with the witches, but she couldn't imagine any of
them doing so. Paul had agreed and that helped him breathe
easier. The dealmaker could be anyone. It didn't have to be his
daughter.

What he found when they arrived at the school sent all these
thoughts fleeing.

"The woman has gone too far," Sylvia said. They had parked
the two cars in the teachers' lot and met at the sidewalk leading
to the school's main doors. "There must be a hundred parents
blocking the door with picket signs."

"They can't legally block the door," Paul said. "The police
would have to arrest them."

"We're not going to go through the blockade, are we?"

"There are other doors," Paul said, "but using one would give
points to the gorgon lady."

"Points?" Sylvia placed a hand on Paul's arm. "This isn't a
game. No one is keeping score."

"Cadwell is. And winning only inspires her to keep it up."

"Is that a news van pulling up?" Sylvia said. "It *is* a news van.
The picket line will be on TV!"

"All the more reason to ignore it." Paul took a deep breath and,
taking Sylvia's arm in his, began walking toward the main
entrance. "Smile for the camera."

A man with a shoulder camera was already panning the picket
line as a woman Paul recognized from the evening news
powdered her nose from a compact.

"Save *Macbeth*?" Sylvia said.

"What's that, dear?" Paul tore his eyes away from the reporter.

"That picket sign. And there's another one. *Kids need
kulture.*"

Paul had looked at some of the signs as they drove up. *No*

Witches at Ashcroft. Macbeth Equals Murderer. And his favourite, *Parents Know Best.* But now the signs all had different messages. *Shakespeare Forever. Save The Bard's Play. We Love Macbeth.* He frowned as he saw a sign that read, *Witches Are Not Prigs*!

"There he is!" someone shouted.

Mrs. Cadwell turned from the parent she had been speaking with and grinned at Paul.

Paul knew he would never get past the gorgon lady without exchanging words, so he altered their course to intercept Mrs. Cadwell on the way to the main doors. From the corner of his eye, Paul saw the newswoman and her cameraman also advancing on the gorgon.

"This is the man responsible for the play," Mrs. Cadwell said to the reporter. "*Macbeth* was Mr. Samson's idea, and he pushed it through despite objections from the principal, Mr. Winston. Paul Samson is his full name. He's the drama teacher."

Paul could see that Cadwell had been going to call him a few other things as well, but she stopped herself, conscious of the camera. In the last few moments, after reading some of the picket signs, Paul had already decided what he would say. He stopped in front of the gorgon lady and ignored the camera.

"Mrs. Cadwell. I have to say that as PTA president you have outdone yourself. Signs. Reporters. I, for one, am more surprised than I can express."

The gorgon grinned and let Paul continue.

"But really, you shouldn't have. I expect that Ashcroft Senior High School's fall performance of *Macbeth* will be as well attended as any production we've done in the past. This extra promotion is unnecessary. Appreciated, don't mistake me, but unnecessary."

He then pressed on toward the door, Sylvia following close at his side.

Paul's one regret was that he only caught a fleeting glimpse of the bafflement on Mrs. Cadwell's face before she vanished behind him beneath a deluge of the reporter's questions.

"I think the parents have begun noticing the wording on their signs," Sylvia said quietly into his ear.

Paul risked glancing back and saw a number of parents arguing with each other. Then he and Sylvia were through the main doors.

"Is what happened what I think happened?" Sylvia asked. She was unconsciously shaking her head from side to side.

"I can't see any other explanation," Paul said. He shrugged. "The signs changed. Just like that. If they hadn't, Cadwell might have succeeded in getting the play cancelled. Depending on what shows up on tonight's news, she may now have no chance, no matter what she attempts in the future."

Sylvia's face drained of blood. "The witches changed the signs? To keep the play from being cancelled?"

Paul nodded. "And no doubt they will do something equally . . . magical, if I try to cancel it."

"Then what can we do?" Sylvia wrapped her arms tightly around her chest.

"I don't know." Paul rested a hand on one of his wife's arms, hoping it would reassure her. Sylvia's skin felt cold and lifeless.

Scene 2: Who Shall Bear the Guilt of Our Great Quell?

PAUL AND SYLVIA walked down the hallway, doing their best to ignore several students who were jabbering excitedly about the events outside. When they arrived at the school auditorium, they told Scarlet what had happened.

"We're going to have to find the student who made the deal with the witches," Scarlet said. "Maybe once we know the destiny the witches have planned, we can use that to avoid any future trouble."

Paul could only agree and repeated the ghost's observation to his wife.

"What if it's not a student?" Sylvia asked. "It could be one of the parents, trying to fast-track young Jane or Joey to stardom."

"That would complicate things," Scarlet said. "I still think we need to start with the students."

Paul had already started that investigation two weeks earlier when Riordan had suggested the same thing. At the time, the most likely candidate had been his own daughter, walking into the female lead after her first twenty minutes in drama class, ever. Paul had agonized over the suggestion. While Susie's sudden interest in drama surprised him, he could at least explain it. He would never be able to explain Susie's consorting with witches. Perhaps it was time to share his fear with his wife.

"I haven't noticed anything overly unusual about the students," Paul said. "They all pretty much have the roles they deserve. Even Susie, despite her inexperience and previous lack of interest in drama."

"Paul!" Sylvia's voice dropped a half octave. "You're not suggesting our Susie has done this?"

Paul shook his head, though his heart wasn't in it. "Susie is the last student I would suspect. But she is the one who stands out the most."

"It must be someone else," Sylvia insisted. "You said that all of your students are doing better than expected."

"They are giving it more effort than any time in the last two years. But I'd hoped to put that down to them finally showing some maturity."

"I thought it was due to my influence," Sylvia said with a crooked smile.

For the next hour, Paul, Sylvia, and Scarlet went through the cast list, discussing each student and trying to recall any unusual behaviour, peculiar utterances, or unexplained absences. Ironically those three attributes were almost the definition of being a teenager. By the time the bell rang, signalling the end of first period, they were no further ahead.

"Let's forget rehearsing the play and focus on the students," Sylvia suggested as said students began flooding into the auditorium. "See if any of them are acting unusual."

Paul nodded and over the next hour, walked the class through the trouble spots in his notes from last week's rehearsals. He found it more difficult than he would have thought to focus on each student's behaviour rather than his or her acting competency. Instead of full scenes, he had them speak mispronounced lines, change specific blocking, and run through set changes that were too slow. No one displayed the cockiness or false confidence one might expect from someone who knew the fix was in. When the bell rang at the end of class, he was still unable to point to a student and say, "That one."

"Tomorrow we start from the top again," he said as the students put away their props. "From now on, we'll physically raise and lower the curtains and time everything."

"Mr. Samson?"

A student Paul didn't know passed him the note he had been expecting. He didn't even open it but sighed at Sylvia and headed for Winston's office.

Mrs. Kennedy greeted him with a laughing smile. "He's expecting you."

Paul walked in and was not surprised to see Mrs. Cadwell standing against one wall, fuming like a smokestack.

"You are aware," Winston said without greeting him, "of the fiasco on the school's front steps this morning?"

Paul feigned surprise. "Fiasco? I admit I was astonished. I had no idea that Mrs. Cadwell had had a change of heart, never mind a newfound desire to promote the play."

"I didn't and I don't." Cadwell half strangled the words. "I don't know how you did it—"

"I?" Paul pressed a hand against his chest. "All I did was show up for work this morning. That there were people, I assume PTA parents, in front of the school holding signs in support of the play surprised no one more than it did me. It almost brought tears to my eyes. When that reporter showed up, well, I was so overwhelmed, I rushed inside."

"Oh, yes, tears. Tears of laughter!" Cadwell shrieked.

Paul forced a puzzled expression onto his face. "I'm missing something here."

Winston let out a heavy sigh. "I think you and I both know that Mrs. Cadwell has not had a change of heart."

"Then why the signs?" Paul asked.

"You changed the signs!" The gorgon stuck a finger in his face.

Paul flinched. "I didn't even know about the signs."

"Mrs. Cadwell," said Winston, "I understand your dilemma. But you can't go accusing one of my teachers of misbehaviour without some kind of proof. Do you have any proof?"

The gorgon swung her finger toward the principal. "Of course I don't have any proof. If I did, then I'd know how he did it. But who else would have done it?"

Winston sighed again. "Who indeed? Fortunately for Mr. Samson, we live in a country where one is innocent until proven guilty, even in high school. Don't darken my door again until you have some evidence."

The gorgon opened her mouth then closed it again and stormed out of the office.

"And you," Winston said to Paul. "I just lied to that woman. You and I both know that the mere appearance of inappropriate behaviour can lead to getting a teacher fired. With everything that's happened in your class so far this year, I think we are well beyond a mere appearance. You're just lucky that when I spoke with the reporter, she told me that you were the only one outside the school with a modicum of decorum.

"But listen to me now, and listen to me good. If you or that woman embarrasses this school again, I'll have the both of you banned from the premises. Is that understood?"

Paul knew that "Yes, sir," was the appropriate response.

"Dismissed."

As Paul left the office, he wondered if Winston had been a drill sergeant in another life.

He hadn't gone ten steps before Mrs. Cadwell was blocking his way. "You think you've won, don't you?" The gorgon lady had never looked less like a human being. Her eyes were twice their normal size, and Paul could swear there was drool running down the corner of her mouth.

"Mrs. Cadwell, I can honestly tell you that I had nothing to do with your failed attempt to crucify me this morning. If someone changed your signs, they have my deepest gratitude. But you'll have to look elsewhere. It wasn't me."

The gorgon lady gave Paul a curious look and marched away. Paul had the uncanny feeling that, for once, she actually believed him.

Scene 3: Bring Me No More Reports

"I DON'T BELIEVE I can eat another bite," said Agatha.

It was lunchtime and a new stack of empty pizza boxes

adorned the table.

"More crust for me," suggested Gertrude.

"I feel different," Netty said. "Like chains that once hung around my neck have been released."

"Like I've lost twenty pounds," said Agatha, who barely weighed more than twenty pounds to start with.

"Like I've eaten more pizza in three days than I usually eat in three years," said Gertrude.

"You haven't eaten any pizza," Agatha said. "All you've had is flour, oil, and cheese."

"With a dash of salt," Netty added. "Possibly more than a dash."

"Pizza is tomato sauce, pepperoni, green peppers, and eye of newt," Agatha said, waving a hand dramatically above a partly eaten pie.

"That can't be right," Netty said. "Green peppers? Why would you order pizza with vegetables on it?"

"That's why I only eat the crust," Gertrude said. "I can't abide vegetables."

"Green pepper is a fruit," said Agatha.

"Yes, but isn't tomato a vegetable?" asked Netty.

"Also a fruit," said Agatha. "But I asked for extra garlic in the sauce because I know Gertie won't eat it."

"Garlic is a vegetable," said Gertrude, "and don't you start calling me Gertie! It's bad enough when Anjennette does it."

"It's business as usual, I see," said Hecate, appearing at their table, dressed all in black. Her eyes were masked with heavy eye shadow, making her look like a raccoon, and she had bits of silver metal sticking through her eyebrows, earlobes, nose, and lips. Her only colour consisted of purple highlights combed through her midnight-black hair.

"My goddess!" Agatha croaked. "You look like one of the students."

Hecate picked up a slice of pizza and began nibbling on it. "I thought I'd look around the school. Since your reports are close to nonexistent, I figured it was time I wrote my own report. Is this green pepper?" She threw the unfinished slice back into the box. "Only a Weird Sister would eat pizza with vegetables on it."

"Pepper is a fruit," said Agatha. "Only a moron—"

"We've given you lots of reports," Gertrude interrupted.

"Steady progress," added Netty.

"Is that so?" A stack of papers appeared on the table in front of Hecate. It was a short stack. Very short. And the pages were mostly ink free. Hecate spread them around with her fingers.

"You've been at this a month and so far, let's see, a broken leg, a fallen canvas wall, and a teacher who has gone insane but is still teaching. Have I missed anything?"

"We had a pitched battle in front of the school this morning!" Netty crowed.

Hecate raised a pierced eyebrow. "Sounds promising. How many dead?"

"Dead!" Netty coughed slightly and swallowed. "No one died. Lots of bumps and bruises. One man left in an ambulance. Tripped over his own picket sign."

"It wasn't our intention to kill anyone," Gertrude said.

Hecate snorted. "Bumps and bruises? You've grown soft." She picked up a fresh slice of pizza, picked off the green pepper, and bit into it.

Agatha ground her teeth. "There are worse things than death."

Hecate spoke while chewing. "Such as?"

"Embarrassment."

Hecate ceased chewing. She wagged her head, as though considering. She swallowed then nodded. "In sufficient quantity."

"I suggest you watch the local news this evening," Gertrude said. "You'll see embarrassment in spades."

Laughter filled the air above the booth. When Hecate ceased laughing, she said, "I never waste time watching the news. Can't believe half of it anyway. Bunch of prigs, those newscasters. If there is anything to see, I'll see it during my tour of the school."

With that, Hecate disappeared.

"Do you think we should have told her?" Netty asked.

"Told her what?" Agatha threw the pizza box Hecate had touched onto the floor and opened a new one.

Netty rolled her bulbous head around on her shoulders. "That students look . . . considerably younger than adults. She had the costume down, but she still looks thirty years old."

The other two witches let out a loud cackle.

"Hecate should learn for herself," Gertrude said, "that high schools are tough nuts to crack."

Another cackle.

"Where were we before we were so rudely interrupted?" asked Agatha.

"Discussing whether tomatoes are a vegetable or a fruit," Gertrude said.

"No, before that," said Agatha. "Ah, yes, we were feeling different."

Gertrude let out a deep snort. "It's obvious. For the first time in four hundred years, we've cursed something besides the play."

"We did?" asked Netty.

"We cursed the gorgon," said Gertrude.

"Not only that," Agatha said. "We helped the play. We anticursed it. That's a first."

"Anticurse?" Netty rumpled her already rumpled forehead. "I'm not sure how I feel about that."

Scene 4: Angels Are Bright Still

IT WAS ONE of those rare Monday evenings when the entire family was together for supper. Sylvia was home early enough to cook. And Susie had deigned to stay in rather than roam the mall with her friends, or whatever it was that teenage girls did these days.

Paul knew it was now or never. After coming no closer to finding their dealmaker during class, he and Sylvia had agreed, and somehow Paul had volunteered to take the lead. He'd rather eat his own liver, but what choice did they have?

"Did you see that weird substitute teacher at school today?" Susie asked. She was on her second helping of meatloaf with mashed potatoes. "Goth to the hilt and not a day under thirty. It was like a bad movie."

Paul glanced at Sylvia. "Um, no. I—uh, rather thought you might mention the PTA picket line this morning."

Susie didn't look up from her plate. "Old news."

"Yes, well, your mother and I and are going to watch the news on TV after supper to see if there is any mention."

"Whatever."

Paul knew he was approaching the topic in the most

roundabout way possible. "Aren't you the least curious about what the PTA was up to?"

This time Susie did look up. "They were picketing the play. As if that's a surprise." Before Paul could speak, she added, "And they screwed up the signs. Again, no surprise there. They didn't even spell all the words right. I swear, the only reason the PTA is interested in high school is because they were all dropouts and they don't want their kids to be smarter than they are."

Paul had never considered that. "An excellent theory. So you don't know anything about the signs being in support of the play?"

Susie twirled her fork, gathering up a cloud of potato. "Sorry, Dad. None of us knew about the picketing. The PTA must have planned it at the last minute and kept it hush-hush."

Paul glanced at Sylvia. "None of us?"

His daughter offered a conspiratorial smile. "The drama class. Ever since we got involved putting the petition together, we've been watching out for other attempts to stop the play."

"Oh." Paul wasn't sure what to say. "I certainly appreciate it."

Susie went back to hacking up her meatloaf so she could mix each forkful to be half meatloaf and half potatoes and gravy.

When Paul first noticed his daughter doing this several years earlier, he had suggested that Sylvia make meatloaf and mashed potato soup. Paul had found the taste and eating experience to be identical to what Susie was doing now, but his daughter refused to even try it. Sylvia had never made that particular soup again.

Paul sighed at the realization that his navel gazing was a stall tactic. His oblique approach had gotten him nowhere, so now he would have to face Susie head on. He could lose everything. But doing nothing could be even worse.

"Uh, Susie, on a completely different topic, I'm wondering what you can tell me about witches."

His daughter looked at him, and a strange smile spread across her face. "Like in the play? Gemma's really into the role now, and so are Teresa and Camille. Gemma doesn't hold my getting the part of Lady Macbeth against me anymore."

"Oh, that is good news." Paul pushed a slice of meatloaf across his plate. "But I was thinking of real-life witches. The kind you might meet in the street. Or on a heath."

His daughter continued to look at him. Her smile got perhaps a bit stranger. "Real-life witches?"

"That's right." Paul continued to rake his dinner with his fork, though he tried to keep his eyes on Susie.

"Oh," said Susie. "Those." She put down her fork and nodded her whole upper torso. "They're just ordinary teenagers with magical powers facing the same teenage angst as everyone else."

"Really?" Paul wasn't sure what answer he had expected, but this wasn't it.

Susie stopped nodding and snorted. "Last time I looked, on television. There's no such thing as real-life witches."

"Oh," said Sylvia, at last joining in. "So you haven't met any witches? Not even three witches?"

Susie's humour turned to concern. "Are you guys okay?"

"We're fine, dear," said Sylvia. "Someone reported seeing three oddly dressed women near the school, and some of the parents are concerned."

Their daughter snickered. "I bet that goth substitute teacher is one of them. I hope the gorgon lady doesn't hear about it. She'll try to close the school." Susie resumed murdering her meatloaf.

Paul let out a slow sigh of relief. He had agreed with Sylvia that they would just probe for answers and see if Susie offered up any hint of guilt. Telling their teenage daughter that the play might be cursed was not on the agenda. As far as Paul was concerned, Susie had passed with flying colours.

But they were still no closer to finding the guilty party. Paul made a mental note to ask Mrs. Kennedy about the goth substitute teacher and turned the conversation to less delicate topics.

Scene 5: How Now, You Secret, Black, and Midnight Hags!

REHEARSAL TUESDAY MORNING included the curtain. This required one of Anna's stagehands to man the pulley without slowing down set transitions. When she'd lose two additional hands to be ushers on performance night, Anna's reduced crew would work up a sweat moving double-time. It was an odd way to orchestrate the stagehands, but the offstage students needed to be kept busy during rehearsals, and it was good experience for them.

Sylvia sat in the second director's chair with a pad of ruled paper and a stopwatch. There was a line for each scene as well as lines for set changes and curtain calls. Everything would be timed, and anything that was too slow would be marked and worked on.

Paul spoke through his megaphone. "This is the phase of production development where the technicians need to stop playing and start working. And by technicians I mean Anna, Jennifer, Sigrid, and Sally. One mistake by any of you, and the play can come to a screeching halt. Not only is there no room for error, but time is of the essence. Too long a delay during set changes or while the curtain is down, and the audience will grow restless. Who knows what a restless audience is?"

When no one raised a hand, Lenny spoke up. "An unhappy audience."

"Lenny is correct. Put the audience in a foul mood, and it may last the rest of the evening, despite our best efforts. Many of you have tasks when not on stage to help the technicians. You can't screw up either. Forgetting to move a chair can be more disastrous than forgetting your lines. Who knows why a theatre company is called a company?"

Again no hands. Again Lenny spoke up. "Because we have to work together."

"Correct, but even that's too simple. Just like in the military, our lives depend on each other. Figuratively, if not literally.

"Okay. Everyone get in position for Act I, Scene 1. Sigrid, you're the curtain man, well, curtain woman. Lower the curtain. I'll give the final welcome line, concluding with, 'Enjoy the show.' Count five seconds and then raise the curtain."

Paul lowered the megaphone and, once the curtain was down, turned to Sylvia. "Ready."

Sylvia smiled at him. "I've got my finger on the trigger."

Paul raised the megaphone and said, "Welcome to Ashcroft Senior High's third-year production of Shakespeare's *Macbeth*. Enjoy the show."

Sylvia clicked her stopwatch, and five seconds later, the curtain rose.

Paul took furious notes as the play progressed through to the end of Act III, Scene 5. He frequently referred to his notes of the previous week's run-through that he had marked up on Monday's spot rehearsal. There were still plenty of problems but fewer than the previous week.

About the only real surprise was that Banquo's ghost failed to show up. Sylvia had even slipped backstage to shake John awake and quickly returned to her chair when the effort wasn't needed.

"Very good, class," Paul said, moments before the bell. "Even after adding the curtain, we finished two additional scenes. Does anyone know why?"

After a pause, Lenny said, "Less dead air."

"Um. Yes, that's one way to put it. In drama terms, you did a better job of stepping on each other's lines. Remember, when people talk, they don't take turns. They speak as soon as possible after someone finishes and often interrupt each other. I don't want you to interrupt each other unless the script calls for it. But you don't want to pause before saying your lines."

The bell rang and the students evaporated almost before Paul had finished speaking. Sylvia handed him the notebook and the stopwatch. "Gotta run. House to show."

Before he had blinked three times, Paul was alone with Scarlet.

"No Banquo." The ghost's smile was bitter.

Perhaps for the first time, Paul saw Scarlet as a sad young woman rather than a vibrant, if deceased, young woman. It occurred to him that Scarlet was only a few years older than Susie. And day after day, except for the time Paul was in the auditorium rehearsing *Macbeth*, she was completely alone.

"Banquo was twice your age," Paul said. "And had bad teeth." Only after speaking, did Paul realize he couldn't have said anything stupider. Still, Scarlet's smile brightened.

"Actually," Paul added, "you are also twice your age. You may look twenty, but you were born four decades ago. I can't imagine what it's like being a ghost, but I suppose Banquo could, so I understand why you miss him.

"You know what?" Having spoken the wrong words, Paul felt he had some right words to say. "I've been so distracted by the play's curse that I haven't spent any time yet figuring out how to get you out of that lamp permanently. Or freeing you from whatever binds you to me."

Scarlet grinned. "So you're an expert on ghosts now, are you?"

Paul shrugged. "Last week I wasn't an expert on curses. Look at me now. I'm a quick study."

Having promised to help the ghost, Paul regretted leaving the auditorium and consigning Scarlet back into Riordan's lamp. But if he was going to solve anything, he had work to do.

Mrs. Kennedy gave him a puzzled look when Paul showed up at her desk. "What did you do now?" the secretary asked. "I know Winston hasn't sent for you."

Paul waggled his eyebrows. "It's you I've come to see."

"Me?" Mrs. Kennedy batted her eyes and waved her hand like a fan to cool her face. She finished speaking in a mock Southern drawl. "No one evah comes to see li'l ol' me."

Paul grinned. "Then people are missing out. Would I be correct in saying that you know everything that goes on in this school?"

Mrs. Kennedy tilted her head, and Paul could see that she was trying to figure out his angle.

"Let me rephrase. If an outlandish substitute teacher showed up, you would know about it?"

All the humour left Mrs. Kennedy's face. "You're talking about the goth woman."

Paul felt a weight hit his stomach. "Oh, so there is such a teacher."

"Absolutely not," said Mrs. Kennedy. "This school may have no written dress code for teachers, but if you broke the unwritten code, you'd be sent home in a heartbeat."

Paul had always assumed as much, but testing his theory had never been a priority. "So this woman, then . . ."

Mrs. Kennedy snorted. "Had a difficult time explaining herself. I'm certain she must be foreign. Eventually she claimed to be a parent investigating likely schools in which to place her daughter. If the daughter is anything like the mother, I'm certain she's been expelled from any number of schools."

Paul couldn't help but laugh. "Mrs. Kennedy, you've been of greater help than I possibly imagined."

"Uh-huh. Why the interest?"

"My daughter mentioned seeing a strange woman in the school and thought she must be a substitute teacher."

The secretary pursed her lips. "If you're looking for strange women, try the Dairy Queen."

"What?"

"It's been the talk of the school all term. Three—I hesitate to use the word *hags*, but that's what the students call them—have been living in the Dairy Queen for weeks. I haven't gone to look for myself, but apparently they've taken over a corner booth and haven't budged."

"Three hags?" If Paul had been limber enough to kick himself, he would have done so on the spot. He noticed Mrs. Kennedy watching him in the same manner that doctors view infections or entomologists the behaviour of drunken ants. He shrugged. "I believe I've seen them."

Paul remembered the photo he had taken with his camera and printed out to show his three witches. He reached into his coat pocket and, with trembling hands, pulled out the folded photo. He handed it to Mrs. Kennedy, who looked at it with an expression of surprised horror then squinted at it closely.

She looked up at Paul. "It's the same woman. Has to be. But the hair is different and the face metal and eye shadow are all gone." More slowly, the school secretary asked, "Why is she in her underwear?"

Paul took back the photo and stared at it, mortified that he had shown Mrs. Kennedy the wrong one. "The same as who?"

"The foreigner who was here yesterday looking at schools for her daughter."

Paul had no idea what to make of that and made a mental note to think about it later. Pulling the second photo from his pocket, he thrust it at Mrs. Kennedy. "The lingerie woman was at Dairy Queen standing next to these three."

Mrs. Kennedy examined the second photo then nodded her head. "The students are right. Hags. No doubt about it." She handed the photo back.

"You . . . um." Paul fidgeted as he put the photos back in his pocket. "You won't tell Mrs. Cadwell about these strange women, will you?"

The school secretary gave Paul a severe look. "Mr. Samson, I make it policy to refrain from telling the gorgon lady so much as the time of day."

Paul nodded slowly. "That's good to know. Mrs. Kennedy, you have been extremely helpful."

"Any time, Mr. Samson. Any time."

After retreating into the empty hallway, Paul opened his cell phone and dialed a number in his call history. When the other end answered, he said. "This is Paul Samson calling. Could you let Mr. Riordan know that there have been further developments?"

Scene 6: Let Not Light See My Black and Deep Desires

WEDNESDAY MORNING CONCLUDED the curtain rehearsal. Sylvia worked her magic with the pad of ruled paper and the stopwatch while Paul jotted comments onto paper already crowded with notes. Everything was running smoothly until Act V, Scene 8. That's when Paul realized he was an idiot.

Locked in mortal combat, hacking at each other with plastic swords, Macbeth shouted at Macduff: "Let fall thy blade on vulnerable crests; I bear a charmed life, which must not yield, to one of woman born."

Paul knew why he had missed it. Assigning Lenny the role of Macduff had been an error on his part. Quite childishly, he had wanted to knock Lenny down a notch. Lenny should have been Macbeth, and one broken leg later, he had the part he should have had all along. So seeing Lenny as Macbeth had not seemed out of place.

Not in a million years could Paul see his daughter, Susie, out on a heath with three witches trading gym class to play the part of Lady Macbeth in her father's drama class. But he had no problem at all seeing Lenny, dressed in the same black clothes he wore now, standing on a windy bluff, selling his soul to play the villain instead of the hero.

When the curtain fell at the end of the play, there were still fifteen minutes of class left.

Once the students had finished their formal bows in front of the curtain, Paul lifted the megaphone to his lips. "Fantastic job, everyone. Tomorrow we'll go over the notes from today and yesterday's rehearsal. Class dismissed."

The students hesitated; teachers weren't allowed to end class early. But as soon as one student moved to leave, the rest followed like lemmings.

Paul returned the megaphone to his lips. "A word, Lenny."

By the time Lenny approached the directors' chairs, his peers had vanished.

Paul took in a deep breath. "I have a serious question for you, Lenny, and I want you to answer truthfully. You're not in any kind of trouble, but I need an honest answer."

Lenny replied with a blank stare.

"Are you aware of the three . . . older women who have been hanging out at the Dairy Queen?"

Sylvia sat at Paul's side, silent. He had told her about his conversation with Mrs. Kennedy the moment he had returned home the previous evening.

Lenny's stare never faltered. "What?"

Paul removed the photo from his pocket, the correct photo, and showed it to him. "These three woman?"

Lenny hardly glanced at the photo. "No."

With almost fifteen years of dealing with teenagers, including his own daughter, under his belt, Paul had picked up certain street smarts. "I'll take that as a yes. What kind of deal did you make with them?"

Lenny scratched his head. "Oh, *those* women. I might have mentioned that I was playing the part of Macbeth in the school play."

Paul put away the photo. "Like I said, you're not in any kind of trouble. But it is important that I know the details of the deal you made."

The blank stare returned, but it carried a hint of bafflement. "Deal? We just talked."

Sylvia spoke up. "It may not have sounded like a deal. Perhaps they mentioned a destiny?"

The bafflement grew and Paul could see a discussion going on behind Lenny's eyes. Apparently the side of the boy's brain that couldn't see how he could get into any kind of trouble won. "Well, the witch I met first did say I was destined to have the lead in the school play, but that was before you even picked the play."

"Before I?" Now Paul was baffled. "You spoke with the . . .

witches . . . before I chose *Macbeth*?"

"Just one of them. On the Saturday before school started. I was riding my bike in the park, and all of a sudden, this homeless woman leaps out of the trees and screeches at me, 'All hail Lenny! Lead of the autumn school play!'

"So, I said, 'Duh, I'm the best actor in school.'

"'The best are not always first, nor the least last,' the woman said. 'Yet Lenny shall lead!'" Lenny frowned. "Her voice was like a radio station buried in static, so it was hard to understand her, but eventually I understood that she and her friends would guarantee me a career in acting."

"And you believed her?" Sylvia asked.

Lenny smirked. "Hell, no. She was a crazy homeless woman. I told her to take a hike. But eventually she said that all I had to do was drop by the Dairy Queen after school the next Monday, so it was no skin off my nose."

"And then?" Paul asked.

"Then Monday after school, I go to the Dairy Queen and she's there with two other homeless women, eating pretty much the entire menu. I have no idea who paid for it. That's when they told me I'd play the lead role in *Macbeth*. Since no one had thrown them out of the restaurant, I thought that maybe they were telling it to me straight. That maybe they were witches."

Lenny's face took on a slight grimace. "I was a little surprised when you cast me as Macduff. It confirmed that the witches were just crazy ladies. But Kim Greyson as Macbeth? That's even crazier."

Paul was thinking up additional questions to ask when the bell rang. He stepped down from his director's chair. "Thank you, Lenny, for being honest with us. Like I told you, you're not in any trouble. But I do suggest that you stay away from the crazy ladies."

Lenny shrugged and walked away.

"Well," said Sylvia. "Now we know."

"Yes. But I don't see how it helps us. It's not like Lenny can call off the curse. He's a victim in this more than anyone." Paul glanced at his watch, even though the bell had already told him what time it was. "And now I'm off to meet another victim."

Sylvia looked at him with concern. "Do you want me to come along?"

Paul shook his head. "It's difficult enough for Riordan to talk to me. I don't dare tell him that I told you anything."

Scene 7: Fears and Scruples Shake Us

THERE WAS NO sign of Riordan at the Dairy Queen. Paul took their regular table near the door and tried not to notice the three witches seated at the booth at the other end of the seating area. With almost an hour to go before the school lunch bell, the place was quiet, the only other customer a young mother with an uncooperative child of perhaps four years of age.

Paul hoped that Riordan wasn't too ill to make the trip. When they spoke on the phone the previous evening, he had sounded okay, but you never know. Hadn't Riordan said that his doctors gave him very little time? Perhaps the opportunity would arise to find out what his ailment was.

A plaid shirt blocked Paul's view of the top of the witches' heads, and Riordan sank onto the opposite bench, setting a tray in front of him that contained a burger of some kind, fries, and a large soft drink. Paul gawked at it. On the previous two occasions they had shared this booth, the man had only drunk water.

Riordan noticed his reaction and grinned. "I've got my appetite back. I can't remember the last time I felt this hungry. One of my doctors says it's because I'm beginning to face my fears." The older man lost his cheer. "Why are you still here? I thought you would have moved to Switzerland by now. Or Antarctica."

"Running won't help," Paul said. "Besides, I'm not the one who consorted with witches. My leaving won't end the curse."

"No, but it may save your family. You said there were further developments?"

Paul nodded. "I found out who spoke with the witches. It was a student, Lenny, the boy playing Macbeth."

Riordan let out a heavy breath. "Not even children are safe. Have these witches no shame?"

"I also found the witches."

Riordan stared at him.

Paul pulled out the photo he had shown Lenny, and Riordan almost crawled over the back of his seat.

"That's them!" The older man calmed himself and looked closer at the photo. "They haven't changed in twenty years." He looked even closer. "That table they're sitting at. It looks just like this one."

"Don't panic." Paul put out one hand and clasped Riordan's forearm, probably in an unconscious effort to keep the man from bolting. "Your curse ended twenty years ago. The witches have no interest in you."

"You can't know that!" Riordan's baritone grew shrill.

"We can ask them."

The older man's eyes nearly sprang out of his head. "Are you out of your mind?"

"Apparently not." Paul couldn't suppress a chuckle. "The witches tried to make that happen and I survived."

Riordan attempted to rise out of his seat, but Paul's grip on his arm prevented him. "You are out of your mind!"

Paul gave the old man a stern look. "What happened to you wanting to face your fears?"

"Twenty-year-old fears." Riordan breathed hard through his nose. "I've no interest in creating new ones."

"Well, I can understand that." Paul let go of his arm. "But if the witches were going to do anything to you, I think they would have done it by now."

Riordan narrowed his eyes. "Why do you say that?"

"Because they're sitting behind you."

Paul could hear Riordan's back crack as he spun around. Even with the older man partially blocking his view, Paul saw one of the hags, the one who looked like a pretzel, lift a wilted hand and wave. "Hello, Simon! You're looking well."

Riordan let out a strangled cry and collapsed onto the bench.

"Oh, my," said the waving hag. "I hope he isn't dead."

Scene 8: There the Grown Serpent Lies

THE BOOTHS AT Dairy Queen were designed to hold four adults or some random number of smaller children. Sitting three adults on a side was uncomfortable at best, disastrous if you were trying to eat anything. The witches were eating pizza.

Paul was fortunate to be sitting on the side with one witch, who called herself Netty. However, Netty seemed to be almost as wide as she was tall, so he didn't feel himself overly fortunate.

Riordan, though not quite as skeletal as he had been the week before, was still wider than the spindly witch who called herself Agatha. Fortunately the older man had merely fainted on seeing the witches, although Paul suspected he might wish he were dead rather than packed in like a sardine between two of them. The third witch, the one who had waved, was named Gertrude and sat at the end of the bench, waging a war against being pushed out into the aisle.

In the confusion of checking Riordan's pulse and getting him a glass of water, somehow the witches had manoeuvred them to the opposite side of the seating area and into their own booth, with Riordan the centre of a witch sandwich and Paul pressed against the window so neither could leave until the witches let them. *If* the witches let them.

Paul's meeting with the witches had hardly begun, and already he was regretting that he had instigated it.

"Simon!" Netty wobbled her round head at Riordan. "It is wondrous to see you again. After all this time."

Gertrude peered up at him from where her crooked head rested on her hunched shoulder. "Those were glorious days out on the heath, weren't they?"

"Ah," said Riordan, his shoulders pulled tight and sitting absolutely still. "You're not going to hurt me, are you?"

Gertrude smiled and let out a loud cackle. "Simple Simon! Why would we hurt you?"

Agatha swallowed a mouthful of pizza. "Your destiny has been fulfilled. Why would we waste our time?"

Paul figured he should say something to get things started. Like, *Is Lenny's destiny also fulfilled? He has the role he wanted.*

But what came out was, "Are those anchovies?"

Netty snorted. "Only a Frenchman would put anchovies on a pizza. That's newt."

Agatha picked up another slice. "Sadly, it's just the eyes. Hard to find a pizza with whole salamanders these days. Try some."

Paul swallowed. "Ah, thank you, no. Are you done with Lenny?"

"Who?" all three witches said together.

"My student. The one playing Macbeth."

"Oh, him." Gertrude waved her fingers in the air.

Paul flinched, expecting some kind of spell.

"Don't mind me, dearie. I'm just drying my hands. The crust has cheese in it. Oily, but that's what makes it yummy. You really should try some."

Paul picked up a piece of crust, gnawed the smallest bit of one end, then put it down again. "Yes. Delicious."

"You were asking about your Macbeth," said Agatha. "The wannabe actor."

"Yes." Paul searched for words. "You said his destiny was to have the lead in the school play. He does. Does that mean the curse is over?"

All three witches cackled.

Riordan did his best to slide under the table, but with two witches pressed against him, he wasn't going anywhere. Paul now regretted asking his old mentor to come. He'd hoped that Riordan's presence would help even the odds, but Paul now knew that bringing an army wouldn't even the odds. These were witches, and Paul felt useless against them. He could tell from just looking at Riordan that his old drama teacher felt less than useless.

"You're here about the curse?" Gertrude again waved her fingers in the air. "And here I thought this was just a social visit."

Agatha pointed a slice of half-eaten pizza at him. "Once begun, a curse must run its course. It cannot be stopped."

Gertrude let out a small, wicked laugh. "That said, we've decided to stop the curse."

"Really?" For the first time in weeks, Paul felt real hope.

"Oh, yes," Gertrude said, still waving her fingers. "We stopped cursing the play ages ago."

"Simply ages!" Netty said.

"Last Friday, to be exact." Agatha laughed out her nose, and that started all three witches cackling.

"In fact . . ." Gertrude played with a slice of pizza on the table, spinning the triangle one hundred eighty degrees. "We've been anticursing the play."

"Anticursing?" Then realization struck him. "So that was you who changed the picket signs."

Another long bout of cackling. Then Agatha caught her breath. "Who else could have done it?"

"Well, thank you," Paul said. "I don't know what to say." And that was true. Paul really had no idea what to say.

"Then say nothing," Agatha said. "We didn't do it for you."

"Then, why?" Paul knew he shouldn't have said it. Never look a gift horse in the mouth. And here he'd looked into not one but three mouths.

It was Gertrude who answered. "Because there is another curse on your play."

Netty joined in. "A curse from someone more fearsome than a witch."

"More fearsome than three witches," said Agatha.

"Don't believe them!" It was Riordan, at last working up the courage to speak. "If you believe them, they'll call it destiny, and you'll be making the deal!"

The three witches cackled. Then Agatha jabbed Riordan in the stomach with a bony elbow. "That's some imagination you've got there, Simon."

Netty was still laughing so hard, she couldn't speak. By some means of magic, she made her words understandable. "We don't need a deal to invoke a curse."

Gertrude was nodding her head. "We can curse whomever we want, whenever we want."

"Now where were we?" asked Agatha. "Oh, yes. More fearsome than three witches."

Paul couldn't help himself. He had to know. "Who?"

The three hags spoke together. "The gorgon!"

Paul sat up a little straighter. "The gorgon? You mean the gorgon lady? Mrs. Cadwell?"

Three hoary heads nodded.

"She is a devious woman," Agatha said.

"With hundreds of minions!" Netty crowed. "Perhaps even

three."

"And," Gertrude added, "she's a prig!"

"A what?" asked Paul.

Gertrude shook her head, or at least Paul assumed it was a shake. "Too horrible to explain."

Paul decided he could look *prig* up in a dictionary. What he couldn't fathom was that Mrs. Cadwell was somehow a bigger problem than three witches. "Does she have some kind of dark powers?"

Agatha wagged her head. "Powers are neither light nor dark. The colour is in the heart of the wielder."

The teacher in Paul told him that *colour* was the wrong word for the metaphor, but he understood what the witch meant.

"Okay, but you're saying that the gorgon lady can do things? Like what you did with changing the signs?"

"Worse," said Gertrude. "We may have changed the signs, but the gorgon created them in the first place."

"And convinced minions to wield them!" Netty said.

"Right. Right." Paul searched for a way to ask the right question. "But is the gorgon lady magical like you? Or just an ordinary person like me?"

The witches rumpled their foreheads and looked at each other, apparently as exasperated as Paul felt.

"For God's sake," said Riordan. "What can we do to stop the gorgon lady from cursing the play?"

Agatha nodded solemnly. "For starters, you can look at this."

From out of nowhere, a handbill appeared on the table. It showed an elderly man with a flowing beard and fiery eyes. The caption revealed his name as Reverend Sebastian Archibald Long and listed him as the author of several books. The titles included *Daughters of the Devil in Our Day*, *There Is a Coven in Your Neighborhood*, and *Samhain Disguised as Halloween*. There was a location and date: Ashcroft Senior High, Friday, October 9.

"That's in two days!" Paul said, his heart slamming into his throat. "Why haven't I heard of this?"

Gertrude waved her fingers in the air and the date changed to October 16. "That was the original date for the reverend's appearance. The handbills were going to come out next week. But with the picket signs failing so phenomenally, the gorgon lady convinced him to reschedule. Oh, this time the fingers were magic. Heh."

The misshapen witch then tapped the handbill with a greasy finger, and the date returned to the ninth. "The reverend was supposed to justify the cancellation of the play after it had already happened. But now the gorgon lady is using him in a last-ditch effort to get the play called off."

Paul couldn't believe it. "But this handbill says that he's going to speak to the school in the large gymnasium over the lunch hour. That goes against school policy. Religion can't be taught in schools."

Riordan shook his head. "But the reverend isn't going to talk about God. He's going to talk about the Devil. And witches. And the evils of Halloween costumes and candied apples."

"But that's the same thing!"

Agatha leaned forward, almost stabbing Paul with her crooked nose. "Not according to your PTA."

Scene 9: The Instruments of Darkness

"I WAS WONDERING when you'd come see me," Winston said. "I saw you on the news two nights ago. I suppose you're looking for extra credit for downplaying the PTA's picketing debacle in front of the media."

Paul blinked with surprise. "That news article was only fifteen seconds long. I'm surprised you noticed me at all."

Winston gave him an uneasy smile. "I noticed because I expected you to strangle Mrs. Cadwell. If it had been me on the school steps, I might have. Has she lost her mind?"

"You mean recently?" Paul asked.

The principal waved his hand. "Point taken. If you're not here about the news coverage, why are you here?"

Paul pulled from his sport coat pocket the handbill he had received from the witches and tossed it onto the principal's desk.

Winston stared at the crinkled sheet then up at Paul. "Where did you get that? They're not supposed to go out until tomorrow."

Paul shook his head. "It doesn't matter where I got it. What matters is what it says. You're really going to allow Cadwell to bring in a bible thumper to speak to the students?"

Winston's sweaty forehead topped his flushed face, and the battle had scarce begun. The heavyset man pulled a handkerchief from his pocket and wiped his brow. "I understand that Mr. Long is a reverend, but he is also an author and will be speaking in that capacity. Mr. Long speaks at schools all over the country in Halloween season, urging students to live clean, respectable lives and stay away from those who would catch them up in lifestyles that include drugs, violence, and the occult."

Paul couldn't believe what he was hearing. "You really have been drinking the gorgon lady's Kool-Aid, haven't you? Reverend Long doesn't write books about drugs or violence. He writes about the occult. Chalk pentagrams and black candles. Neither of which have ever been seen within a hundred miles of Ashcroft Senior High. The reverend's talk is only going to bring such things to the kids' attention and inspire them to try them out."

Winston's mouth gaped open, and his skin flushed even further.

"You know I'm right," Paul said.

Winston threw his handkerchief down on the desk. "Of course you're right. The reverend is a nut bar, and the only people he inspires are other nut bars. Unfortunately that group includes Mrs. Cadwell and many of the members of her PTA. The way I hear it, they worship the man. I'm not bringing him in; the PTA is. And until the reverend tells the students to get baptized or join a church, there's not a damn thing I can do about it."

It was Paul's turn to stand open mouthed with flushed skin. "She can really do this?"

Winston picked up his handkerchief. "She *can* do this. And she *is* doing this."

THAT EVENING Paul and Sylvia retired to the living room to watch some television. At least, that was what they told Susie.

"So tell me about your meeting with Riordan," Sylvia asked before they had even sat down. "And the witches."

"You won't believe it," Paul said. "But before I get into that, you should look at this."

Sylvia stared at the handbill. "Isn't it illegal for a minister to preach at a school?"

Paul shook his head. "There seems to be a loophole. If you're arguing that Satanism is real and should be avoided, it's not considered religion."

"That's ridiculous."

"So say all right-thinking men and women. The thing is, if I can't think of a way to stop him, the witches might steal his gizzard or have a cat rip out his tongue."

"What?" Sylvia sat down heavily in her favourite armchair.

Paul sat in the chair across from his wife. "Oh, did I forget to mention? The witches have decided to switch sides."

Sylvia frowned. "What you told me over the phone was that you and Riordan had met with the witches and that the meeting went well. Then you hung up, saying that you had to speak with Winston and that you'd fill me in tonight."

Paul spent the next few minutes recounting what he could remember of what the witches had said. For some reason, the conversation swirled elusively around his mind. Much like Riordan's account of his dealings with the witches twenty years ago, it seemed more confusing than it should have been. Perhaps because they were witches, memories of them didn't stick like regular memories.

"So," said Sylvia. She tapped a thumb against her chin. "You're saying that the witches are afraid of Mrs. Cadwell?"

Paul almost laughed out loud. "Not afraid. I don't think they know the meaning of the word. Respect perhaps? They've watched Cadwell's attempts to stop the play and are impressed."

"And the witches changed the slogans on the picket signs Monday morning?"

Paul nodded. "Near as I can tell, instead of trying to stop the play, the witches now want to see it succeed."

Sylvia blinked her eyes. "Why?"

Paul blew a gust of air between his lips. "No idea."

"Well," said Sylvia. "Best not to look a gift horse in the mouth."

Paul cleared this throat. "My thoughts exactly."

Sylvia turned her attention back to the handbill. "So what are we going to do about the reverend?"

Scene 10: If Thou Speak'st False

PAUL COULDN'T REMEMBER the last time he had seen the gymnasium so crowded. Since he didn't have a class in third period, he was able to arrive at the gym well before anyone else and spend a good twenty minutes helping the caretaker, Jerry Noonan, and several student volunteers set up chairs before taking a seat in the front row.

As the students poured in to waste a valuable lunch hour listening to a lunatic, Paul noticed that many of those gathering weren't students. A good number of the teachers were showing up, more likely out of curiosity than anything else. He recognized a number of faces from the PTA legion who had invaded his auditorium several weeks earlier.

Paul laughed to himself, thinking that the Ashcroft-Tate Auditorium would be perfect for Long's talk. Of course, Mrs. Cadwell wouldn't dare try to use it. The auditorium was Paul's turf. She wouldn't need his permission, strictly speaking, but Paul would have found out about Long's visit well before yesterday's official announcement. Besides, the gorgon was used to using the gymnasium for her PTA meetings.

At ten minutes after high noon, Mrs. Cadwell stepped up onto the large dais that had been erected at the front of the gymnasium. The portable platform was the modern equivalent of a soapbox, an apt name for what was about to happen. The gorgon lady looked out at the sea of expectant faces and tapped the microphone. She then gave what Paul believed was an introductory spiel common to schools all across the nation whenever a PTA guest speaker was introduced. After a brief smile, she welcomed best-selling author Reverend Sebastian Archibald Long.

Mild applause greeted the aging minister who Paul knew, after several hours of Internet research, could only dream of having a best-selling book. Despite a plethora of rave reviews and overstated cover blurbs, the man's books sold infrequently, and then only to a niche market within the lunatic fringe.

What the man did have, however, was charisma. Paul had read about it. And he experienced it himself after only a few minutes of the man's speaking. Long took the microphone out of its stand and sat in a chair then warmed his audience with a few jokes and an anecdote from his childhood. His face then grew serious as he told the story of a college girl who joined a sorority with rather peculiar hazing rituals. Paul's hair literally stood on end as the tale degenerated into horrific acts of violence and implied sexual degradation.

Paul was so caught up in the story that he almost forgot to slip his hand into his sport coat pocket and press the button on the small transmitter concealed there.

As Long continued his cautionary tale, a barely perceptible heartbeat added itself to the sound system. *Thump-thump.* The reverend didn't seem to notice, and indeed, Paul wouldn't have noticed either if he hadn't been listening for it. The heartbeat grew gradually louder until Paul couldn't not hear it. Muttering from the audience confirmed that others were having the same problem.

The reverend continued his delivery, oblivious. He'd finished the college tale and had started in on some horrible misdeed that happened somewhere, some when, on Halloween. Paul was having trouble paying attention, the *thump-thump* distracting him from the tale each time he tried to listen.

During his research, Paul had discovered that the reverend's hearing was failing. He was now deaf in one ear and relied on a hearing aid in the other. However, he had trouble with the lower end of the spectrum. Even with the hearing aid, the old man couldn't hear the low-pitched heartbeat.

As his talk continued, people began leaving the gymnasium. For some, the steady heartbeat was giving them a headache, possibly a migraine. For others, they had simply grown bored, unable to concentrate on what the reverend was saying.

Long was beginning to look uncomfortable, not because he could hear anything wrong, but because he was losing his audience.

Mrs. Cadwell stepped back up onto the dais and gave the reverend a different microphone.

Paul managed not to laugh. He tried to tune out the heartbeat and listen as Reverend Long described the true cost of being a daughter of the Devil. He listed several physical and mental horrors before concluding with the loss of the soul.

When Paul couldn't take the audial assault any longer, he rose from his seat and walked out of the mostly empty gymnasium. Movement caught his eye, and he looked up to the top of the folded bleachers, where he saw three hags kicking their feet and cackling.

Keeping an eye out for Mrs. Cadwell and any of her PTA cronies, Paul walked straight to Winston's office. When Mrs. Kennedy rose from her desk to knock on the principal's door and announce him, Paul slipped his hand into his pocket and passed her the small transmitter.

He couldn't have pulled it off without the help of Mrs. Kennedy and the music teacher, Art Perry. Mrs. Kennedy had recommended Art when Paul told her his idea, and Art was only too happy to make the needed recording, tap into the gymnasium sound system, and rig the transmitter to start the playback. When the coast was clear, Art would untap the sound system.

Winston looked up from his desk as Paul entered. "I thought you'd be listening to the reverend, making notes on how to combat the mass hysteria that will arise from his infecting the minds of innocent students."

Paul decided to do something then that he never did, but figured that since he hadn't actually been summoned and wasn't embarking on a confrontation, felt its time had come. He flopped himself down into one of Winston's two visitor chairs.

The principal's jaw dropped.

"I listened for a while," Paul said, "but left when I got a headache." He rubbed his temples. "I actually kind of like the old gaffer. If he wasn't off in la-la land, I could listen to him for hours."

Winston recovered from his initial shock and pursed his lips. "You're not concerned that the reverend's comments will inflame the school to cancel your play?"

Paul shrugged. "The reverend was talking Amityville Horror. I swear he gets his material from the movies. The kids will see through that, even if some of the parents don't."

Mrs. Cadwell chose that moment to barge in through the door. She glared at Winston then, seeing Paul seated in one of the visitor chairs, glared at him twice as hard. "What did you do?"

Paul squeezed his eyes shut as the shout bounced around inside his head.

"Mrs. Cadwell?" Winston's voice was soft. "Is there a problem?"

"He did something!"

Paul opened his eyes to find the tip of the gorgon lady's finger just inches from his face.

"Indeed," said Winston. "He went to listen to your witch-hunter and then came here to tell me that he didn't think your latest attempt to cancel his play is as big a problem as he feared."

"He—he did what?"

"I was in the audience." Paul raised his hand and gently pushed Mrs. Cadwell's finger away. "I kind of like your Reverend Long. His obsession with Satan leaves a bad taste in my mouth, but otherwise he's an affable old guy."

"You were in the audience?"

"I also found it odd that all of Long's tales and cautions were about teenage girls. Aren't boys equally susceptible to the dark side?"

Winston cleared his throat. "Recent statistics show that boys are thirty percent more likely to get into trouble than girls. Something to do with gender expectations."

The gorgon regained her voice. "If you were in the audience, then you know there was no audience."

Paul blew air out of his lips. "It was a full house! At least when it started. You're right, though. People did drift off. I didn't stay until the end either. It was rather repetitious, don't you think? After Long's third yarn of nubile young women being ravished and tortured, I didn't think I could listen to another."

"He said what?" Winston's voice was no longer soft.

Paul waved his hand. "Long was discreet. Kept graphic detail to a minimum. He's quite the storyteller." Paul looked at Mrs. Cadwell. "But that's all they are, stories. I did some reading about your Mr. Long last night. Seems a good number of people take issue with his so-called facts. They say he cherry-picks questionable witnesses and takes quotes from newspapers out of context, bending accounts and calling his version the only version."

"That's slander," said Mrs. Cadwell.

Paul nodded. "Perhaps. We'll know next week when my findings are published in the school newspaper. If I'm half as good at cherry-picking the public record as Long is, I should be okay."

The gorgon's expression resembled a snake choking on a too-large mouse. "You're printing a story on Reverend Long in the school newspaper?"

Paul looked at Winston. "Didn't I just say that?"

Mrs. Cadwell ground her teeth. "This isn't over."

The last time the gorgon lady spoke those words, Paul had let it go. But Paul was no longer the same man, and this Paul wasn't going to let it go. "Mrs. Cadwell, allow me to make a suggestion. Let the students perform the play. Come and see it. Take lots of notes on how damaging it is to the student psyche, and then have your own review printed in the school newspaper. If you like, have your Reverend Long come and write a review."

Winston stood up from his desk. "Mr. Samson makes a good point. The school newspaper exists as a forum to discuss public opinion. While the intent is for students to submit articles, the occasional article from a teacher or parent shouldn't be a problem."

The overweight principal then shooed the gorgon out the door and turned to look at Paul. "I'm impressed. Most of the teachers overreact when the gorgon lady gets them in her sights. That most usually includes you. But lately you've kept your nose clean. You may just have your *Macbeth* after all."

Paul would have accepted the praise if he hadn't covertly sabotaged the reverend's talk. Instead, he felt guilty. Not long ago he had accused the gorgon of high-tech espionage. Not only was that a false accusation, but now here he was, doing exactly what he had accused her of. He had started all this trying to teach a lesson about cheating, and here he was, the biggest cheater of all.

"No need to blush," Winston said, easing himself back into his chair.

Paul stood but said nothing. He wanted to tell Winston that the red in his face was an entirely different shade of embarrassment, but doing so could be disastrous. He had cheated then lied to cover it up. Somehow he was going to have to learn to live with that. He gave the principal a grim smile and left the office.

-ACT VI-

Scene 1: How Now, Hecate! You Look Angerly

ON MONDAY MORNING, a seventeen-year-old girl with purple-black hair and enough face metal to build a Cadillac walked into the Dairy Queen, strode to the back of the seating area, and tossed a thin newspaper onto the witches' table.

Agatha glanced down at the Ashcroft Senior High School newspaper then up at the student. "Hecate. That's a new look for you."

The student frowned and aged a dozen years in a matter of moments. Then the senior witch sat down. "I'm not impressed."

"I agree," Gertrude said. "It's hardly worthy of the name newspaper. It's mostly ads and announcements for things the students are already perfectly aware of. It contains hardly any news at all."

Netty sniffed at Hecate. "I thought you weren't interested in the news?"

Hecate thinned her lips. "I'm talking about you."

"Oh!" Netty said. "Well, that's hardly news either."

Hecate smiled. "I've been hanging around this school of yours for the past week."

Agatha lifted a French fry off her plate, rolled her eyes at it, and watched it catch fire and burn until it was a cinder. "I understand that hanging around schools can be hazardous to your health. You could accidentally learn something."

Hecate glared at the burnt fry, and it burned in reverse, becoming a light golden brown. "I learned plenty. Mostly that I've been right about you three all along. The play has been hardly vexed, never mind cursed. Have you forgotten how to curse?"

Agatha cast a long stare at Gertrude.

"Oh! My turn." Gertrude scowled at her near-empty plastic cup, and the plastic began to darken. Then cola began bubbling out of the top of the straw and flowing out onto the table, making a small, dark brown lake.

Hecate sighed and the lake froze, turned into mist, and disappeared into the atmosphere.

Netty made a choking sound and spit a gob of half-chewed French fries onto the table. Her eyes rolled in their sockets. "Are you three going to play with your food all morning, or are we going to say what needs to be said?"

Hecate waved her hand, and the table was suddenly bare of food. The only thing left was a slightly damp school newspaper. "But I was so enjoying your petty attempts at intimidation."

"I wasn't finished with my breakfast!" Netty waggled her fingers in the air, and her tray reappeared. On it sat a half-eaten hamburger, a Styrofoam plate of fries, and a hardly touched soft drink.

"What's with the finger waggling?" Hecate asked.

Netty growled deep in her throat. "It amuses me."

"I see." Hecate waggled her own fingers, and Netty's fries became a puddle of soup.

Netty stared at it, dipped in a finger, tasted it, and grimaced. "Don't give up your day job."

Hecate smiled. "And why would I? It's the greatest job in the world. Too bad you three have given up yours."

"What do you mean?" asked Agatha.

The senior witch let her gaze drift out the window. "You haven't cursed the play in over a week. And from what I can tell, you've hardly cursed it at all." Hecate tapped the newspaper. "This is not a curse."

"It also wasn't us," Netty said. "It was our drama teacher what cut Reverend Witch-hunter off at the knees."

"Witch-hunter?" said Hecate. "Reverend Long is a recruiter! Nothing tastes as good as forbidden fruit, and Mr. Long is an effective fruit salesman. In the past ten years, he's lured more women into our ranks than anyone else."

Gertrude cackled. "So you see what we've been up against. Mr. Samson is no slouch."

Hecate slammed a fist onto the table. "He's just a man. And a mortal man at that. I suppose he's also the one who made a disaster of the PTA picket line last Monday?"

Gertrude grinned. "No. That was us."

The senior witch grabbed a swatch of her own hair and pulled it out of her head, then threw the black strands onto the table. "You should have arranged the picket line, not stopped it."

Agatha let out a short cackle. "This is our play to curse. We'll do it our own way, thank you very much."

"Your own way?" Hecate glared at the school newspaper. It spontaneously shredded itself into confetti and blew around the table. "There is no such thing as your own way. You work for me!"

"Worked," Gertrude said. "You're fired."

Hecate's eyes bulged out of her head. "You can't fire me. I'm your boss. If there is any firing to be done, I'm firing you!"

"We accept!" crowed Netty.

Agatha held out a burning French fry. "It's about time we set out on our own."

Gertrude held out a burning finger. "We don't need you telling us what to do. Oh my!" She extinguished her finger. "I thought that was a fry."

Hecate ground her teeth. "If you do this, you'll be on your own. Completely cut off. Your names will be stricken from the Order of Witches. You'll be barred from coven gatherings."

"Yee-hee-hee-hee!" Netty screeched. "We haven't been invited to coven gatherings in centuries."

Agatha nodded. "And we haven't missed them."

"Then we are done here." Hecate vanished.

There was a brief silence while the Weird Sisters waited to ensure they were really alone.

"Well," Agatha said. "That went smoother than I thought it would."

"I thought she'd boil us in oil," Gertrude admitted. "I even wore my swimming suit beneath my knickers."

"She did ruin my fries," said Netty.

Then, just as suddenly as she had disappeared, Hecate was back. "One more thing. Since you three appear incapable of cursing the play, I'll do it." Then she was gone again.

"Oh, booger," Gertrude said.

Scene 2: The Instruments of Darkness Tell Us Truths

NOT A SINGLE student mentioned Reverend Long's visit on Friday. "Old news," Susie had said. And that was on Friday evening.

It was now Monday, and Paul was once again running the students through full rehearsal. They'd worked on weak spots last Thursday and Friday, and Paul had asked them to complete their costumes and props over the weekend.

"This is it," Paul said through his megaphone. "From now on, we have full-dress rehearsal, including costume changes. Sally will stop helping the stage technicians and will work the lights instead. So you are all going to have to work harder. Let's see if we can't improve on some of those problems we discussed last week."

When the bell rang, signalling the end of class, Paul had a shorter list of notes than previous weeks. But he did notice that some of the students seemed to be getting bored from the constant repetition. That was not unexpected. These were students, after all, not professional actors. He decided they'd take a break from rehearsal and spend the next two classes watching and discussing the Orson Welles film version of *Macbeth*.

"Mr. Samson?" A student he didn't recognize stood before him with a note.

"Now what?" Paul opened the note, expecting two familiar words: *Principal's Office*. What he found were two different words entirely: *Weird Sisters*.

Paul wondered if he should call Riordan. Then he laughed, certain that Riordan had no inclination to meet with the witches again. Sylvia was busy with a showing and hadn't been able to join him, so he couldn't ask her, not that introducing anyone else to the witches seemed a good idea. Lenny? But the boy was already off to his next class. He also couldn't imagine what help Lenny could possibly be.

It seemed he was on his own.

The witches were in their usual booth. Paul ordered a cola from the bored-looking woman running the cash register then joined them. "No pizza today?"

The witches' table was decorated with normal DQ fare, except for a Styrofoam plate that contained something that looked like creamed corn. Netty was waggling her fingers over it and frowning.

"Time for a change," said the tall witch named Agatha.

"Besides," Gertrude said. "Pizza gives me gas."

"I'm so glad you told us," said Netty, still waggling her fingers. "It's not like we haven't noticed."

Paul spotted a school newspaper on the table. It appeared to have been shredded then glued back together. He did a double take when he saw today's date. "Is that out already? They don't usually put it out until lunchtime."

Agatha glanced at it. "Hecate must have acquired an advance copy."

"Hecate?" Paul stopped looking through the paper for his article. "The fourth witch from *Macbeth*?"

Netty finally stopped waggling her fingers. The cream corn still looked like cream corn. "She used to be our boss."

"By 'used to be,' Netty means as recently as fifteen minutes ago," Gertrude said.

"We fired her," Agatha said.

Paul recalled a line from the play. "Beldams as you are, saucy and overbold?"

The three witches cackled.

"She called us much worse than that," said Gertrude.

"And did much worse," Netty added. "Look what she did to my fries!"

"I take it that Hecate didn't take it well," Paul said. "The firing, I mean."

"That's why we sent the student with the note," said Agatha.

Gertrude let out a halfhearted cackle. "Hecate said something about cursing the play herself."

Paul swallowed. "Hecate is going to curse the play?"

The three witches nodded.

"That's not a small problem," Netty said. "As you can see from my fries, Hecate's curses tend to be rather blunt."

"Can't you stop her?" Paul demanded. "From cursing the play,

219

I mean."

Netty let out a howl that made Paul's heart rise into his throat. "The play? We can't even stop her from cursing my breakfast!"

Paul slumped back against the bench seat. "I'll have to cancel. I'll go to Winston right now and tell him the play's off."

The three witches cackled.

Agatha snorted. "I'm not sure that will do any good. Hecate's in a mood. She's bound to cause trouble no matter what."

Paul threw his hands in the air. "I can't think of anything else. I have to cancel. The kids will be disappointed. They've worked so hard. I'll try to make it up to them."

"I'd be more concerned with just keeping them alive," Gertrude said. "Hecate's got a violent streak wider than China."

The other two witches looked at her.

"What? China is rather wide."

Paul's stomach churned. His kids could be killed? He thought about Scarlet. The witches sitting at the table with him had killed the young actress without a second thought, and they considered Hecate unnaturally violent?

Thinking about Scarlet reminded him about his promise to her. "If you can't stop Hecate, can you at least do something else?"

Agatha cast him a look of interest. "Something else?"

"Can you bring a ghost back to life?"

The three witches cackled. Then Gertrude said, "No one can bring a ghost back from beyond."

"Once a ghost, always a ghost," said Netty. Her expression turned curious. "Did you acquire a fondness for Banquo?"

"Not Banquo," Paul said. "Scarlet."

When the witches looked baffled, he said, "The actress you killed when you cursed Simon Riordan's play?"

"Oh, that Scarlet," Agatha said. "Why would you want to bring her back?"

"I don't think Simon would appreciate the gesture," Gertrude added.

"She already is back," Paul said. "She's haunting one of the props in the play. I was hoping you could do something for her."

"A ghost is haunting the play?" asked Netty. "A ghost that we didn't put there?"

Paul explained everything he knew about Scarlet, and as he

spoke, the witches grew more and more excited.

"Yes," said Agatha. The tall witch tapped her fingers together. "I think we can work with that."

"Don't cancel the play," Gertrude said. "We need to use it as bait."

"Bait?"

Agatha hunched down over the table and lowered her voice. "Let me tell you about witches and the haunts of ghosts."

Scene 3: Double, Double Toil and Trouble

PAUL ARRIVED AT school Tuesday morning after a long, sleepless night. It had taken most of the previous evening to talk Sylvia out of taking Riordan's advice and moving to Japan, or India, or anywhere but here. "You can't outrun a curse," Paul had argued. They then spent the remainder of the night discussing the witches' plan and speculating on all the things that could go wrong.

To be honest, Paul didn't think much of the Weird Sisters' plan. It relied on a number of assumptions, some of which baffled him. But the witches said they knew Hecate well enough to be able to guess how she might go about cursing the play. The first assumption was that she wouldn't make a move until rehearsals resumed. The second assumption was that Hecate would strike during rehearsal, repeatedly if necessary. The witches were counting on repeatedly.

Simon Riordan met them in the school parking lot. The skeletal old man looked frightened but carried with him a nervous energy.

Paul shook his mentor's hand. "I'm glad you agreed to help, though I'm a little surprised."

Riordan nodded and greeted Sylvia.

"When you said that this would help Scarlet, how could I refuse?"

Paul had explained the witches' plan over the phone. "You never met Hecate when the witches cursed you those many years ago?"

Riordan shook his head. "I remember her from the play, of course. Some kind of senior witch. I seem to recall that while the Weird Sisters mostly just talked, it was Hecate who performed what appeared as actual magic. It was Hecate who summoned three apparitions from Hell while hiding offstage. That's who we're expecting this morning?"

Paul nodded and pulled a printed photograph from his coat pocket.

Riordan gawked at it. "Are you sure this is the right photo? This is that lingerie model you showed me."

"I'm sure. The witches guarantee she'll be dressed differently, but her face will have the same general characteristics. Her hair is usually black. Oh, and she was last seen as a seventeen-year-old with a full set of facial piercings."

Riordan handed back the photo. "I don't think this is going to help us identify her."

They reached the auditorium, and Paul took a cautious look inside: empty. Then he thought he saw three shadows reclining in the back row of the theatre seats. A hand waved.

Scarlet appeared and Paul whispered just loud enough for her to hear. "The Weird Sisters are here." Scarlet froze where she stood. The ghost's eyes looked terrified.

Paul had gone over the plan with Scarlet the previous afternoon after reciting some lines from The Bard's Play to free her from the lamp, all the while hoping that the witches were right and that Hecate wasn't eavesdropping. One of the witches' assumptions was that Hecate didn't know about Scarlet and would believe that the ghost was one of the Weird Sisters' lame attempts at cursing the play. Not that the sisters had used the word *lame*.

The students arrived, seeing nothing amiss. Paul and Sylvia were in their customary directors' chairs. Riordan was hiding backstage. Some of the students noticed the small audience sitting in the far shadows and stared for a moment.

Paul raised the megaphone to his lips. "Class, I noticed yesterday that some of you are looking bored running through the same scenes over and over. So today we'll try something different. I have arranged for a series of distractions to occur during rehearsal. Your job is to ignore them or work around them to the best of your ability. Ad-lib, if necessary. What's the actor's creed?"

Several students surprised Paul by shouting, "The show must go on!"

Paul grinned. "That's right. Places, everyone. The curtain rises on Act IV, Scene 1. Enter the three Witches."

The curtain rose and three witches stood centre stage. The witch stirring the cauldron spoke: "Thrice the brinded cat hath mew'd."

"Thrice and once the hedge-pig whined," answered the second.

Then the third witch, Gemma Henderson, stepped to one side and called to the audience, "Harpier cries 'Tis time, 'tis time!"

The first witch continued stirring and gave her verse; then all three witches chorused the famous line, "Double, double toil and trouble; Fire burn, and cauldron bubble."

Paul thought he heard a muffled cackle from the back of the theatre seats. The three stage witches ignored it.

Witches two and three gave their verses, with all three repeating the chorus each time, then witch two concluded with, "Cool it with a baboon's blood, then the charm is firm and good."

Hecate then stepped onto the stage.

Not the real Hecate. It was Val King, dressed as the oft-forgotten fourth witch of Shakespeare's play. "O well done! I commend your pains," Val chanted. "And every one shall share i' the gains; and now about the cauldron sing, live elves and fairies in a ring, enchanting all that you put in."

Hecate then stepped back behind a stage curtain.

Paul had been sure that the real Hecate would try something. Perhaps step on stage herself and proceed to raise Hell, literally, but so far, nothing. Perhaps the Weird Sisters were wrong and Hecate wouldn't show up. Perhaps Hecate's promise to curse the play herself was just an idle threat. He could hope.

The second witch stepped forward and recited another well-remembered line. "By the pricking of my thumbs, something wicked this way comes. Open, locks, whoever knocks!"

That was Lenny's cue. Macbeth walked onto the stage. "How now, you secret, black, and midnight hags! What is't you do?"

The three witches chorused: "A deed without a name."

The scene continued, and it occurred to Paul that the apparitions were another good opportunity to wreak havoc. But the student playing the first apparition appeared onstage and delivered her line without flaw. "Macbeth! Macbeth! Macbeth! Beware Macduff. Beware the thane of Fife. Dismiss me. Enough."

The second apparition also went smoothly. "Be bloody, bold, and resolute; laugh to scorn the power of man, for none of woman born shall harm Macbeth."

Likewise the third apparition. "Be lion-mettled, proud; and take no care who chafes, who frets, or where conspirers are: Macbeth shall never vanquish'd be until great Birnam wood to high Dunsinane hill shall come against him."

Macbeth exchanged words with the witches, and the scene played out with still no sign of Hecate. Then the witches withdrew, and Macbeth pontificated to the audience. "Where are they? Gone? Let this pernicious hour stand aye accursed in the calendar! Come in, without there!"

Lennox stepped onto the stage, but before Bruce Filman could deliver his line, the cauldron began spewing a volcano's worth of smoke. Paul thought he could see flames as well. Lenny froze where he stood, staring at the cauldron, while Bruce turned and almost fell down backward. Then a skeletal old man rushed out from backstage and began blasting the cauldron with a fire extinguisher.

Paul was about to use his megaphone when Bruce shook himself and, doing his best to ignore Simon Riordan's attack on the cauldron, gave Lennox's line. "What's your grace's will?"

Lenny turned away from the cauldron and, after a moment, found his place. "Saw you the weird sisters?"

"No, my lord," said Lennox.

"Came they not by you?"

"No, indeed, my lord."

By now the cauldron was extinguished and Riordan ducked back between the backstage curtains. Paul risked looking around the auditorium for signs of Hecate but saw no one.

"Infected be the air whereon they ride," said Macbeth. "And damn'd all those that trust them! I did hear the galloping of horse: who was't came by?"

"'Tis two or three, my lord, that bring you word. Macduff is fled to England."

Macbeth was in the middle of ordering Macduff's family executed when Riordan suddenly dashed from behind the curtains and tackled Lennox, pushing him out of the way of a falling stage light. The bulb burst with a cannon-sized *pop* as the light hit the stage, the metal casing gashing a shallow wound in the hardwood floor.

"Sorry!" came Sally's strangled voice from the lighting booth at the back of the auditorium. "I don't know how that happened. I wasn't even touching the controls."

"The show must go on!" Paul shouted through the megaphone, his own voice sounding just as strangled.

With the scene more or less ended, Anna and Jennifer rushed out to replace the cauldron with two chairs. They also carried the broken light offstage. Meanwhile, several of the actors carried off the scenery flats depicting the Scottish heath, revealing the castle walls that covered the flats just behind them. Paul was not surprised that Sigrid forgot to lower and raise the curtain during the set change. Given the witches' plan, that was all for the best.

Without fanfare, Lady Macduff and her eldest son entered stage left and sat in the chairs. Thane Ross then stepped out and stood before them.

"What had he done," asked Lady Macduff, "to make him fly the land?"

"You must have patience, madam," Ross said politely.

Lady Macduff cast Ross a look of disdain. "He had none: His flight was madness: when our actions do not, our fears do make us traitors."

While Lady Macduff complained about her husband's less attractive traits, Paul detected the scent of ozone in the air. He sniffed and turned around to see thunderclouds forming above the theatre seats. To her credit, Julia Asher continued with Lady Macduff's lines, showing almost no hesitation.

The ozone grew suddenly sharper, and what Paul could only describe as a bolt of slow-motion lightning appeared and flew toward the stage.

Julia, losing her Lady Macduff persona, shrieked and knocked over her chair in an attempt to flee. Billy Tiptree, playing the son, just sat there, mouth agape. Showing all the quick action expected of a Scottish lord, Thane Ross dived off the stage into where an orchestra pit would have been had the auditorium been larger. Riordan rushed onto the stage and flailed his hands. What could he possibly do about lightning?

Then Scarlet appeared, standing in the centre of the stage, dressed as Lady Macbeth. She looked at the approaching lightning with large, round eyes, and quickly shut them and ducked her head slightly.

The lightning veered away from Julia and Billy and headed straight for the ghost.

There was a rattling sound, and Paul watched as Riordan's lamp flew off the castle wall and into the path of the lightning. There was a bright flash, and when the spots cleared from Paul's vision, he saw the lightning was gone, as was the lamp, nothing left but a few scraps of burned metal littering the stage.

Scarlet, still standing, hesitantly opened her eyes.

A seventeen-year-old goth girl appeared in the air where the storm clouds had been. She floated in place but expanded out until she was perhaps five times the size of a normal person. "Who dares to interrupt my curses?" she roared.

That was more than the students were prepared to handle. With a few frightened shouts and one hasty, "I'm outta here!" Paul heard them scuffle out the stage doors and into the supposed safety of the larger school. Paul would have given anything to be able to run with them. But this was his mess to clean up, one way or another.

A loud cackling went up from the last row of seats. "Interrupt your curses? Why would anyone do that? We were so enjoying the show."

The house lights went up halfway, exposing the Weird Sisters. Paul glanced over at the lighting booth, but it was empty. Sally had also made her escape.

Hecate shrieked. "Don't think I didn't know you were there!"

"We wouldn't dream such a thing," Agatha said.

"Hecate knows all," Gertrude added.

"You ruined my fries!" said Netty.

Hecate pointed a ruler-length finger at Riordan. "Who is this man who extinguished my fire and dodged my falling lamp?"

Riordan's face turned pale, but he stood firm.

Gertrude let out a wicked laugh. "Oh, my. I was wrong. Hecate doesn't know all. That's Simple Simon. He once had a destiny."

"Simon was going to be a hero," said Agatha.

"And today he is!" Netty said. "Who knew?"

Hecate deflated to a slightly smaller size, but Paul could see her clench and unclench her fists and glare at the Weird Sisters. "You switched ghosts. You said you summoned Banquo's ghost. If that's Banquo, I read the wrong play."

"We had to dismiss Banquo," Agatha said.

Netty snorted. "He wasn't working out."

"Who's this, then?" Hecate demanded.

"Just a dead actress," Gertrude said.

"Imagine our surprise," said Agatha, "when we found her haunting this auditorium."

"Lucky for us," Netty said, "that we didn't do anything to . . . Hmm, how can I put this?"

"Interfere," suggested Agatha.

"Ah, yes." Netty showed her gap-toothed grin. "Interfere with a ghost's haunted territory."

Hecate's eyes grew round as oranges, and she shrank another two sizes. "You didn't mention in your reports that the auditorium was haunted."

The witches cackled.

"We found out yesterday," Agatha said.

"After you fired us," said Gertrude.

Hecate was now a normal-sized seventeen-year-old. She even pouted like a teenager, if they could pout while floating in mid-air. "How convenient."

More cackling.

"That's not the convenient part," said Agatha.

"The ghost will tell you," added Gertrude.

"Go ahead, young miss," Netty said. "Tell our friend here what you were haunting."

Hecate narrowed her eyes. "You said she was haunting the auditorium."

"Not the whole auditorium," Scarlet said, her voice hesitant. "Just the prop lamp."

"What prop lamp?" Hecate demanded, turning to face the ghost.

Scarlet poked the remains of the lamp with her toe. "Now what am I supposed to do?"

"Oh, my," Gertrude said. "Is that your lamp?"

"Looks like it was struck by witch's lightning," said Agatha.

Netty let out a gasp. "What witch in her right mind would throw lightning at a haunted object? Isn't there a rule against that?"

"I didn't throw lightning at a haunted object," Hecate argued. "I threw lightning at the ghost."

Agatha let out a piercing cackle. "That technicality is sure to get you off the hook at the coven tribunal." She then spoke in a perfect imitation of Hecate's voice. "I wasn't trying to destroy the haunted lamp. I was trying to destroy the ghost that haunted it."

Gertrude shook her crooked head. "I think there's a rule against harming independent ghosts as well."

"I didn't know the ghost was independent," Hecate whined. "I thought you had summoned it."

Agatha snorted. "You could have taken a moment and asked us."

"We were sitting right here," Gertrude said.

"You even said that you knew we were sitting right here," Netty added.

Hecate clenched her fists and looked ready to throw another bolt of lightning.

"Do you think they'll ask us to testify?" Gertrude asked. "Heh. I've never testified at a coven tribunal before."

"Three eyewitnesses," Agatha said. "Four when you include the ghost. I imagine the tribunal will be quite short. Not a lot of room for argument."

"Will there be tea?" asked Netty. "I hope not. I can't abide tea."

Paul waited for Hecate to respond. When she didn't, he looked up to where the goth witch had been floating in the air. There was no sign of her.

"Is she really gone?" asked Sylvia.

The voice next to his ear was so sudden that Paul almost leaped out of his chair. He had forgotten his wife was even there.

"Perhaps," said Agatha. "Either way, the young miss must be quick. You did tell her what to do?"

"He did," said Scarlet. "Are you certain this is going to work?"

"So the stories go," Gertrude said.

"I've never seen it done," said Netty.

"Okay," said Scarlet.

The ghost tensed visibly in concentration, and Paul saw spots before his eyes. Then he realized that the spots were really the ashes and fragments of the prop lamp rising up off the stage. Scarlet suddenly threw wide her hands, and the fragments flew in all directions, striking the walls, floor, and ceiling of the auditorium, embedding themselves permanently into every corner of Ashcroft-Tate Auditorium.

The witches cackled with glee.

"It's official," said Agatha. "Now you do haunt the entire auditorium."

"We'll make sure word spreads," Gertrude said.

"At Hecate's trial," said Netty, "if not before."

"What about the other part?" asked Scarlet. "Do you really think I can do that as well?"

The witches cackled once more.

"Dearie," said Agatha, "ghosts have been doing the other part since Cain murdered Abel."

"All you've lacked is confidence," said Gertrude.

"If you want a mortal to see you," Netty said, "all you have to do is let them see you."

Once again, Scarlet closed her eyes and concentrated.

Beside Paul, Sylvia said, "Oh!"

Then there was a thud, and Paul turned to see Simon Riordan lying across the stage.

"Oh my," said Gertrude. "I hope he isn't dead. Again."

Scene 4: I Am Sick at Heart

FORTUNATELY RIORDAN HAD merely fainted. Again.

When Sylvia roused the older man, he looked about and his eyes locked on Scarlet. "My dear, you haven't changed a bit!"

Scarlet's smile was like the sun rising.

"If I'm not mistaken," Riordan continued, "you're even wearing the same dress."

"My wardrobe these days is rather limited," Scarlet admitted.

The old man's face grew suddenly grey, and Paul felt he knew what was coming.

He turned to Sylvia. "We'd better start cleaning up. It's only a matter of time before someone comes around to investigate the tales the students must surely be telling."

Sylvia seemed to understand that Riordan and Scarlet needed

a few moments. After all, Paul had told her all about how Riordan blamed himself for Scarlet's death. "Perhaps the Weird Sisters can help put things back to normal," Sylvia suggested. But the witches were gone.

The papier-mâché cauldron was beyond salvaging, so they hauled it out to the garbage bin. Sylvia said she would make a replacement in the art room later that day.

The light fixture was a write-off, but no record had been kept of the state of the stage lights. The fixture's remains also found a home in the garbage bin. However, there was still a sizable dent in the hardwood floor of the stage. Sylvia retrieved a can of floor polish from Jerry the caretaker and succeeded in at least making the damage look older than it was.

The final problem was the prop lamp, which had been all but destroyed. That damage, at least, had been planned for. Riordan, who had bought the original lamp decades earlier, had somehow managed in the time between Paul's phone call the previous afternoon and arriving at the school this morning, to find one very similar to it. Paul had scarce hung the new lamp on one of the scenery flats when a student he didn't recognize was at his elbow with a note.

The summons was expected, and Paul told himself that he still had every reason to believe that the Weird Sisters' plan was intact. He kept telling himself that all the way to Winston's office, right up until he saw, sitting in one of the detention seats, a girl with black hair, heavy mascara, and sixteen pounds of metal piercing her face.

Hecate cast him an amused grin as Mrs. Kennedy knocked on Winston's door.

"You have some explaining to do, Mr. Samson."

The words were spoken by the gorgon lady rather than the principal, who sat behind his desk, sweating as usual and looking as if he might be having trouble breathing. The gorgon did have that effect on people. Paul was only thankful that Lenny wasn't with her. Her son was in a position to add some unhelpful commentary.

Paul tried to smile. "Perhaps you could drop me a hint regarding what's bothering you today."

Mrs. Cadwell looked near apoplectic. "Your students ran screaming from your classroom."

Paul let out a soft laugh. "I'll ignore the hyperbole, but, yes, that was the intent. And I did warn them in advance."

The gorgon stared at him.

"It was an exercise."

"An exercise?"

"In distraction." Paul was tempted to sit, especially as Winston had opted to stay out of the confrontation, but he didn't want to look up to Mrs. Cadwell. "I instructed my students to continue performing as best they could despite a series of distractions. Those do happen in real life, and actors need to learn to work through them."

The gorgon lady's face darkened. "You call fires, falling stage lights, and whatever that light show was 'distractions'?"

Paul waved a hand. "Smoke and mirrors. Literally."

Mrs. Cadwell shook with rage, or excitement, or adrenalin, or whatever it was that powered a woman intent on making other people's lives miserable. "You could have set fire to the school. Or injured one of the students. You scared half the kids to death. Mr. Winston, don't you have anything to say about this?"

Mrs. Cadwell turned toward Winston, and her expression of righteous indignation became one of astonishment. Despite the amusement the gorgon's apoplexy was giving him, Paul turned to see what had so alarmed the woman. His stomach hit the floor. Winston was slouched in his desk chair, clutching his hand to his chest. His face had gone white, and sweat poured down as though he had just got out of a hot shower.

Paul pushed open the door to Winston's office and shouted to Mrs. Kennedy. "Call for a paramedic and get the school nurse. Principal Winston is having a heart attack!"

The nurse arrived almost before Paul had reentered the office, which was a good thing, as he had no idea what to do to help a heart attack victim. Mrs. Cadwell appeared to have even less of an idea. She just stood in a corner of the office with one hand over her mouth.

In fifteen years, Paul had never had occasion to learn the school nurse's name, but thank God she knew what she was doing. In no time at all, Winston was breathing better, but he still looked as white as a sated vampire's victim. A few minutes later, two young women who looked as fit as firefighters came running into the office, carrying four large red bags. They took an oxygen mask from one of the bags and placed it over Winston's mouth. Then one of the paramedics pulled out a stethoscope and listened to the principal's chest while the other wrapped a blood pressure cuff around his arm and began pumping.

The taller of the two paramedics left the office and returned a few minutes later with one of those wheeled stretchers like the one that had hauled away Kim Greyson. Together, they lifted Winston onto the bed, threw their red bags on top of his legs, and rolled him out of the office.

Mrs. Cadwell hadn't moved the entire time and still stood in a corner with her hand over her mouth. Paul briefly considered requesting a second ambulance for her but decided to leave that up to Mrs. Kennedy.

Outside the office, a large number of teachers and students had gathered. Most of them stood watching the paramedics roll their principal down the hallway. One student was not watching. She walked over to Paul and spoke to him in a barely audible whisper. "Unless *Macbeth* is finished, this is just the beginning." Then Hecate walked back to stand with the other students and smiled as Winston was hauled away to the hospital.

Scene 5: Embrace the Fate of That Dark Hour

AFTER THE FOUR p.m. bell sent his second-year drama students running from the Ashcroft-Tate Auditorium to their after-school activities, Paul went out to the parking lot, climbed into his car, and drove to Hinton Valley Hospital.

He had already told Sylvia, Riordan, and Scarlet what had happened to Winston as well as what Hecate had said. They'd then gone looking for the Weird Sisters at the Dairy Queen, but for the first time in six weeks, the witches' table was unoccupied. One of the restaurant employees was scrubbing the table with strong-smelling liquid from a bucket and looking none too pleased about it.

Regrouping at the auditorium, where Scarlet had waited for them, they'd agreed that they had saved the play from unimaginable odds but would have to cancel it anyway. They couldn't predict what Hecate might or might not do next.

Paul already knew from Mrs. Kennedy what room Winston was in and that visitors were allowed. That Mrs. Cadwell was already there, still complaining about events in the auditorium that morning, didn't surprise him.

"And here he is now," said Mrs. Cadwell. "Care to try that smoke-and-mirrors story again now that Mr. Winston is able to comment?"

There was a nurse in the room attempting to shush the gorgon lady, but she was getting nowhere. Paul ignored both of them and walked to Winston's bedside. The large man was awake, looked irritable, and had a tube sticking in his arm.

"They tell me that you're going to be all right," Paul said.

Winston wagged his head toward Mrs. Cadwell. "All right is a relative term. The heart attack was a mild one, as far as heart attacks go. But the diet these doctors are putting me on is sure to finish me off."

That Winston could joke, in a hospital bed, with the gorgon lady ranting in his ear, was a promising sign that Winston would be okay—provided Hecate didn't come at him again.

"You listen when I'm talking!" Mrs. Cadwell snapped. "It's your fault that Mr. Winston is in this hospital. You and your Satanic play."

Paul drew in a deep breath and turned to face the gorgon lady. "Mrs. Cadwell, I'll make a bargain with you. If you leave this hospital right now and don't come back and give Mr. Winston half a chance to recuperate, I will cancel the play."

"You'll do no such—" Mrs. Cadwell froze. "You'll do what?"

"You heard me." Paul raised his arms and waved them fervently. "It is sheer nonsense that Shakespeare writing a play about Scottish politics could turn students into Satanists or put high school principals in the hospital, but you appear to be obsessed with nonsense. For the sake of Mr. Winston's health, if not his sanity, I am willing to ask the students to perform a different play."

Winston tugged at Paul's sport coat. "You can't. There's less than three weeks until midterm. If you're going to cancel, cancel. But don't try to do a different play."

Paul shook his head. "These are the best students I've ever had. It's bad enough that all the hard work they've put in so far is going out the window. Not getting to perform anything at all will totally demoralize them. We'll have to substitute in a different play."

"What play?" said Mrs. Cadwell, her voice as well as her eyes filled with suspicion.

Paul continued to wave his hands in the air, feigning deep thoughts. He'd already prepared what he was going to say before arriving at the hospital. Then he froze and looked up into space. "*Much Ado about Nothing.*" His hands began moving again. "It's a short play. The dialogue is fairly straightforward and should be easy to learn." He nodded his head as though mentally seeing keys click into locks. "Most of the costumes and sets will still work, if perhaps a bit odd at times."

"I've never heard of this play," said Mrs. Cadwell. "It's not Shakespeare, is it?"

"A romantic comedy," said Winston.

That got the gorgon lady's attention. "That sounds safe. There aren't any witches in it, are there?"

Paul shook his head. "It's set in Italy, land of the pope."

"Well . . ." A thick smile marched across the gorgon lady's face. "I'm glad you've finally seen reason. But if you go back on your word and try to trick me, there'll be hell to pay."

"It's a deal, then?" Paul asked, lowering his arms. He knew better than to try to shake on it.

The gorgon lady stared at Paul with eyes bulging with suspicion. "Deal." She turned to leave. "My business here is done."

"Oh, and Mrs. Cadwell." Paul finally allowed a smile to grace his own lips. "I will make sure that you receive full credit for *Macbeth* being cancelled."

When the gorgon lady was gone, Winston said, "You didn't have to do that."

Paul sighed and sat in the visitor's chair. "Yes, I did. Look at the trouble that woman has caused. And could continue to cause over the next three weeks."

"Story of her life," said Winston. "I do appreciate you getting her out of my hospital room. *Much Ado about Nothing*? Not exactly Shakespeare's most popular play."

Paul laughed. "We performed it when I was in high school. I was Verges."

Now Winston laughed. "Not the most popular role."

Paul sighed. "My only real regret about cancelling *Macbeth* is having to tell the students."

Scene 6: When the Battle's Lost and Won

PAUL ARRIVED AT school early Wednesday morning and hauled a near-empty box out of the trunk of his car. It contained a script and several pages of notes. A visit with Mrs. Shean in the school library and twenty minutes lingering by the photocopier produced thirty copies of the script, adding considerable weight to the box.

He found Scarlet waiting for him in the auditorium. Since Hecate had destroyed Riordan's lamp, the ghost no longer vanished whenever Paul was away. And now that she could make anyone see her whenever she wished, Scarlet was also free of any ties to Paul. Not that she was truly free of Paul. They would see each other every school day as long as Paul continued to teach drama.

Paul had asked Sylvia not to join him today. Telling the students that *Macbeth* was cancelled was going to be difficult, and he didn't want Sylvia to share in the blame or the pain.

"Do you think the students will show up?" he asked Scarlet. "Yesterday's rehearsal was pretty rough. And then Winston's heart attack."

Scarlet laughed. "Most of them probably ignored the school principal's heart attack. Winston is an adult, too far removed from the important things in teenagers' lives. A lot of them have yet to learn how fragile life is and can't differentiate between a heart attack and the flu. To them, Winston's just taking a few days in bed with a box of Kleenex."

While a month ago Paul might have agreed with the ghost, today he'd give his students more credit. The younger generation might have a different way of expressing themselves and dealing with emotion, but Paul was pretty certain that being oblivious wasn't one of them. After dinner last night, he'd had a brief chat with Susie about Winston, and her signature claim of old news hadn't rung true. He could tell his daughter was shaken.

Lenny Cadwell was the first student to arrive, dressed all in black and carrying Macbeth's crown in his left hand. "My mother says you're cancelling the play."

Paul nodded. "I do have some news I need to share with the class."

The boy pouted. "The witches promised me that I would be Macbeth."

Again, Paul nodded. "You've been Macbeth for almost six weeks. A fine Macbeth, if I do say so myself."

"It's not fair."

"Life isn't always fair," Paul said. He stopped himself from adding, *Especially when your mother is involved.*

Lenny tossed his crown into a prop box and sat on the stage, his face a storm cloud.

The second-period bell rang, and other students began arriving, some, like Lenny, in costume. Seeing Lenny's demeanour, they all realized that something was wrong and ceased talking. Many joined Lenny on the floor. No one mentioned the distractions from yesterday's rehearsal.

When Paul saw that they had all arrived, he picked up the megaphone and sat in his director's chair. "I'm afraid I have some troubling news. As all of you know, the PTA has had some concerns about Shakespeare's *Macbeth* being performed at Ashcroft Senior High." This evoked a few snickers.

"These concerns have resulted in the PTA taking several escalating actions to suppress the play, all of which failed to achieve their goal." This evoked several cheers.

"The PTA's concerns, however, have not gone away, and yesterday it was decided that it would be better for all concerned if *Macbeth* was cancelled."

Stunned silence.

"Not better for us," someone yelled.

Paul looked around and saw that it was Kim Greyson. The boy had abandoned his wheelchair after his first day back but still leaned on crutches, one of which he waved like a sword in battle. Paul had smiled each and every time he had watched Kim rehearse a battle scene.

He also saw Susie glaring at him. Feeling it unfair to inform some students before others, Paul and Sylvia had been forced to hide what had happened from their own daughter. He was not surprised that Mrs. Cadwell had felt no such compunction.

Then he nearly fell off his director's chair when he noticed an extra student standing against one wall: black hair, heavy mascara, a face full of metal. Hecate. He quickly arranged his thoughts and continued speaking, raising his hands to quell the complaints that had followed Kim's objection.

"Please, kids. You have all done a fantastic job rehearsing your parts. I have never been more impressed by any class at this school. And because I am impressed, I have every confidence that we can still put on a midterm play on the thirtieth. How many of you have read *Much Ado about Nothing*?"

When no one raised a hand, Paul looked at Lenny. The boy shrugged.

"Tomorrow we will watch the 2012 film version of the play directed by Joss Whedon. I think you will like it. It's a comedy."

"Is it Shakespeare?" Gemma Henderson asked.

Paul paused to take a breath. "Yes."

"Good."

Several students echoed the sentiment.

Paul looked over at Hecate and saw that she was no longer in the auditorium. That, too, was good. Paul didn't know if he could stall the discussion much longer.

"How are we supposed to learn a whole new play in two weeks?"

"I'm glad you asked, John. Two weeks is asking a lot. Many professional actors wouldn't be able to learn a new script in two weeks." While he spoke, Paul searched for signs that Hecate was still lurking in the auditorium. "That's why I spent last night modifying the original script so that it would be easier to learn. Lenny, could you hand out the scripts and the highlighters so that everyone can mark their lines."

"We're not going to audition this time?" Lenny asked, his expression still dark with anger.

"Not necessary. When you review your script, you'll see why." Paul could see no sign of Hecate. Either way, he was committed now.

"Hey," said Camille, looking at the script's opening page. "This is my line. But Leonato is speaking it. Who's Leonato?"

Paul drew a deep breath. "You have all done a commendable

job learning your lines for *Macbeth*, and we don't have time for you to learn a whole new play. So I've adapted as much of the *Macbeth* script as I could to replace lines from *Much Ado*. What you will have to learn over the next two and a half weeks are new character and place names, some unavoidable changes to some of your lines, and a few new lines. Most of the blocking remains the same. Unfortunately I couldn't keep the murders and the battles. *Much Ado* is, after all, a romantic comedy. Instead, we have some duels, break and enter, and a considerable amount of spying."

That caused some grumbling, especially from the boys.

Paul looked at Lenny. "Macbeth, you are now Benedick, a witty, aristocratic soldier who is married to Beatrice."

He turned to Susie. "Lady Macbeth, you are now the pleasant-spirited, though sharp-tongued Beatrice, or Lady Benedick.

"Duncan is Claudio, a soldier whose suspicious nature makes him quick to believe evil rumours.

"Banquo is Don Pedro, an important nobleman.

"Macduff, you're Dogberry—"

"Dogberry!" William looked scandalized. "What kind of a name is that?"

"It has to be Dogberry. Dogberry's the hero. He's the constable in charge of the watch. And the witches now have names instead of numbers. You are Conrade, Borachio, and Margaret."

"Isn't Conrade a boy's name?" asked Teresa.

"Then use Conrada when your name is spoken. Camille, use Borachia."

"What about me?" asked Gemma.

Paul looked at her. "If you don't like Margaret, use Margrata.

"Hecate, you are Don John."

"But—" said Val.

"Don John is the villain," said Paul. "His name is too well known to change."

"But I should be the villain," said Lenny. "Not this Benedict Arnold fellow."

Paul shook his head. "Benedick is the lead and delivers Macbeth's copious lines. Don John delivers Hecate's two monologues. Do you really want to switch?"

Lenny shook his head but not as furiously as Val.

Teresa Van Pelt raised her hand.

"Yes, Teresa."

"I've been looking at the script. I still have the same lines, only the tag says Conrade instead of First Witch."

Paul let out a deep breath. "Not quite the same lines, Teresa. Instead of a witch, you are now a greedy nobleman." He consulted the script. "Camille's first line now says: 'When the hurlyburly's done, when the duel is lost and won.' And Gemma's second line is: 'There to meet with Benedick.'"

A chorus of confused grumbling arose from the gathered students.

Paul raised his megaphone. "You all know what a mash-up is." It was a statement. He knew better than to make it a question. "We have to do a different play. One without witches and cauldrons and destinies. One that is different enough from *Macbeth* that it can't be called *Macbeth*." He paused. "But we don't have time to learn new dialogue and blocking, or to make new costumes. So what do we do?"

Seconds ticked by while Paul waited for an answer.

Finally, Kim Greyson lifted a hand from one of his crutches. "We cheat?"

Paul rubbed his face. He had started all this as a lesson in honesty, as a response to the cheating on exams that had occurred last June. Was this any different? Paul didn't have time to think about it.

"No, Kim," he said at last. "We don't cheat. Technically I am probably cheating. And I'm prepared to suffer the consequences should anyone take offence. But you and the rest of the class are definitely not cheating. I'm your teacher. This is the assignment I'm giving you. You're expected to complete the assignment. Any questions?"

Silence filled the auditorium.

Then a hand went up. "What about me, Mr. Samson. What's my new name?"

Paul ran a finger down his list. "Seyton. You're *Boy*."

"Boy?"

"Perfect name for a servant."

It took several minutes to run through the remainder of the cast name changes.

"Remember," Paul said, "the play now takes place in sunny Italy rather than wintry Scotland. You're not in Dunsinane;

you're in Messina. All of the place name changes are also in your new scripts."

Several of the students were flipping through the script and laughing.

"Care to share the joke, Lenny?" Paul asked.

"You've replaced the word *murder* in all of my lines," Lenny said. "It now says *marriage*. 'My thought, whose marriage yet is but fantastical.'" He flipped a few pages. "'The curtain'd sleep; the dark night celebrates pale Don John's offerings, and wither'd marriage.'"

Paul nodded. "As I said at the beginning, the play is now a romantic comedy. You have two weeks to relearn your lines. Many are unchanged, but most have subtle changes. Incorporating the changes won't be as hard as you think. We'll still have battles, only they'll be polite duels and no one will die. The winner gets the girl. The loser leaves the scene to go sulk with his friends. But remember, as far as everyone outside this class is concerned, the play is *Much Ado about Nothing*. That is the play the PTA expects, and that is the play they are going to get."

Scene 7: *Much Ado about Macbeth*

PAUL PEEKED BETWEEN the curtains and looked out on row after row of filled theatre seats. Those who couldn't find seats stood along the back and side walls, in blatant violation of the fire code. In his fifteen years of teaching at Ashcroft Senior High School, Paul had never seen a better turnout for a school play. His one hope was that they'd make it through to the end.

He'd seen no sign of Hecate during the twelve days of rehearsal, and no disasters had befallen anyone in the cast or elsewhere in the school. The kids had worked hard, and he didn't think anyone unfamiliar with Shakespeare would realize Paul had cheated.

Yes, cheated. There was no other way to describe it. He had disguised *Macbeth* as a different play. And it wasn't even a clever disguise. Anyone familiar with either play would catch him in the act, so to speak, and a wrong word to the gorgon lady could bring the house down, and not in a good way.

But it wasn't the gorgon lady who worried him. Mrs. Cadwell could scream and shout and collapse with epilepsy for all he cared. The days of fencing with the PTA were over. Paul didn't need to play games or win arguments. He would do what he thought best as a teacher, and if the gorgon lady disagreed, she could choke on it.

What worried him was Hecate. What his students were about to perform was arguably not The Scottish Play. The name Macbeth would never be used. Nor would any other character or place name from that play. There were no witches, no cauldron. Don John and his minions would enact their deceptions around a campfire outside the city of Messina. No one would be murdered in beds, in homes, or on the field of battle. The cast would not be concerned with political advancement, but instead seek flirtatious misadventure, happy marriages, and houses filled with the patter of tiny feet.

The script was, admittedly, a poor one. Paul had never published a script, but he'd tried his hand now and then. Plagiarism aside, his liberal adaptation of *Much Ado about Nothing* would receive an *F* from any drama teacher with the stomach to read it. But that was not the point.

The students had worked hard, and they deserved to put on a play. This was the best Paul could do for them. Whether the audience was familiar with Shakespeare or not, they should get a laugh, if for different reasons. And he hoped it was sufficient to satisfy the wicked witch; a witch too wicked for even the Weird Sisters. But Paul had no way of knowing. He didn't think he could win an argument with Hecate no matter how right he was. But it was too late to worry about that now.

The house lights were still up, so Paul had no trouble seeing faces in the audience. He searched for anyone recognizable from the PTA, but succeeded only in finding Mrs. Cadwell sitting near the centre of the auditorium. He swallowed as he noticed the notebook computer on her lap. He had been joking when he suggested she write a review of the play for the school newspaper, and he could only imagine what it was going to say. But at least she couldn't say there were witches.

In the front row, Winston sat, looking fitter than Paul had seen him in years. The school principal had been on his new diet for only a couple of weeks, but already he was a new man.

Speaking of new men, next to Winston sat Simon Riordan, a skeleton no longer and looking ten years younger. In other words, Simon Riordan as he should look at sixty years of age. Unburdening himself of guilt over Scarlet's death had saved Paul's old mentor from an early grave. Helping Paul with the mash-up play the past couple of weeks had reinforced his new vitality.

Privately Paul considered himself a new man as well. Only by witnessing the shell of a man Riordan had become had Paul realized his own shortcomings. Year by year he had steadily failed to live up to the ideals he had adopted from Riordan in high school. He had grown cynical, and that had affected not just work but his home life as well. His family had been growing apart.

Susie had found her own solution to her father's descent into ill-being by manoeuvring herself into his drama class. He hadn't called her on it, but he knew it to be true. If her father wouldn't show an interest in what she was doing, then she would show interest in his life.

Sylvia, sitting next to Riordan with a program in her hand and a wide grin on her face, had done the same by volunteering herself as his helper at school.

It had occurred to Paul that mother and daughter might have conspired together to use the play to save their family. Well, it was about time Paul joined the conspiracy. From now on, they'd have a weekly family night. Susie could pick an evening that fit her schedule, and as a family, they'd watch movies, go bowling, or do whatever normal families did. Perhaps they'd take in a play.

Seeing that the seats were full and the audience was growing restless, Paul decided he could delay no longer. He took three deep breaths then stepped out in front of the curtain to introduce *Much Ado about Nothing*.

"THAT WAS A decent enough prologue," suggested Agatha. "If brief."

The drama teacher had left the stage, and the curtain was rising.

"Oh, my," said Gertrude. "Three despotic noblemen gathered around a campfire outside a sixteenth-century Sicilian city. Heh. I didn't see that coming."

"Noble?" said Netty. "They're dressed like hags! Look at that frumpy hat. And they're wearing boots!"

"Shh!" said a man with psoriasis and a bad toupee who was sitting in front of them.

"They do seem a tad underdressed for their station," Agatha agreed. "Fallen on hard times, I imagine."

"Speaking of falling on hard times," said Gertrude, "has anyone heard from Hecate?"

"I haven't seen her since the tribunal," Netty said.

"Shh!" the man repeated.

Netty ignored him. "Heard she was transferred. Antarctica or some such place."

The three witches cackled, causing half the row in front of them to turn and make shushing noises.

"Ah, well," said Agatha. "Best we sit back and enjoy the show. I've never seen *Much Ado about Nothing*. Although it does seem very familiar."

–THE END–

Acknowlegements

I would very much like to thank my publisher, Tyche Books, and editor Andrea Howe for painstakingly massaging the pages of this book to make it as solid a work as possible. Thanks also to the many pre-readers who provided helpful feedback, including Tereasa Maillie of Gas & Light Productions for her theatre expertise; Kim Greyson, high school teacher extraordinaire; award-winning fantasy author David B. Coe; and fellow writers Howie Erickson, Monica Plamondon, and Val King. Any errors remaining in this book are solely my own and I beg forgiveness.

Author Biography

RANDY MCCHARLES is a writer of speculative fiction, usually of the wickedly humorous variety, with short stories and novellas available from Edge Science Fiction and Fantasy Publishing, House of Anansi, and Reality Skimming Press. He is the recipient of several Aurora Awards (Canada's most prestigious award for speculative fiction). In 2013, his short story Ghost-B-Gone Incorporated won the House of Anansi 7-day Ghost Story Contest.

In addition to writing, Randy chairs the award-winning When Words Collide Festival for Readers and Writers as well as organizing various reading and craft events for writers.

www.randymccharles.com

CPSIA information can be obtained at www.ICGtesting.com
Printed in the USA
LVOW08s0629011015

456476LV00002B/10/P

9 781928 025290